"Have you seen this?" Edna demanded when Marie opened the door and got out of the way. Edna had the look of a woman not to be denied.

"We'll have tea," Marie said, snatching off the bandanna and freeing herself of her cleaning apron.

"They're going to close St. Hilary's! They're going to tear down the church, the rectory, everything."

"What on earth are you talking about?" Marie asked, following Edna into the kitchen.

Edna slapped the newspaper onto the kitchen table and stood staring at Marie, angry tears in her eyes.

"Nonsense!"

"Read it."

"I'll put on the water."

While she did, Edna began reading the story to her. Belatedly, Marie felt the force of Edna's message. She stood at the sink with water spilling over the top of the kettle, mouth open in disbelief. The information was attributed to "reliable sources," and the story concerned the archdiocese's need to close half a dozen parishes that had been isolated by demographic changes. There, undeniably, the third on the list, was St. Hilary's of Fox River.

"Where is Father Dowling, Marie?"

"This is his monthly day of recollection."

"Get hold of him!"

"Interrupt his only day off in the month? Edna, he's saying his prayers."

"He'd better be or else he may have lots of days off soon."

★

STAINED GLASS

RALPH McINERNY

WORLDWIDE®

TORONTO • NEW YORK • LONDON
AMSTERDAM • PARIS • SYDNEY • HAMBURG
STOCKHOLM • ATHENS • TOKYO • MILAN
MADRID • WARSAW • BUDAPEST • AUCKLAND

Recycling programs
for this product may
not exist in your area.

STAINED GLASS

A Worldwide Mystery/August 2011

First published by St. Martin's Press

ISBN-13: 978-0-373-26762-0

Printed in U.S.A.

For Mary and Bill Dempsey

PART ONE

ONE

TETZEL OF THE *FOX RIVER Tribune* sat morosely in the press-room at the courthouse seriously contemplating taking the pledge. He could remember the night before up to a certain point and then things went blank. He had come awake with a sore neck and a throbbing headache sitting at his desk in the pressroom and had no idea how he had ended up there. His hand lifted to massage his brow and tipped his hat from his head. When he stooped to pick it up off the floor, he nearly blacked out. The hat kept moving away from his groping hand. He sat back in his chair, hatless, and closed his eyes. Someone entered.

"The top of the morning to you, Tetzel."

There was no need to open his eyes to know that it was Tuttle. He heard the little lawyer collapse in a chair whose squeak went through Tetzel's nervous system like a laser.

"Stop rocking, damn it."

"You're not feeling well."

"Could you whisper?"

"You should have left when I did, Tetzel."

The reporter opened one eye, the one nearer to Tuttle. "Were you there?"

"Everyone was there."

"When did you leave?"

"Just after my curfew."

Tetzel considered asking Tuttle where "there" was, or had been, but he was at enough of a disadvantage already. "I feel awful."

"Better come across the street."

For a remedial drink? Minutes before, Tetzel would have found the suggestion emetic. Now it seemed only sensible. "Hand me my hat."

Tuttle swept it up and stood. He put the hat on Tetzel's head and helped him rise. He guided the reporter down the hall to the elevator, steered him inside, and pressed a button. Tetzel felt that he was leaving his stomach on the floor they had left. His body broke out in a cold sweat. Vague memories of sobriety teased his mind. Once he had been a clear-headed reporter, a model for youngsters, a legend because of the novel he was allegedly writing. They arrived safely on the ground floor; the doors slid open, and Tetzel hung back. Before him, in the lobby of the courthouse, were busy men and women, hurrying this way and that. Tetzel was sure that each and every one of them could give a clear account of the way he had spent the previous night. Tuttle urged him forth, and they crossed the black-and-white marble squares to the revolving doors. They actually entered together, a tight fit, but Tetzel wondered if he would have dared the door on his own.

Outside was more normalcy, sunlight, traffic, horns, the usually inaudible roar of the city. Tuttle wisely took his charge to the corner, and they crossed with the light. Ahead lay the friendly confines of the Jury Room.

Once inside, Tuttle's grip on his arm loosened and Tetzel moved like a zombie toward a far booth, as far from sunlight as any in the room. At the bar, Tuttle ordered a Coke for himself and a Bloody Mary for Tetzel. The bartender was watching Tetzel. The reporter looked as if he were one of the Flying Wallendas negotiating a rope high above a circus audience. His arms were extended for better balance.

"He going to be sick?"

"He is sick."

"Put him in the men's room."

"Now, now, Portia, that's no way to treat a steady customer."

"He isn't steady."

"He will be."

Tuttle swept up the drinks, called, "Tetzel's tab," over his shoulder, and walked carefully to the booth. He put Tetzel's drink before him and slid into the seat across from him. The reporter was contemplating the Bloody Mary.

"Tell me about last night."

"What's to tell?"

"You don't remember," Tetzel said accusingly. He lowered his lips to the plastic straw and his cheeks hollowed. He inhaled half the drink before sitting back. A moment passed. Color came back to Tetzel's face. Another moment and he sighed. "I needed that."

Tuttle advised against a repetition of the remedy. With his synapses responding, Tetzel was inclined to dispute the point. Tuttle opened the newspaper he had taken from the bar, turning the pages with an indifference that annoyed Tetzel.

"Good Lord," Tuttle cried.

"What?" Tetzel asked, trying to signal Portia.

"They plan to tear down St. Hilary's."

TWO

Amos Cadbury was the dean of the Fox River bar, seventy-nine years old and thus, as he insisted to himself, in his eightieth year. He was the sole surviving partner of the colleagues with whom he had formed the firm many, many years ago. He had stopped taking new clients a decade before, but he still brought business into the firm, passing new clients on to others with the assurance that they would benefit from the counsel of the oldest member.

The oldest member. Amos was a lifelong fan of P. G. Wodehouse, and the author's golf stories had become even more delightful since Amos had put away his clubs and, like the narrator of the Wodehouse stories, was content to sit on the clubhouse veranda watching golfers come and go on the course before him. Just below the veranda was the eighteenth green and, to the right, the first tee. The contrast between those beginning their round and those ending theirs seemed an allegory of life. The first tee is a symbol of hope, the triumph of expectation over experience; the eighteenth green was the supreme moral test as players frowned over their cards and fought the temptation to alter the record of their play. When they directed their electric carts up the path to the clubhouse, the idealists who had driven from the first tee were once more realists, the notion of par a mockery of their skills.

A foursome had just left the eighteenth green when a ball lofted from the valley below dropped neatly onto the green and then spun backward, stopping mere inches from the hole.

Amos waited for other balls to appear, but none had when a young man, his bag slung over his shoulder, came into view. He seemed still fresh and spry, unlike the members of the foursome, who, although they had gone round in carts, might have been breasting the tape at the end of a marathon. The young man was Hugh Devere. He took out his putter, dropped his bag at the edge of the green, and walked to his ball. He left the flag in as he tapped the ball into the hole.

Hugh was one of the few golfers who would have been allowed to go round as a singleton. His play was sure and swift. Amos wondered how many groups had waved Hugh through, if only for the pleasure of watching the young man play.

Amos lifted his gin and tonic in a toast as Hugh approached and was delighted when the young man joined him on the veranda. He took a chair and lit a cigarette.

"An athlete smoking?"

"I'm not an athlete, I'm a golfer."

"Let me see your card."

"Oh, I keep score in my head."

"And?"

"Three over."

"Very good."

"Probably my last round before I head back to South Bend."

Several generations of Deveres had been clients of Amos's, and all the males, like himself, were alumni of Notre Dame, Amos a double domer, undergraduate then law school. Hugh had gone off to Thomas Aquinas College in California but now had entered the architecture school at Notre Dame, thus salvaging the Devere record. Architecture is an undergraduate program, but, as Hugh put it, now that he had acquired an education, he would prepare himself for professional life. Relieved of the necessity of taking courses outside the architecture school, he would finish his studies at the end of the coming year.

"Did my dad get hold of you?"

"This is my day away from the office."

"He's madder than hell."

"At not finding me in?"

"The story in the *Tribune*."

Amos drew on his cigar. It was a feature of his Wednesdays that he read no papers and listened to no news broadcasts. He spent the mornings reading and then had lunch at the club, after which he took up his station on the veranda, where watching other golfers reconciled him to the fact that he himself no longer played. He waited to see if Hugh would pursue the subject, hoping he would not.

"I can't believe they will tear it down."

Amos remained silent, wishing the alarums and excursions of what was taken for news into deserved oblivion.

"What will happen to Father Dowling?"

"Father Dowling?"

"So you haven't read the story."

"You have the advantage of me there, Hugh. Tell me about it." Amos listened in disbelief. There had been a story in the *Tribune* concerning the closing down of certain parishes in the archdiocese, and St. Hilary's in Fox River was on the list of those slated for closing.

"Dad is up in arms."

"Of course. He is a parishioner at St. Hilary's."

"His grandfather donated the windows."

Hugh's was alarming news indeed. The peace of the day dissipated, and Amos finished his drink and got to his feet.

Hugh did the same. "Well, I'm off to the showers."

Amos watched Hugh as he walked away, young and carefree, as if he had not just destroyed Amos's peace of mind. The venerable lawyer went inside, found a copy of the paper, and read the story, finding it even more upsetting than Hugh's account. He went into the bar and telephoned Father Dowling.

THREE

FATHER DOWLING WAS OFF on his monthly day of recollection and Marie Murkin, a bandanna around her head and wearing an ankle-length apron, was giving the rectory a thorough cleaning. Each time she passed the closed door of the pastor's study, she fought the temptation to ignore the fact that it was the one room in the house on which she could not unleash her energy. Finally she opened the door and looked in, frowning at the stacks of books on each side of Father Dowling's reading chair, the chaos on the desktop, the aroma of pipe smoke. That, at least, she could do something about. She marched across the room and pulled up the window, letting in the humid August air. When she turned on the air conditioner in the other window, she noticed Edna Hospers hurrying along the walk from the school where the seniors of the parish whiled away their day.

What on earth was Edna's hurry? Clearly she was headed for the rectory, and Marie felt a surge of the old undeclared war between them, the rectory housekeeper and the director of the senior center. Edna had a rolled-up newspaper in her hand, carrying it like a weapon. With some trepidation, Marie went to the front door.

"Have you seen this?" Edna demanded when Marie opened the door and got out of the way. Edna had the look of a woman not to be denied.

"We'll have tea," Marie said, snatching off the bandanna and freeing herself of her cleaning apron.

"They're going to close St. Hilary's! They're going to tear down the church, the rectory, everything."

"What on earth are you talking about?" Marie asked, following Edna into the kitchen.

Edna slapped the newspaper onto the kitchen table and stood staring at Marie, angry tears in her eyes.

"Nonsense!"

"Read it."

"I'll put on the water."

While she did, Edna began reading the story to her. Belatedly, Marie felt the force of Edna's message. She stood at the sink with water spilling over the top of the kettle, mouth open in disbelief. The information was attributed to "reliable sources," and the story concerned the archdiocese's need to close half a dozen parishes that had been isolated by demographic changes. There, undeniably, the third on the list, was St. Hilary's of Fox River.

"Where is Father Dowling, Marie?"

"This is his monthly day of recollection."

"Get hold of him!"

"Interrupt his only day off in the month. Edna, he's saying his prayers."

"He'd better be or else he may have lots of days off soon."

Marie went back to the sink, lowered the level of water in the kettle, and put it on the stove. Later she would remember that her first concern had been herself. She had been housekeeper here before Father Dowling came, a survivor of years under Franciscans she preferred not to think about. The rectory was as much her home as Father Dowling's, maybe more. The thought that she might be turned into the street after her years of service filled her with dread, and then anger. "Over my dead body, Edna."

"What good will that do?"

"Get out the cups, will you? I have some cherry pie."

"Cherry pie! Marie, this is the end of the world and you're talking of cherry pie."

"I wonder if I *should* call Father."

"Of course you should. They can't do this to him."

Father Dowling was spending the day at Mundelein, where he had been a seminarian and which was peaceful and empty before the resumption of classes. He had been assigned the bishop's room for the day, and the chapel would be all his. Marie remembered the look with which Father Dowling had gone off, several books under his arm, his breviary in his hand. She had asked him if he had his pipe and tobacco.

"Not today, Marie."

That was all, no explanation, but Marie hadn't needed one. Honestly, she didn't know what she would do if he didn't smoke. He ate like a bird, he didn't drink, he didn't golf or pal around with clerical friends. The man was an anchorite. Thank God for Phil Keegan's frequent visits.

The problem was that she had no telephone number for his room at the seminary. When had she ever had to interrupt his day of recollection? She explained this to Edna. They were at the table now, the tea settling in the pot, slices of cherry pie before them. Edna ate half of hers before she pushed it away. "How can I eat cherry pie?"

"You were doing pretty well."

"I don't know what I'm doing."

It helped to have Edna acting outwardly as Marie felt within.

Still, she wasn't used to being the calm and rational one in a crisis—and this was a crisis. Marie turned the paper toward her, started to read the story, then pushed it away. She would rather eat cherry pie. In her nervousness, Edna assumed the role of hostess and poured out the tea.

"Lemon?" Marie asked.

"Nothing. I'll drink it straight." She made it sound like liquor.

"Edna, I can't read that story to him over the phone. I can't just tell him that they're going to close the parish."

"Well, have someone else do it."

"Would you want to?"

Edna assumed a look of dread. "No!"

Phil Keegan? He was possible, but Marie didn't like the thought of Phil Keegan running interference for her with the pastor. Then the phone rang, and the problem was solved.

"Marie," Amos Cadbury said. "Is he there?"

Marie could have cheered in relief. Amos Cadbury, of course. He was the perfect one to bring the bad news to Father Dowling.

"He won't be back until suppertime, Mr. Cadbury."

"You've seen this story in the *Tribune?*"

"Yes."

"What time is supper, Marie?"

"Can you come?"

"Marie, I couldn't stay away."

FOUR

THE SPIRITUAL EXERCISES of St. Ignatius were not designed for a one-day retreat, but, for all that, Father Dowling found the little book written by the founder of the Society of Jesus a good companion as he spent hours in the chapel and other hours reading in his room. The campus was all but deserted, and on his walk from room to chapel and back again he was assailed by sweet memories of student days. Nevertheless, it was all the days between then and now that formed the subject of his meditations. What had the young man he was at the time of ordination thought the future held for him? In retrospect, he seemed to himself a somewhat shallow man, caught up in an unformulated dream of clerical advancement. He had been sent on to graduate school to get his degree in canon law. He had returned to Chicago and an appointment on the marriage court. That experience had been his personal undoing in one sense and the making of him in a more profound sense. Dispirited by those who came petitioning to have their marriages dissolved, annulled, declared never really to have happened, and at a time when annulments were rare to the point of nonexistent, save after years of waiting, he had sought refuge in alcohol. At the time he had been spoken of as a future bishop, first an auxiliary in Chicago, then on to a diocese of his own, and then—excelsior, who knew how high he would rise? He had learned how low he could fall.

Looked back upon, the time he had spent in a Wisconsin haven for priests with a drinking problem had been a second

seminary for him. When he emerged, he sensed the attitude
of former friends. The offer of St. Hilary's in Fox River had
been made almost with averted eyes. Here was the ultima
Thule of the Archdiocese of Chicago, at its far western bor-
der, being offered to the former white hope of the Chicago
clergy. It was a parish that had been enclosed by roaring interstates, abandoned by most of its parishioners, all but mori-
bund—and it was there that he had flourished. Signs of life
appeared, signs appropriate to the parish. The school was no
longer necessary to accommodate the children of the parish;
there weren't enough children there. So he had asked Edna
Hospers to turn it into a meeting place for the many seniors
in the parish. It had been an unequivocal success, drawing
old people from beyond the borders of St. Hilary's. The population of the parish stabilized; flight to the more congenial
suburbs slowed, then stopped. Young couples began to buy
the large houses at bargain rates. It was possible to imagine
a new day for St. Hilary's.

It had certainly meant a new day for Roger Dowling. Freed
from any remnant of clerical ambition, able to see where he
was as where he was, the place where his soul would be saved
by giving his all to what most of his fellow priests would have
regarded as a Mickey Mouse assignment, that was the grace
he had been given. So, on this day of recollection at the seminary where he had studied, his heart was full of thanksgiving. That failure should be its own kind of success seemed
the essential message of Christianity.

In midafternoon, he lay on his bed for forty winks. It was
a day to refresh the body as well as the soul. But he could not
sleep. He lay on his back, looking at the ceiling, aware of the
stir of trees at the window and the song of birds everywhere,
full of a euphoria that almost frightened him. We have here no
lasting city, he reminded himself, not even Fox River, Illinois.

At the time it seemed merely a pious reminder. When he got home to his rectory the thought seemed almost prophetic.

THE FIRST SURPRISE WAS THE sight of Amos Cadbury's automobile in the driveway. When he pulled in beside it and looked toward the school, there seemed to be a cluster of old people watching him.

Then the front door opened and Marie Murkin, with a stricken expression, came running toward him. "Have you heard?"

"Good Lord, what is it?"

"Mr. Cadbury will tell you." Marie burst into tears. Father Dowling took her arm and led her into the house, full of foreboding.

Amos Cadbury came out of the study, apologizing for invading the inner sanctum. "Marie insisted, Father Dowling. Besides, I wanted to smoke a cigar."

Amos's manner calmed Marie. Edna Hospers looked out of the kitchen, her hand to her mouth, eyes wide with anxiety.

Father Dowling went into the study, and Amos followed, shutting the door behind him.

"So what is it, Amos?"

For answer, Amos handed that morning's *Chicago Tribune* to Father Dowling, indicating what he should read.

The story was by the religious editor of the paper and began with a sweeping account of the altering character of the archdiocese, changes that were characteristic of other large cities as well but especially visible in Chicago, the largest diocese in the country, some said in the world. The writer described with some unction driving from the Loop to O'Hare and seeing on either side of the interstate massive churches, only a few blocks apart. A dozen at least, maybe more. He had not counted them. Those churches, larger than most cathedrals, were monuments to the ethnic groups that had built them, clustering around their parish plant, a little world of their own in the wider world of Chicago. A few blocks away, a similar little world, and another and another. The question the archdiocese faced was what to do with these huge churches and parish plants now that their parishioners had deserted them for the suburbs. Their schools were now open to any children in the neighborhood but could scarcely be called parochial schools anymore. They represented a significant contribution to the education of the young of the city, but who was to bear the financial burden?

The conclusion to this overture seemed obvious. It was unrealistic to imagine that such parishes would know a rebirth. The expense of keeping them up was now borne more by the archdiocese than those living within the parish confines. The financial burden was becoming too much. There would have to be a closing of some churches, a consolidation of parishes, a more justifiable use of resources. Then came a list of churches to be closed, based on "authoritative sources."

Father Dowling looked at the name of his parish on the list.

He realized that Amos was waiting for his reaction. He sat forward and rummaged around on his desk. The day's mail was still bundled together and enclosed in a rubber band. He slipped it off and shuffled through the letters. There was no letter from the archdiocese.

"It's all speculation, Amos. I wonder who his 'authoritative sources' are."

Amos was not a man given to expressing surprise—he had seen too much over a long life to find anything truly novel—but Father Dowling had surprised him. "You don't think it's true?"

"Amos, the only authoritative sources I know would communicate with me directly and give their names. There's no point in getting upset by a newspaper story."

That was the line he took, and he stuck with it. Amos, Marie, Edna, and Phil Keegan, when he arrived in time to be asked to supper, fell in with him, or pretended to, but he sensed that they thought he was deluding himself. Perhaps he was. Thank God he had a day of recollection behind him when he received the news. In the end, it proved to be an almost convivial occasion. When they rose from the table and Edna and Marie went into the kitchen, the men repaired to Father Dowling's study. Cigars were lit, and the pastor's pipe. Phil Keegan mentioned that the Cubs were on, but that was that. Getting interested in a ball game would have required more pretense than Father Dowling was capable of.

After Edna left to go back to her family, Marie brought Phil a beer and handed Amos a glass of Courvoisier. The pastor was content with coffee. The great topic was forgotten when Phil brought them up-to-date on current crimes and murders, and both the lawyer and the priest showed professional interest. Of course, it was Phil's phlegmatic account of a woman's body that had been found hanging in a garage that particularly caught their attention.

"What a horrible thing," Amos said.

"Horvath is on the case," Phil said. "He and Agnes Lamb."

When his guests rose to go, Father Dowling went with them to the door.

"I DON'T THINK THE DEVERES will take the threat to the parish as philosophically as you do," Amos said.

"I thought I was taking it theologically."

Amos smiled a wintry smile and followed Phil down the front walk.

Father Dowling watched them drive away. Marie had gone up to her apartment, reached by a staircase in the back of the house. Father Dowling returned to the study, sat at his desk, and looked bleakly about. *"Nunc dimittis servum tuum, Domine,"* he murmured. For the first time he confronted the real possibility that his days as pastor of St. Hilary's could be coming to an end.

FIVE

HUGH DEVERE IN THE LAST few days before returning to school felt pulled in opposite directions. On the one hand there was the undeniable attraction of immersion in his family, his siblings, his parents, his grandmother Jane, the matriarch of the family, as old as the hills, as she seemed to her grandson, and yet with an almost mystical connection with a past he had never known, the past of the Deveres. It was impossible to sit with her and not feel the contagion of that family pride. On the other hand, of course, was the eagerness to return to South Bend, complete his studies, and become established as an architect. He was, there was no other way to put it, a disciple of Duncan Stroik and Thomas Gordon Smith, two men who while still very much professors were supervising the building of their architectural dreams across the country. Ecclesiastical architecture. Smith had designed the magnificent church of the newly founded Clear Creek monastery outside Tulsa; Stroik was responsible for the church rising on the campus of Hugh's alma mater in Santa Paula, California. A young man needs models, and these two men were his models, a fact he manifested by refusing to show them any servile deference. There was also, though, the undeniable fact that he was a Devere.

Jane Devere dwelt in matriarchal splendor on the third floor of the Devere home, by and large out of sight but never out of mind. In the great house below, there was only Mrs. O'Grady, the housekeeper, cook, and whatever, and the intermittent presence of Mrs. Bernard Ward, Jane's widowed daughter. Jane's son, James, after his wife died, had come back to the old house, too, bringing two of his children with him. The wonderful old woman was the genius loci, and, with more docility than Susan, his sister, Hugh visited her often and sat quite literally at her feet in her sitting room, where she was surrounded by photographs and other artifacts that recalled her long life.

After his round of golf, he went home and climbed to the third floor.

"They're going to tear down St. Hilary's," Hugh said.

"Nonsense."

"It was in the *Tribune* this morning."

"The *Tribune!*"

"Why did Mom and Dad move out of the parish?"

"For that they will have to answer to God. Of course, your father brought you back."

Grandma Jane insisted on being driven to St. Hilary's each Sunday, and during the summer vacation that happy task had fallen to Hugh. A month ago, after the church had emptied, they had stayed on, and his grandmother had gone slowly up and down the aisle drawing his attention to the stained glass windows.

"I trust you do not find them ordinary, Hugh."

"Who did them?"

"Good heavens, you don't know?"

"Tell me."

She sank into a pew, resting her hands on her cane, and looked from him to the windows. "Does the name Menotti mean anything to you?"

"I wish it did."

The old woman sighed. "Hugh, it is the bane of age to live into a time that one was not perhaps meant to see. Oh, how the mighty have fallen. Here you are, at the dawn of life, intent on doing great and significant things. It would not occur to you that, if you were fortunate enough to do those things, time would pass and eventually no one would know or care that you had lived. Let alone that you were the creator of a beauty that would have become commonplace to them, because of familiarity. These windows, Hugh, are works of genius."

She rose once more, took his arm, and then began to discourse on the theme of the windows, those on the left commemorating great figures of the Old Testament, those on the right events of the New Testament. Those along the left featured prophetic scenes from the Old Covenant.

"Do you see the thematic unity of those on the right?"

All he had to do was wait. The seven windows depicted the Seven Dolors of the Blessed Virgin. The prophecy of Simeon, the flight into Egypt, the loss of the child Jesus in the temple at twelve, and then, as if fast-forwarding, Mary encountering her son as he carried his cross to Golgotha, Mary at the foot of the cross (*Stabat Mater dolo-rosa,* his grandmother fairly crooned the hymn), Jesus taken down from the cross—the Pietà—and finally the burial of Jesus. Grandma Jane's eyes were moist as she recalled those great moments in Mary's life that linked her indissolubly to her son.

Before they left the church, Hugh's grandmother led him to a small octagonal chapel entered from the apse. "We had this added after August died."

Inset in the floor was a pale marble slab on which was engraved AUGUST DEVERE.

"Is he buried here?"

She nodded. "So is your grandfather."

A family mausoleum as part of the parish church. Did Jane plan to be buried here herself?

NOW HE WAS IN HER SITTING room telling her of the newspaper story about the closing of St. Hilary's. He might have been telling her that key articles of the Creed were being discarded. He tried to redirect the conversation he had started. "Tell me about Menotti."

The old woman stirred in her chair. "What do you mean?"

"The man who designed the stained glass windows."

"They were a special gift to the church from the Devere family."

"Grandfather?"

An impatient noise. "His father. August Devere."

"My great-grandfather?"

"Of course."

"So you must remember the building of the church?"

"Your great-grandfather, as I suppose we must call him, visited the building site every day. I accompanied him. The architect was not without merit, but you could find the twin of that church in half the towns of Illinois and Wisconsin. No, it was the windows that made it special."

"I suppose Menotti was Italian."

She dipped her head and looked at him over her glasses.

"Did he live in Italy?"

"His studio was in Peoria."

"Peoria!"

"And what is wrong with Peoria?"

"I've never been there."

"You should go."

"When did Menotti die?"

"Die? Did I say he died? He is scarcely older than I am."

Hugh observed a moment of silence. How old would Jane Devere have been when St. Hilary's was built? She must have been a young wife then, newly swept into the Devere family and acquiring an unrivaled pride in it.

"If I ever go to Peoria, I will look him up."

The old woman looked away, as if searching among the bric-a-brac in the room for some other subject. Hugh rose, leaned over his ancient relative, and pressed his lips to her cheek. When he straightened, he was surprised to see that her eyes were filled with tears. He bent to kiss her again, but she waved him away.

"That's enough of that, young man."

SIX

AFTER SPENDING HALF AN HOUR urging Father Dowling to make an appointment with Bishop Wilenski, Marie Murkin went out the kitchen door and headed for the church. It was her intention to spend at least an hour on her knees before the Blessed Sacrament, praying to the Lord to put some fight into the pastor.

"We'll see, Marie" had been his final word, and she knew what that was worth.

Her pace slowed as she neared the side door of the church. She pondered her decision. She didn't want to be a show-off. When she reached the walk that led away to the school, she took it. God would understand. She would drop in on him after she had visited Edna Hospers. After all, if God had intended her to be a contemplative nun he would have issued her a veil. At the moment, she just had to talk things over with someone who would talk back.

On one of the benches beside the walk a figure sat. Willie, the alleged maintenance man, who occupied an apartment in the basement of the school. He gave Marie a tragic look.

Marie stopped. To say that she did not approve of Willie would have been an understatement. He was the most recent in a line of parolees for whom Father Dowling had found employment in the parish, making St. Hilary's a kind of halfway house between Joliet and the wider world, not that he had ever got much work out of any of them. On this score, Willie was a clear-cut winner. According to Edna, for an hour or so each day he pushed a broom around the area of the school used by the seniors, and that was about it. Willie had brought the broom with him to the bench.

"I knew it couldn't last," he said.

"You need a new broom?"

Willie shook his head sadly. "Don't try to spare me."

"I never have."

"Is it true we'll soon be out of a job?"

That her plight could be compared with Willie's filled Marie with anger. She was about to say something cutting, something cruel, but suddenly she was drained of rancor and collapsed on the bench beside Willie. "Father Dowling is seeing the bishop now."

"Will it matter?"

"How can we know? You might say a prayer about it."

"I already have," Willie said, moving the brush of his broom from one shoe to the other. The handle he gripped firmly in his left hand.

"Good." Marie found herself doubting Willie. Good Lord, what a trial the man was. A minute in his presence and she felt like a pharisee. She remembered the story of the rich man entering the temple to thank God that he was not like the rest of men; the contrast was with the poor wretch who barely entered and prayed, "Have mercy on me, a sinner." The parallel was too close for Marie's comfort. "Your prayers will go right to God's ear."

"He doesn't need ears," Willie said.

Once more anger flared up in Marie. Was this parolee presuming to instruct her in such matters? "I had no idea you were a theologian."

"I'm not, but I studied a bit in Joliet. With the chaplain."

"Father Blatz?"

"This guy was a Baptist. He knew the Bible backward and forward."

"I thought you were a Catholic."

"That's what it says in my records."

"Have you forsaken the faith?"

"You mean quit?"

Marie inhaled. "Did you become a Baptist?"

"What was the point? You don't have to be a Baptist to read the Bible."

Marie gave up. She stood. Impulsively, she took Willie's broom and began to shake it vigorously. Little puffs of dust and lint flew away in the slight breeze. She tightened the handle before giving it back, twisting it into the brush.

Willie looked on with admiration. "You must have worked as a janitor once."

"My aspirations never rose that high."

INSIDE THE SCHOOL, THE FORMER gym, which was the chief meeting place for the seniors, was strangely quiet. No one played shuffleboard; no cards had been dealt for bridge; the television set was a gray eye in the corner. There were groups clustered about, whispering as if they were at a wake. At the sight of Marie, they surged toward her.

"What's the news, Mrs. Murkin?"

Marie just waved in what was intended to be a reassuring way and continued to the staircase. Edna's office was on the second floor, what had once been the office of the school's principal, when it had been a school.

Edna was seated at her desk doing nothing. She stared at Marie when the housekeeper entered. "Is he going to talk to the bishop?"

"He hasn't decided yet." She said this matter-of-factly. It was one thing for Marie Murkin to be critical of the pastor, but it wouldn't do to have Edna follow suit.

"Marie, is there any hope?"

"There is always hope." Suddenly Marie felt like a pillar

of strength, the one person in the parish who kept her wits about her and her chin high. "Make some tea, Edna."

Doing something is always better than doing nothing. Marie was awash in tea, but it was the principle of the thing. Edna was soon on her feet and a bustle of activity. Marie felt that she had already done good.

Once the water was on, she suggested that she and Edna go downstairs and perk up the old people. "They're just moping around, Edna."

"Do you blame them?"

"Of course I blame them. They're old enough to know that life has its ups and downs. Anyway, we aren't down yet, not by a long shot."

When they came into the gym, they were soon surrounded, and Marie made a little speech, a pep talk. What did they think Father Dowling would feel if he saw them like this? Was he brooding in his study, waiting for the other shoe to fall? You bet he wasn't. He was going to go downtown and confront the powers that be. They were in good hands with Father Dowling. Everything was going to be all right.

"So let's get with it! Let's..." Marie paused and then in a high voice cried, "Let's have fun!"

From the doorway where he had been listening, Willie began a cheer, pounding the floor with the handle of his broom. The cheer was taken up, and Marie and Edna were lifted by it as they went back upstairs for their tea.

"How long have you been in the parish, Marie?"

Marie pondered the question and the reason for its being asked. In the circumstances, it seemed understandable, but her old rivalry with Edna made Marie wary. She didn't like to think how much older than Edna she was. Her fiction was that they were contemporaries, matched opponents in age at least. Was Edna suggesting that Marie's career had been so long that having it stopped would mean less anguish?

"It seems like yesterday I came here," Marie said.

"I know. I feel the same way. I have gotten so used to it. It just never occurred to me that it could end."

"Now, now, cheer up."

"You were wonderful downstairs, Marie."

Marie harrumphed. "Well, Willie seemed to like it."

ON THE WAY BACK TO THE rectory, she realized that she had not set her phone so that it would ring at the school; of course, when she left the house her destination had been the church. She went along the walk to where it intersected the walk coming from the rectory to the church. She stopped and looked at the side door of the church. Go inside and pray? That seemed self-indulgent, a retreat from battle. You couldn't expect God to do things you could do yourself. Besides, she had to check her phone to see who might have called in her absence. There had been several calls from Jane Devere.

SEVEN

THE GROUSING IN THE SENIOR center about the threatened closing of St. Hilary's took some days to find an appropriate form of expression. Marie Murkin's pep talk had equivocal results.

"Have fun?"

"Dancing on the *Titanic*."

Massimo Bartelli kept his peace, appraising the bewildered men and women around him. They were old, that was clear, creaky of limb, hunched, weighed down by a lifetime of ups and downs. Massimo, too, was old, but in this group he felt young. It was when old Reynolds announced that he was not coming back to the center, it was as good as closed already, that Massimo stepped forward.

"Nonsense! We must organize." Long ago, he had led his fellow workers at Fox River Punch and Drill into the union and reigned for years as shop steward before rising into the upper ranks of the union, never more to operate a punch press. Silence fell, and he was surrounded. He smiled confidently into their anxious faces. "In union there is strength."

"Bah," said Reynolds.

Massimo ignored him and outlined his plan. The first thing was to elect a leader. He looked around, waiting.

"It's your idea," Reynolds said.

"Is that a nomination?"

It was. Massimo was elected by acclamation and turned immediately to the question of what the group would be called.

"SOS," Reynolds said, chuckling. This was greeted by baffled expressions. "Save Our Seniors?"

Massimo suggested a broader designation. "It is the parish, not just ourselves."

"What's in a name?"

Eventually, Massimo's suggestion was accepted. Save St. Hilary's.

"Ssssh," said the disgusted Reynolds, but he was ignored.

Marge Wilpert was elected vice-chairman and O'Rourke, once a CPA, treasurer. Massimo withdrew to a corner with his fellow officers.

"First we must let Father Dowling know," Marge said.

O'Rourke agreed.

To Massimo, Father Dowling represented management. "Father Dowling has enough things on his mind. We want to surprise him with the support we can give him."

"What exactly will we do?" Marge asked.

"Publicity," Massimo said. "A public outcry."

"The parish bulletin?"

Massimo smiled. "I have a better idea."

The *Fox River Tribune* was a force for reaction, but who is more full of grievances than a reporter? Massimo had contacts in the courthouse, and he knew Tuttle, whose father had joined the union after retiring from the post office and going to work for a private delivery service, needing added income to finance his son's long march through law school. The union had covered the funeral expenses of Tuttle Sr., and the son had wept with gratitude. Massimo told his fellow officers he would seek legal advice, a soothing phrase, as he had known it would be. No need to mention Tuttle's name.

After ten minutes of waiting for the elevator that never came, Massimo mounted the four flights to the lawyer's office. Tuttle's secretary said that the lawyer was expected momentarily and asked his business.

"What sort of benefits does he give you, Hazel?" Her nameplate was on her desk.

"Benefits?"

"Medical care, retirement…"

Hers was an unattractive laugh, exhibiting a small fortune in dental work. "I'm lucky to get my salary."

Massimo shook his head. On another occasion he might have evangelized Hazel on the power of organization. For the moment, he considered the implications of her remark. If Tuttle were in need of business, he might balk at the proposal that he represent Ssssh (Reynolds's revenge: His hissing acronym was hard to forget once he had made it) pro bono. Such doubts fled when the lawyer arrived, looked at Massimo for a moment, and then swept him into his arms. He remembered his father's funeral.

"Come in, come in," he cried, opening the door of the inner office. "No calls, Hazel." Tuttle's office looked like a landfill, papers, plastic cups, Styrofoam boxes, trial records, books everywhere. Tuttle made a ringer with his tweed hat on the top of the coat stand and gestured Massimo to a chair. "Just put that stuff on the floor." Before sitting down himself, Tuttle retrieved his Irish tweed hat and put it on.

"I assume you have heard of the closing of St. Hilary's, Mr. Tuttle."

"An outrage!"

"I have been deputized by those who frequent the senior center at the parish to do something to prevent that outrage."

"Good."

"I wish we could afford your professional advice."

Tuttle leaned forward, making room for his elbows on the desktop. "Mr. Bartelli, I am eternally in your debt. How could I ever forget your support when…" The lawyer's eyes filled with tears and he looked away.

Massimo noticed the framed photograph of Tuttle Sr., positioned above the law degree. "In union there is strength."

Tuttle nodded, wiping his eyes. "What are your plans?"

Massimo approached the point of his visit gradually. Of course the news of the threatened closing had appeared.

"In the *Chicago Tribune*," Tuttle said, frowning.

"You are close to reporters on the Fox River paper, I believe."

A hand lifted to tip back the tweed hat. Tuttle's sparkling eyes indicated that he had made the logical link. Within minutes, they were busy composing the statement Tuttle promised to get prominently into the local paper.

"What are their ad rates?"

Tuttle smiled. "I plan an end run. Does the name Tetzel mean anything to you?"

Massimo sat back. "I am sure it is going to."

Hazel tapped up the statement on her computer and printed a copy for Massimo. Tuttle folded his copy twice and put it into his tweed hat.

"Mr. Bartelli asked about my medical benefits."

"Thank God for them, Hazel. Medicare is a marvelous system."

As they went down the four flights of stairs, Massimo asked about the elevator.

"It hasn't worked for years."

"Have you complained?"

"It's useless."

"We could picket the building. Close it down."

"No! Good Lord, no. Where could I match the rent I pay here?"

EIGHT

MENTEUR'S RESIDUAL METHODISM sufficed to leave him unmoved by the prospect of Catholic churches folding. On the other hand, local loyalty suggested that the paper should object to St. Hilary's being threatened. Father Dowling was one of the few priests Menteur had ever felt comfortable with, but Bartelli seemed to be asking that he run an ad protesting the closing gratis.

"Talk to the business office," he suggested, frowning at Tuttle, who had brought Bartelli to him.

"Mr. Bartelli is active in local unions," Tuttle said, addressing the remark to the ceiling.

Menteur began to chew his gum furiously. Several years before, his soul had been seared by a strike at the paper. Circulation was dropping, advertising revenue was at an all-time low, editorial was under constant pressure from the business side, and the printers wanted a hefty raise and lots of new perks. Menteur, like an idiot, had pleaded with them, calling the paper a family whose members had to stick together in trying times. His remarks were considered patronizing as well as a ruse to keep a bigger slice of the pie in editorial. They didn't believe him when he told them what the entry-level salary for reporters was.

The strike strung on. They were down to a single sheet, a damned newsletter, before management caved and the presses began to hum again. Menteur's father had been a plumber, he considered himself a man of the people, but after that strike he seriously doubted the intelligence of the common man. Now

Bartelli was looking at Menteur across the editorial desk as if it were a bargaining table.

"Of course, we could feed what you want to say into a news story," Menteur said.

"Good idea," Tuttle cried. Menteur would have liked to pull that tweed hat down over his ears.

Bartelli slid a sheet across the desk to Menteur, then began to pat his shirt pocket. "Okay to smoke in here?"

"No!"

"You can't smoke in your own office? I thought this was a newspaper."

Menteur could have wept. Bartelli's remark called up the wonderful days of yore when newspaper work had been done in clinging clouds of smoke. "It's a city law."

"How can they enforce it?"

"Spies. Informers."

Bartelli shook his head. "You should have picketed the courthouse."

"You can smoke in the courthouse."

"And not here?"

"It's not as bad as it sounds," Menteur said, chewing furiously. He rose. "Let's go outside for a smoke."

They went down in the elevator and huddled in a shadeless corner, exposed to a brisk breeze. Menteur lit Bartelli's cigarette for him, then his own, but the smoke was whipped away before he could inhale it. He turned with hunched shoulders to the wall and filled his lungs with soothing smoke.

Bartelli was shaking his head when Menteur turned back to him. "How can you enjoy a cigarette like this?" He tossed his into the street. "I'd rather quit."

Menteur had brought the sheet Bartelli had given him. He assured him he would get out the news of the formation of Save St. Hilary's. They actually shook hands, and the triumphant Tuttle led his client up the street.

Menteur tried without success to derive some satisfaction from his cigarette, then flung it down angrily and started, accelerating as he went, toward the courthouse. He spat out his mouthful of gum.

He rushed through the revolving doors and then across the black-and-white marble squares as if engaged in a game of hopscotch to the elevators. From the moment he had entered the building, he imagined that he could smell tobacco. When he got out of the elevator and headed for the pressroom he was shaking a cigarette free. He stopped in the doorway.

Tetzel sat at his computer, wreathed in smoke.

Rebecca Farmer, at the sound of footsteps, put something in the bottom drawer of her desk before turning. "Mr. Menteur!"

Tetzel swung in his chair and had to brake it before he turned 360 degrees.

Menteur busied himself lighting his cigarette. He took a chair and dragged blissfully on his Pall Mall. "You lucky bastards," he breathed. "Sorry," he said to Rebecca.

She made a dismissive wave with her nicotine-stained hand.

"You two know about the threat to St. Hilary's? Okay. A group has been formed to protest it." He gave Bartelli's sheet of paper to Rebecca. "Write it up. Wring the reader's heart. Appeal to local pride. More than religion is involved here." He might have been addressing the shade of his Methodist father.

Rebecca read the sheet, nodding.

"You came over here just to tell us this?" Tetzel said in a wondering tone.

"And to have a goddamn cigarette."

"Let's go over to the Jury Room," Tetzel suggested.

"Can you smoke there?"

Tetzel shook his head. Rebecca opened the bottom drawer

she had just closed and brought out a bottle of Johnny Walker Red and several glasses. She poured a generous amount and handed the glass to Menteur.

He took it with tears in his eyes. "Why did I ever want to be an editor?"

He had another bump and two more cigarettes while Rebecca went to work on a sob story about St. Hilary's.

"Is it just the seniors?" she asked.

"Call them concerned parishioners."

Rebecca turned back to her keyboard.

He had her first draft when he rose to go. He stood for a moment, looking around the smoke-wreathed room, shaking his head sadly. "You lucky bastards," he growled.

NINE

WITH JANE DEVERE, AMOS had adopted the attitude of Father Dowling toward the threatened closing of St. Hilary's. "There is no final list, Jane."

"A list was published with St. Hilary's on it."

"Apparently there are several lists."

"The Devere family has been in St. Hilary's parish for generations, Amos. I consider this an attack on us."

"We must see how things develop."

"Nonsense. We must make sure that things don't develop. Those old people at the parish center are showing the right kind of gumption. You're a lawyer, Amos. How can we stop them?"

"There are several possibilities," he said carefully, "but anything you do could backfire."

"Remember when those idiots in city hall announced they were going to tear down the old courthouse? The one building for blocks around that isn't an eyesore and they wanted to reduce it to rubble. An injunction stopped them."

Amos remembered. The old courthouse was an impressive building. It now served as a local museum instead of making way for the parking garage the mayor's son-in-law had planned to build there.

"The chancery office is not run by politicians, Jane."

"Ha. Anyone will bend to the will of the people."

The will of the people in this case meant the wishes of the Devere family. Young James, as Jane called her son, came to

Amos's office. Spurred by his mother, he had brought himself up-to-date on the threat to St. Hilary's.

"Is there a statute of limitations on gifts, Amos? Are donors to understand that after the passage of a few years what they have contributed to will be torn to the ground? Is that the message the cardinal wants to send?"

"Your mother is thinking of the Menotti windows."

"Of course she is, but there is more. My father and grandfather are buried in the side chapel of St. Hilary's. It would be like desecrating graves."

"I hadn't thought of that."

"My mother intends to be buried there. It is like a family vault." James paused. "I may end up there myself."

"I wonder if there was any special agreement about those graves."

"There must have been."

"I'll look into it."

"We're counting on you, Amos."

THE PIECE IN THE LOCAL PAPER about the group organized by the seniors in the parish center was maudlin. You would have thought that a homeless center was being shut down and its clients thrown into the street. Tuttle, it emerged, had been advising the group, and that in Amos's mind tainted their efforts. Perhaps there could be a dignified and legal way to dissuade the archdiocese from closing St. Hilary's.

When Father Dowling showed Amos the condition of the parish records, Amos blanched. Several old wooden file cabinets whose drawers required real muscle to open were in the basement of the rectory, where the Franciscans who had preceded Roger Dowling had moved them. There were dividers in the drawer they opened, but papers seemed to have been stuffed in any which way.

"Of course, the records of marriages and baptisms and funerals are in my study."

"Let's start there," Amos said, putting his shoulder to the drawer and getting it closed.

They did find the records of the funerals of August Devere and of Jane's husband, but there was no notation suggesting that their burial in the church was due to a formal agreement.

"I could send one of our paralegals out here to put order into those records."

"Why don't we ask Marie about it?"

The housekeeper was wearing an apron when she came into the study. At the sight of Amos Cadbury she tried to take it off without calling attention to what she was doing. She ran a hand over her hair. Father Dowling feared that she might simper.

The question she was asked brought an angry flush to Marie's cheeks. "Jane Devere's father-in-law! How long do you think I've been in this parish, Father Dowling?"

Amos, ever diplomatic, managed to calm her. "Marie, surely you don't think anyone would imagine that you were here when…" He laughed a dismissive laugh.

"Apparently someone does," Marie said, refusing to look at the pastor.

"We wondered if you had ever heard any reference to the graves in the side chapel of the church."

Marie threw up her hands. "Heard anything! On their anniversaries, Father Placidus pulled out all the stops. A solemn high requiem Mass, the old kind, black vestments, yellow candles, the Dease Erie."

It took a moment before Amos realized that Marie was referring to the lugubrious hymn, the Dies Irae, that had once been sung at funerals, with all the consolation of the first two canticas of the Divine Comedy. Nowadays, of course, the soul of the deceased was assumed to have winged its way to heaven before the funeral Mass.

Amos promised to send someone from the office to organize the parish records while looking for any agreement between the Deveres and St. Hilary's about those graves in the side chapel. "I'll also find out what public notice may have been given that they would be buried here."

LATER, AFTER DINNER, lounging in Father Dowling's study, Amos was reluctant to pursue the subject that had brought him here. It was clear that the pastor of St. Hilary's was of two minds about fighting the chancery office. No one knew more than Amos how much the parish meant to Father Dowling, but of course he understood as well that a priest would not want to quarrel, or seem to quarrel, with his religious superior.

They talked of other things, and when Amos rose to go, Father Dowling accompanied him to the front door.

Amos took the priest's hand. "None of this need concern you, Father. Any more than it already does, of course."

"*Ubi vult spirat,*" Father Dowling murmured.

Amos, no mean classicist, smiled. The Spirit blows where it wills. Did Father Dowling mean that it would blow down St. Hilary's?

TEN

IF A BOAT IS SAILING eastward at ten miles per hour and on its deck a passenger dashes westward at the same rate of speed, has the passenger moved at all? Father Dowling smiled, remembering the half-serious discussions of such puzzles at the seminary.

"The earth, too, is rotating westward, Father Dowling." Amos Cadbury drew on his cigar, his expression mischievous. "The whole solar system involves constant harmonious but opposed movements."

"Do law students raise such issues, too?"

"Oh, far worse. Is a ship that docks at Southampton, having been rebuilt during the crossing, the same ship that left Hoboken?"

"What is the answer?"

"One can defend either the affirmative or negative equally well." Reasoning, the glory of the human race, lends itself to trivial uses, and language is abused with puns. He said this aloud.

"Crossword puzzles?" Amos asked.

"Now, now."

Sometimes Father Dowling regretted having told Amos of his addiction to crossword puzzles, and of his pride in doing them with a ballpoint pen. Ah, the pleasure in completing a crossword, which is swiftly followed by a realization of its silliness. An end in itself?

It was the endless discussions of moral problems in the rec

room so long ago that he remembered now. His present unease was what he wanted to discuss with Amos. The lawyer
had come to tell him of the legal steps he was taking.

"I cannot oppose whatever decision the cardinal might
make, Amos."

"You can be a silent partner."

"If I say nothing, the chancery will assume that I am behind it."

"You are not responsible for their assumptions."

"Do you agree with the family, Amos?"

Amos displayed his palms. "I am merely their lawyer." He
brought his hands together. "Of course, I was married in that
church."

The Deveres, prompted by Jane, had decided to make a
public protest of the threat to St. Hilary's. For Father Dowling
to remain silent would seem to be collusion with the Deveres,
and yet to announce his opposition to them would be regarded
as a betrayal. Amos had come to the rectory to tell Father
Dowling of the injunction he would file seeking to prevent
the razing of St. Hilary's.

Marie was delighted. "Imagine thinking they can decide
something like that in an office downtown. Why don't they
come out here and see what they're talking about?"

"Perhaps Mr. Cadbury would like some tea, Marie."

"Of course he would like some tea," Marie snapped.

"I won't be having any."

"Hemlock?" Marie had surprised herself. She smiled wick-
edly and stormed off to her kitchen.

Amos explained to Father Dowling what he planned to do.

"Church and state, Amos."

"A noble principle," Amos replied. "When convenient."

The Deveres wished to base their complaint on the family
graves in the church. Apparently there were legal restrictions

on the relocation of cemeteries, and the injunction would be based on those rather than the Menotti windows.

"Susan Devere wants to have the church declared a historical landmark and thus untouchable."

"Historical?"

"A repository of Menotti's stained glass windows."

"Wouldn't that make more sense?"

"The family will pursue that, as well. Susan is going to take photographs of the windows to accompany the application."

"Won't that take time?"

"Of course. Hence the injunction."

"What a revolutionary you've become, Amos."

"Churches are too important to be left to the exclusive care of cardinals."

THE FOLLOWING DAY, in midmorning, Father Dowling went over to the church. As the door closed behind him, he stood for a moment, enjoying the silence. As he went into the sacristy, the silence gave way to creaks and snaps and the other sounds with which old buildings sigh away their days. He knelt at a prie-dieu that gave him a view of the sanctuary and of the tabernacle on the altar. As pastor, he was the creature of the cardinal, bound by the promise of obedience he had made at ordination. His own reaction to the famous list was one he tried to keep to himself. For years, the parish, this church, had seemed the permanent setting of his priestly life, but he had no permanent claim on it. Quite apart from the fate of the church, he could be reassigned by the cardinal at any time—but reassigned where? Would he be given a new parish at his age? Perhaps he would be asked to take a chaplaincy, at the hospital, in a convent, at a retirement home. He brought his hands to his face and prayed for the grace of obedience. Of course, he need not like what he was asked to do. When he had been assigned to St. Hilary's, he had had no premonition of how satisfying he would find the assignment. Over time, in his own mind, a seemingly unbreakable bond had formed between himself and St. Hilary's parish in Fox River, Illinois.

He removed his hands and stared at the tabernacle. How ridiculous it was to elevate his problem into such importance. Think of the difficulties others faced, sickness, family problems, worse. Think of priests in many countries of the world, as much at risk as the earliest Christians. He remembered a story of what an African bishop at one of the synods in Rome had said when Americans were fussing about altar girls, women's ordination, inclusive language in the literature: "In my diocese, the problem is to keep girl babies alive." The remark had put the problems of the so-called first world into an unwonted perspective. Something like that perspective had eased Father Dowling's mind before he rose and left the church.

On a bench along the path to the rectory a disconsolate Willie sat.

"Will you give me a letter of recommendation, Father?"

"If you ever need one." He sat beside the little maintenance man.

"I feel more at home here than I did in Joliet."

"Do you miss prison?"

"You know what I mean."

"I know what you mean."

"How long we got, Father?"

"Nothing is settled."

Willie just looked at him, the expression of a man for whom the possibility of bad news had always turned out to be true. "I can always rob a bank and go back."

"Is that what you did, rob a bank?"

"Well, I tried."

"Wait until I've talked to the bishop." He seemed to have made that decision while he prayed in the church.

Willie sat forward. "You going to do that? Give 'em hell, Father."

"You've been reading Dante."

"Who's he play for?"

Father Dowling's laughter lasted him almost to the rectory door.

ELEVEN

TED WILENSKI WAS THE youngest of the auxiliary bishops of the Archdiocese of Chicago who eased some of the burden from the shoulders of the cardinal. One of Wilenski's charges was the vexed issue of closing inner-city parishes, or combining old rivals into a new unity to cater to the altered population. It had been observed that no Polish parish had made it onto the list that appeared in the *Tribune* story. When he telephoned, Roger had been told to come along as soon as he liked, and now they were seated in Bishop Wilenski's office.

"My cousin was a classmate of yours, Father Dowling."

Roger Dowling tried to remember a Wilenski in his ordination class.

"George Salter."

"Salter!" The name had given rise to any number of what passed for witticisms in clerical circles. Roger smiled. "I haven't seen him in years."

"He's still in Rome."

George Salter had taken a degree from the Jesuit university in Rome and then stayed on, giving courses here and there about the city, ending finally at the University of Santa Croce. Naturally, his academic speciality was Scripture.

After an exchange of pleasantries, Wilenski sat back. "Of course, I know why you're here."

"That story in the *Tribune* has caused quite a stir in the parish."

"I'm sure of that."

"I wanted you to know that the protests were done without my knowledge."

"You realize that story was not official, Father."

"No 'authoritative sources'?"

"Oh, the list is genuine enough. So are three or four other lists that differ from it. The cardinal has made no final decisions."

"Am I safe?"

"I can't say that." He paused. "Do you really like being at St. Hilary's?"

"I do."

Wilenski seemed surprised. "One of my advisors suggested this might be a way to find you a more appropriate parish."

"Good Lord. My hope is to die as pastor of St. Hilary's. Or at least to stay there until I am put out to pasture."

"A pastor to pasture." Wilenski had a round head and short-clipped blond hair. Here in his office, wearing a suit, apart from the discreetly displayed chain of his pectoral cross, he might have been any other young priest. Of course, there was also the rather prominent ring on his right hand. The hand seemed to lift under Father Dowling's notice as if an episcopal blessing were in the offing. "Tell me about St. Hilary's." The ringed hand dropped to a folder on the desk.

"It has been my salvation."

"Ah."

Wilenski would likely know of Roger Dowling's long-ago disgrace. He did not allude to it, of course. Looking at the young bishop, Roger could not help thinking that there but for the grace of God go I. Dutifully, he began to describe the parish, its altering character as young people moved back in. The remnants of old families who had not moved away, families like the Deveres.

Wilenski perked up. "A wonderful family," he said. "Very

generous. Why are they so reluctant to be rewarded for the help they have been to the archdiocese?"

Roger knew that James Devere had politely turned down offers of knighthoods in the Order of St. Gregory and in the Order of the Holy Sepulchre. He was, however, a Knight of Malta.

"Their generosity built St. Hilary's church, Bishop."

"*Did* it? I don't think I've ever seen it."

"You should pay us a visit."

"Tell me about it."

"Architecturally, it is not much. It is the windows that are our pride. A special gift of the Deveres, designed by Menotti."

Wilenski pushed away the folder. "I didn't know that. *The* Menotti?"

"Angelo Menotti, yes."

"The man is a legend. When did he die?"

"As far as I know he is still alive."

"Good heavens." Wilenski sat forward. "Yours is not the only Chicago church that has windows of his. Has Carl Borloff been in touch with you?"

It seemed that Carl Borloff, an art historian, planned to publish a handsome volume containing reproductions of the local work of Menotti. He had not been in touch with Father Dowling.

"He will be, I'm sure. I can't believe that he does not know that you have Menotti windows. Father, I am glad we've had this visit. Your Menotti windows are news to me, as well as the involvement of the Devere family."

The remark signaled the end of the appointment. Before leaving, Roger bowed his head for a blessing, and Wilenski was momentarily embarrassed. When he had traced the sign of the cross over the pastor of St. Hilary's, he smiled. "Now it's your turn." He bowed his head for Father Dowling's blessing.

As they said their goodbyes, the bishop returned to the matter at hand. "I wish I could be more reassuring, Father. The decision is the cardinal's, of course."

"Would there be any point in talking to him?"

The suggestion alarmed Bishop Wilenski. "Probably not. He has so many things on his mind."

"Of course."

As HE DROVE BACK TO Fox River, Roger Dowling wondered if what he had regarded as a fool's errand had been after all inspired. Yet his satisfaction in the outcome of the visit to Bishop Wilenski prompted unease, as well. From the time of his fall, Roger had dropped all efforts to try to influence his own career. This had been made easier by the fact that his assignment was considered a place of exile, the remotest parish, unlikely to be the object of anyone else's covetous glances. But it was more than that. His earlier self had been—in retrospect this became clear to him—ambitious, calculating, weighing his deeds in terms of their probable effect on his future. A careerist, in short. That his ambition and prudent behavior had ended in collapse and the ignominy of the stay in Wisconsin seemed to contain a lesson vital to his life. Had he reverted to his earlier self today?

It was easy to persuade himself that his concern for St. Hilary's was not concern for himself. He had thought of the effects of closing the parish on Marie Murkin, on Edna Hospers, on those parishioners who had retained their roots in the parish, and, of course, on the old people who spent their days in the senior center that the parish school had become. Still, he could not deny thinking of his own tenure there, the quiet exultation of his daily Mass in the church, the comfort of the rectory, his books, Phil Keegan…

He had gone to Bishop Wilenski with the intention of arguing the case for St. Hilary's, of staving off the threat of

closure, and that was in effect to seek to guide the trajectory
of Roger Dowling. But a priest serves at the pleasure of his
bishop. Not a vow of obedience, of course, but close enough.
In recent years, priests had been vocal about their rights, and
among them was included the right to advise and consent to
clerical assignments. Once a priest simply went where his
bishop sent him. Now there was a board that advised the
bishop. Good grief. If he were indeed relieved of his post at
St. Hilary's, he would have to appear before that board. It
would be like appealing to an unemployment bureau. One
of the great attractions of St. Hilary's was that he had been
appointed there at the direct pleasure of his bishop.

THE NEXT DAY he went over to the senior center.

Marie was astounded when he asked that no further protests be made. "You accept it, Father?"

"Nothing is decided. Besides, this is not the way the decision will be made, in response to public complaints."

"Aren't you going to do anything?"

The old faces looked at him as if he were betraying them.

"I will stay in contact with the chancery. I will find out
what I can."

"Give 'em hell," Bartelli urged.

"That is not in my gift," he said, smiling.

TWELVE

CARL BORLOFF WORKED OUT of his apartment, one of whose two bedrooms served as the editorial office for *Sacred Art,* the little journal of limited circulation that had been meant to lift him out of obscurity into the rarefied upper atmosphere of Church circles, those circles that revolved around ecclesiastical art. Others had specialized, confining themselves to the liturgy and even subdividing into those monitoring English translations of liturgical texts and those insisting on Latin; or into music, and here, too, there were subspecializations, some promoting Gregorian chant and others directing attention to the horrors in the hymnbooks cluttering the pews of the country. Of course, there were those whose passion was church architecture and who were striving to wean the Church from the Pizza Hut constructions of the past half century to something resembling houses of worship. All these narrow paths Carl had eschewed. Many facets of Catholic art there might be, but they were facets, not the whole, and any reader of Chesterton must know the results of substituting the part for the whole. No, Carl Borloff was a generalist who welcomed into the pages of *Sacred Art* any and all of the above. He thought of *Sacred Art* as a clearing house, an arbiter, the repository of the full view.

Pity the poor founder of a magazine or journal. The format and layout of *Sacred Art* were, by common consent, marvelous. The paper was thick and shiny, the reproductions of art true, the photographs of churches and shrines works of art in themselves. Nevertheless, subscriptions had been inching toward two thousand for years and never reaching it. To publish is to make something known to the public, but first one must have the attention of the public. Who knew how many would eagerly subscribe to *Sacred Art* if they only knew of its existence? Carl could easily imagine ten thousand, twenty thousand, more, but to make those potential readers aware of the publication cost money—for advertisements, for mailings. Mailings! The postal rate had soared for such publications as his, and he did not dare to raise the annual subscription rate, already at fifty dollars—$49.99 plus postage and handling— making it too much of a luxury even for the few who knew of it. Thank God for those loyal 1,739 subscribers! Thank God, too, for the Deveres, above all Jane, their matriarch. He shuddered to think what his fate would be if left in the hands of the volatile Susan. Without that annual subsidy *Sacred Art* would have disappeared long ago. With it, the work went on. Of course, it was necessary for Carl to schmooze the Deveres, and he was a frequent presence at their home and a devotee in the upper chamber where Jane Devere dwelt.

There he could forget his humble origins, the seventh son of a family in Austin, Minnesota, where his father had worked at Hormel's and many of his siblings were employed at Marigold Dairy. It was only when Carl came home between semesters from Mankato State that he became aware of the heavy aromas that filled the town, from the packing plant and the counter olfactory assault from the ethanol plant on the other side of town. What as a child had been simply the air he breathed now offended his senses. He had majored in art history; vistas had opened before him. After graduation he fled to Chicago with the vague thought of continuing his education, and so in a sense he had. He became a pilgrim of the churches in Chicago; he spent days in many of them, making notes on the architecture, the appointments, the windows.

How easily he might have narrowed his interest to stained glass. Stained glass was a passion with Jane Devere.

"Angelo Menotti," she had cried when Carl spoke to her of a particular church. It was a cry he heard more than once. In fact, he made it a practice to elicit it at least once during each visit to Jane.

The beautiful reproductions of several Menotti windows in *Sacred Art* had been the seed of Jane's suggestion. "They should all be made available to those who do not have the time to make the rounds of all those churches."

Carl had smiled sadly. "That would be a most expensive undertaking."

"How much?"

"I would have to look into it."

He looked into it; he drew up a plan; he estimated costs; he generously provided for himself as editor of the proposed book. Jane looked it over, her glasses sliding down her thin nose to its tip. She nodded and looked at him. "Do it."

It had been a delicate matter to draw up terms of agreement. For this Jane had enlisted the help of her attorney, Amos Cadbury. The lawyer's manner made it difficult to tell whether he approved or disapproved of the proposed outlay of Devere Foundation money. Cadbury inserted a clause calling for half-yearly reports that Carl must make to Jane with a copy going to the lawyer. All this took months during which Carl tried not to hope, was too distracted to pray, and fell behind in preparing the next issue of *Sacred Art* for the printer. Jane Devere had assured him that the Menotti project would not affect her support for *Sacred Art*. Finally the papers were signed, and Carl celebrated with a solitary bottle of Marsala and found it in him at last to pray, sending up thanksgiving to heaven for his great good fortune.

The beauty of the agreement was that it was open-ended, no deadline. Jane had dismissed Amos Cadbury's suggestion.

"I want this done right. I do not want it rushed. This must be a work of art in its own right."

Over and above his semiannual written report, Carl kept Jane abreast of his progress on the Menotti book.

"Where did you learn of Angelo Menotti, Mrs. Devere?"

"When he designed and installed the windows for the parish church."

"What was your parish then?"

She frowned at him. "The same as now. St. Hilary's."

"Here in Fox River!"

His tone of incredulity had been a mistake. The remark seemed to suggest that nothing worthy of aesthetic attention could possibly be found in Fox River. Carl had been surprised that the Deveres still lived there, despite the triangulation of the area by eight-lane highways and interstates along which vehicles hurtled night and day. For all that, it was a little oasis, a memorial to a better day.

"The Menotti windows in St. Hilary's may be the peak of his achievement. I know he thought so."

"You knew him!"

"He was still a young man at the time, not much older than myself." She paused. "My father-in-law, August, underwrote the expense of the windows and became his champion. My enthusiasm came to rival his. I suppose we must have been a nuisance to Angelo, bothering him in his studio and then showing up every day while the windows were being installed."

"How wonderful to have known the man himself."

"You must visit him. He should know of your project."

"Visit him."

"Of course, he is an old man now, but he has remained in Peoria, surrounded by mementos of his long career."

Was the old woman confusing the present and the past? During the anxious months when the agreement for the Menotti volume was under way, Carl had sometimes suspected that Amos Cadbury doubted that the old woman was compos mentis enough to dole out the huge sum. Was she simply imagining that Angelo Menotti was still alive? When she told him that the artist was not much older than herself, it had given Carl a point of reference to guess the old man's age. Angelo Menotti, if he were still alive, would be ninety-two at least.

When the story appeared about the closing of several Chicago parishes, Carl hoped that Jane Devere did not read the *Tribune.* He decided to visit her and find out.

She knew. "This is outrageous. They must be stopped."

"There are three churches on the list that have Menotti windows."

"It must be a conspiracy!"

"Hell hath no fury like a bureaucrat, Mrs. Devere."

"I would buy St. Hilary's rather than let them tear it down."

Coming from anyone else, this might have seemed whimsy.

"In that awful event, you could turn it into a Menotti museum, provide refuge for his windows."

She threw up her hands. "Windows are meant to stay in the churches for which they were designed."

"I couldn't agree more."

"You haven't been to see Angelo Menotti?"

"Not yet. I intend to drive to Peoria later this week." He had formed the intention as they spoke.

She sighed. "If only I could go with you."

"A wonderful idea. Of course you should go."

The old eyes sparkled at the suggestion. She began to nod. "Perhaps I will."

PART TWO

ONE

AGNES LAMB WAS AN EXPERIENCED detective, but not the veteran Cy Horvath was, so it was understandable that she reacted as she did when they arrived at the scene of the crime, answering the call from the cruiser that had been first on the scene.

"Homicide?" Cy had asked.

"At least. It looks like a ritual killing."

Cy did not comment but collected Agnes and took off. All cops were influenced now by television, horror films, and maybe comic books—graphic novels, in the phrase—and were prone to importing the categories of fantasy into their work. Ritual killing!

Agnes was surprised when Cy asked her to drive.

"I forgot to renew my license."

"You're under arrest."

Cy liked Agnes. He hadn't at first. She had seemed pretty clearly a beneficiary of affirmative action, and police work was no place for ideologues. For one thing it was dull, a matter of routine—and disappointment. Most investigations ended up in a tie. Agnes had turned out to be a natural cop, though, one of the best.

It was not the sort of thing you would want to come upon right after having lunch. The body was in a garage, nude, hanging from the cross strut on which the door lift was mounted. There was a cloth laundry sack over the head, cinched tight around the throat. The body had looked as if it were being readied for quartering, or open heart surgery.

The car in the other stall was still running when the cruiser answered the 911 call.

Agnes walked into the garage with Cy, then wheeled and went right outside again. There was a woman cop in uniform out there, probably affected as Agnes was.

Riley stood with his hands on his hips, studying the body. "When the wind is southerly I can tell a hawk from a handsaw."

Cy ignored him, going to examine the body more closely. "Hamlet," Riley said. "You stare at it for a while and you notice it rotates."

"You call the coroner?"

As if in answer a vehicle came into the driveway and squealed to a stop. Dr. Pippen got out. She came toward Cy with her lab coat floating around her, her ponytail floating behind, her eyes on the body. "My God in heaven."

Riley said, "It looks like a ritual killing."

Pippen was giving orders to her crew. "Cut her down."

This was done, and the mutilated body laid in a gurney. Pippen arranged a blanket over it. For the first time, she inhaled.

"The motor of the car was still running," Riley said.

"You turn it off?"

Riley looked from her to Cy. "It seemed the right thing to do."

"Where's the ignition key?"

"In the car." Riley looked as if he wished he were somewhere else.

Cy said, "Call in as complete a report as you can right now. You can edit it when it's typed up."

Riley hurried out to his cruiser, happy to escape.

Pippen asked, "What do you make of it, Cy?"

"A ritual killing?"

"What's that?"

"Ask Riley."

THE GARAGE WAS ATTACHED to a house, entrance to which was gained through a door in the garage. It was closed. Cy eased it open and waited. He put his hand in, groped around, found the light switch, and flicked it. A laundry room. He told Agnes to check downtown to find out who lived at this address. Agnes got out her phone but followed Cy through the rest of the house. Thus began the slow, dull process of trying to figure out what had happened in the garage and who the woman was to whom it had happened.

The house was owned by Amy Gorman, a widow who worked as a legal secretary downtown. The body, it was established after many hours, was that of Madeline Schutz. Clothes and a purse found in the trash can in the garage established her identity tentatively. Cy and Agnes found Amy Gorman about to leave her office for the day. She looked at them quizzically when they asked if they could have a few words with her.

"You've been at the office all day?" Agnes asked.

"What an odd question."

"Is there any coffee here?" Cy asked.

Agnes said, "Something terrible has happened at your house."

"Terrible."

Agnes looked at Cy. "A body was found in your garage when a cruiser answered a 911 call."

Well, how would anyone react to a remark like that? The laugh seemed appropriate, but then she asked Cy who he was. He told her, showed her his ID. Agnes did the same.

"A dead body?"

Cy nodded.

"Come with me." Amy Gorman marched down a hall and into an office whose door was open. "Emil, I want you in on this."

Emil Sooner looked like one of the contestants in a television fat reduction show, before. He was in shirtsleeves and seemed to spill over the arms of his chair. His tie was loosened, and his shirt pocket was full of pens and pencils.

"Hello, Horvath. What's going on?"

Amy Gorman said, "A body has been found in my garage."

Emil might once have been capable of surprise, but years of legal practice had cured him of it. Cy knew him as a formidable defense attorney, more often in white-collar crimes, but from time to time in grislier cases.

"Does the body have a name?"

"Madeline Schutz." Cy looked at Amy Gorman when he said it, but there was no reaction.

"Why don't you all sit down," Emil suggested.

Emil listened while Cy told him what they knew. It was the car that piqued his curiosity. "Registration?"

"Amy Gordon," Agnes said in a flat voice.

If she could be believed, Amy Gorman had no idea who Madeline Schutz was or why she should have been found hanging in her garage with the motor of Amy's car still running. Her keys? They were hung on a hook in the laundry room. Amy had been downtown all day. She seldom drove to work.

After twenty minutes, Emil thanked them for coming here to tell all this to Amy. "I don't suppose you should stay in your house tonight, Amy."

"Good idea," Agnes said. "Good idea not to." She added, "Who knows when the lab people will be done."

"You could stay in a hotel," Emil said. "Or call a friend?" Amy thought about it. "I'll call Susan Devere."

TWO

MENTEUR SUMMONED TETZEL from the pressroom in the court-house to give him the assignment.

"That's religious news," he protested. "Give it to the religion editor."

"Then you haven't heard?"

"Heard what?"

"Bipple insists that the charges are false. He says it is retaliation."

"What charges?"

Bipple in the past had been an assistant Scout leader, and now many years later some of his troop, since grown old, were remembering odd activities around the campfire and in the tents. No journalist had been more zealous than Bipple in publicizing the misdeeds of some of the Catholic clergy. His series in the *Fox River Tribune* had been called "Suffer Little Children" and had been reprinted far and wide. Bipple had always been a pain in the ass, but he became insufferable with fame. Tetzel settled in a chair across the desk from Menteur and wanted to hear all about it. He shook his head and tried not to smile.

"I never put much stock in the rumors myself," Tetzel said with a virtuous look.

"About the Boy Scouts?"

"Menteur, I never made it to Tenderfoot. I couldn't tie the knots. No, I meant here." He lifted his brows significantly.

"Here!"

Tetzel cleared his throat. "The men's room. Should I write it up?"

"Over my dead body."

"I'll keep your name out of it."

Despite himself, Menteur laughed. "I almost hope the charges are true. We could use a new religion editor."

"Don't look at me."

"I'm thinking of you for obituaries."

This was the most congenial conversation Tetzel had had with Menteur in months. He was almost cheerful about being assigned to look into the closing of St. Hilary's. "What's going on?"

Menteur chewed his gum and glared at Tetzel. "If I already knew, why would I send you? Rebecca's story on the seniors drew a lot of letters."

Going down in the elevator, Tetzel was thankful that Menteur, sitting there in his smoke-free office, had gotten over his obsession with the fact that they could still light up in the courthouse pressroom. Or was that the motive behind this freak assignment? Was it a subtle revenge? Then Tetzel thought of Bipple and chuckled, somewhat to the alarm of his fellow passengers in the elevator. Before exiting, he took a cigarette from his pack and put it unlit in his mouth. If chuckling got attention, the sight of a man with a cigarette in his mouth filled observers with shock and horror, some perhaps with envy. Tetzel strolled through the revolving doors and outside to freedom. He lit up.

The funny thing about the assignment was that every time Tetzel had heard St. Hilary's mentioned it was as a booming operation. He might ask Rebecca about it, but he feared she would laugh at the thought of Tetzel being assigned to religious news. Besides, she was trying to find a way to write about what had shocked her when she had been traveling in Europe. Female attendants in men's rooms! Sitting there at little tables just inside, dispensing towels, a dish for tips before them.

"How'd you find out about it?" Tetzel asked.

She glared at him. "It is common knowledge."

"Maybe they have boys in the ladies' rooms."

Rebecca turned away in disgust and fumbled in her drawer, perhaps to find her Tetzel doll so she could stick a few pins in it. She huddled over, using her back as a shield against Tetzel, then after some moments settled back, kicking the drawer shut. She lifted a glass and tossed it off. Say what you would about Rebecca, at least she smoked and drank. Nonetheless, Tetzel decided that Tuttle would be a better source about St. Hilary's.

Tuttle's office was located midway between the *Tribune* building and the courthouse, so Tetzel thought he would just drop in.

Dropping in did not seem the appropriate way to describe the long climb up four flights of stairs. The temporarily out of use elevator hadn't moved in years. Only on the third landing did it occur to him that the prudent course would have been to call first. He took out his cell phone and glared at it, then dropped it back into his shirt pocket. There was only one floor to go, and he would continue to gamble.

The legend on the door read TUTTLE & TUTTLE, a touching tribute to the late Tuttle père, who had been a mail carrier. Tetzel tapped and pushed. The door opened to reveal in profile the formidable woman at her computer.

"Yes?" she said and only then turned. Her nose wrinkled.

"Tetzel of the *Tribune*. I'll start with you, if you don't mind."

"Start with me?" The frostiness fled and she put a hand to her hair. "What do you mean?"

Tetzel pulled a chair up to her desk and got out his notebook. "How do you spell your name?"

For a few minutes Hazel was putty in his hands. He could have asked whether she dyed her hair and gotten an answer. A door behind him opened.

"Tetzel, what are you doing here?"

"I'm going to do a series on the secretaries of our most successful men."

"Don't tell him a thing, Hazel. He gives new meaning to the phrase 'the freedom of the press.'"

"He said it was…" She was so furious she threw her mouse at Tetzel. He retreated into the inner office, followed by Tuttle.

"Thanks a lot, Tetzel. She's been almost human for days."

"Maybe we ought to get out of here."

"I was about to suggest the same thing."

SETTLED IN A BOOTH IN THE Jury Room, Tetzel got the story from Tuttle, who spoiled things a bit by adding it was all in the *Tribune*. Had Bipple been on this before his fall?

"The *Chicago Tribune*."

Tetzel scowled. What he thought of the *Chicago Tribune* was not fit to print, but then anyone there who had heard of him might have reciprocated the sentiment.

"How do you shut down a church, Tuttle?"

"It's not going to happen. I have it on impeccable authority."

"Father Dowling?"

"No. Willie, the maintenance man. If you want the real scoop, go to the man who pushes a broom."

"I think Hazel must fly on one."

"Only in the full moon, Tetzel. Only in the full moon."

THREE

FATHER DOWLING TOLD MARIE of his exchange with Bishop Wilenski, and the housekeeper let out a whoop of triumph. "People say that prayers aren't answered."

"Don't make too much of it, Marie. If anything saves us it will be the stained glass windows."

Marie plunked into a chair. "The stained glass windows." After a moment's silence, she began to nod. "Of course you're right. Our Lady is our refuge."

He let it go. He spent a day searching for any records of the building of the church, but the files were still such a mess that that didn't prove anything at all. He told Amos Cadbury this when they met at the University Club that night.

"Your best source on that would be Jane Devere."

They were having a preprandial drink in the library. At least Amos was, unless tomato juice counts as a drink in such a context. The venerable lawyer tasted his scotch and water with the concentration of a connoisseur.

"Tell me about the Deveres, Amos."

Amos affected surprise. "They're your parishioners."

"And your clients."

"Meaning that each of us might be restricted in what he would say."

"I meant just a sense of the family, the generations. Even Marie is vague on the matter."

Amos put his drink on the table beside him and settled in his chair. "August Devere," he began.

If August were considered the first generation, there were

four generations to be taken into account. Jane, wife of William, the late son of the late August, would be the sole representative of the second, but she had three children, with the oldest of whom, James, and his sister, she shared the house that August had built and in which she had lived most of her long life. Then there was the latest generation.

"Hugh?"

"And Susan," Amos said after a pause.

"Their father, James, has two siblings?"

"He had two. Only one, a sister, is still alive. His younger brother was a naval officer, a pilot, who was reported missing in action in the Middle East. His sister, Margaret, is Mrs. Bernard Ward."

"Mrs. Bernard Ward."

"Yes."

Margaret Ward was what is now called a paleoconservative, a staunch and vocal critic of the so-called neocons, her wit legendary, her aristocratic dismissal of dubious converts to the conservative cause enjoyed even by its victims for the unforgettable English in which it was expressed. "A liberal, like lilies that fester, is odious under any name." Her half-dozen books all continued to sell in respectable numbers; the latest, *Narcissus in Niger,* was still among the top ten on the bestseller lists, almost a year after its publication. She was a formidable foe, a loyal ally, and a ferocious Catholic to boot.

"What is a ferocious Catholic, Amos?"

"Margaret would say that she has modeled herself on Chesterton and Belloc. Others find her more akin to Patrick Buchanan."

"I don't know him."

"Never say that to Margaret."

"I doubt that I will have the opportunity."

"She speaks very highly of you."

"I scarcely know the woman."

"As I said before, the Deveres, some of them, are your parishioners."

"Yes. Margaret is one of them." One he seldom saw. Her work involved incessant travel.

Over their meal, Father Dowling briefed Amos on his conversation with Bishop Wilenski. The lawyer nodded through the narrative as if arriving at a judgment. "The Deveres are your armor and shield, Father Dowling."

"I got the impression that it was the Menotti windows in the church."

"That is very much the same thing."

Later, in a lounge, with Amos sipping brandy, Father Dowling got the lawyer's account of the commissioning of the stained glass windows by August Devere. "It was Jane who made him aware of the work of Angelo Menotti. The artist was not well-known then. Jane had made his acquaintance as a student at Rosary College."

"Surely he wasn't a fellow student."

Amos smiled. Of course, Rosary had been exclusively a women's college.

"He was artist in residence there. It would not be too much to say that Jane launched his career in stained glass windows."

"He did other things, as well?"

"Oh, yes. Paintings, some sculpture. Stained glass was important to his career, but not everything. He did a portrait of my wife."

"The bishop told me that someone intends to reproduce all of Menotti's stained glass in a book."

"Yes. Carl Borloff. I drew up the agreement between him and Jane Devere. Of course, he will also need permission from you and the other pastors in whose churches Menotti windows are found. It is one of the ironies of such things that the artist's permission is not required."

"Is he alive?"

"Indeed he is. In his presence I feel like a young man again, not that I could compete with him in agility. He is older than Jane by a year or two."

"Then you see him?"

Amos drew on his cigar, and his words seemed to ride exhaled smoke as if he were a Plains Indian sending signals. "He is a client of mine."

"For someone in alleged semiretirement, you seem to have a host of clients."

"But of an age, Father. Of an age. By and large, that is."

"I know Hugh, of course. He came by before setting off for South Bend. He wanted me to bless his car. One doesn't get many such requests nowadays."

"He is a good boy. A credit to his family and his school, and a scratch golfer. If he were less serious, he might earn a fortune playing golf."

"Did you ever tell him that?"

"He hardly needs anyone to tell him, but, yes, I did. His reply was, 'But where are the pars of yesteryear?'" Amos smiled at the memory. It was clear that he thought the world of Hugh Devere. "He will make an excellent architect. His mentors at Notre Dame, Stroik and Smith, are designing buildings across the country. Their speciality is church architecture."

"Hugh has a sister."

"Yes."

Father Dowling waited. Finally he said, "You seemed hesitant to mention Susan."

The smile faded. "That is a matter into which I cannot presently go, Father Dowling."

FOUR

AMOS DID SEND YOUNG Maurice Cassidy out to St. Hilary's, to bring order out of the chaos in those file cabinets in the basement of the rectory. His reception might have been chilly if it hadn't been for Marie Murkin's susceptibility to good-looking young men. Cassidy, all five feet nine of him, curly black hair, wide face, and bright blue eyes, made Marie nostalgic for an Ireland she had never seen.

"Watch your step," she warned as she led the young man down the basement stairs.

"I always watch my step, Mrs. Murkin."

To describe the housekeeper's laugh as a giggle would have been unkind. She turned and looked up at him. "Do you plan to become a lawyer?"

"I am a lawyer."

"No!" It was Marie who lost her footing then, not seeing that she had yet a step to go. Cassidy reached out and steadied her and then put his arm about her and they moved across the floor. In a moment, they were dancing. Marie could imagine what Father Dowling would think if he came upon this scene. She freed herself, reluctantly. "You don't look old enough to be a lawyer."

"Well, I'm young enough to be one."

"Where did you go to law school?"

"Notre Dame."

Marie frowned. "When are they going to get a decent coach?"

"Decency has nothing to do with it. They want a winning coach. Do you watch the games?"

"It's become a Lenten penance. These are the cabinets."
Cassidy got out his laptop and placed it on one of the cabinets. Next came the power cord, and Marie connected it for him. Maurice took off his suit jacket, and she took it.

"I'll hang this upstairs. Why would Amos Cadbury give you a job like this?"

"I'm his favorite."

"Would you like coffee?"

"Maybe later."

"Just call me."

He opened a drawer, stepped back, made a face, and then began to riffle through the contents of the drawer. Marie glided up the steps. When was the last time she had danced?

Father Dowling was in his study, his breviary open, lips moving as he read the liturgy of the hours. Marie stood in the doorway. After a moment, Father Dowling laid a ribbon aslant the page and closed the book.

"The boy Amos sent is starting on those file cabinets," Marie said.

"Boy?"

"Young man. Maurice Cassidy. He looks like an altar boy."

"If he was an altar boy he'd be middle-aged or more."

"You know what I mean."

"I wonder if he'll find anything about those Devere graves in the church."

"If they're there, he'll find them."

Half an hour later, Father Dowling came through the kitchen and went down into the basement. Marie stood at the open door, listening to the murmur of their voices. Then she went back to her work, doing a waltz step across the kitchen floor.

TWO DAYS LATER MARIE WAS in the basement, putting in a load of laundry, when Maurice cried, "Eureka!"

"I use a Hoover." She hurried over to see the papers he was flourishing. The day before, after he left, she had come downstairs and slid open a cabinet drawer. Everything in it was neat as a pin.

"This is what Mr. Cadbury hoped I would find. Is Father Dowling in?"

Marie went upstairs with him. She liked the way they got along, the pastor and the young lawyer.

Father Dowling took the papers Maurice handed him and leafed through them, nodding. "Good work."

"I'll take them to Mr. Cadbury."

"Maurice must want some refreshment, Marie."

Maurice was picking up the telephone as Marie left the study. When she came back with the soft drink, he looked at her. "Mr. Cadbury's coming out here." He seemed surprised that the senior member of his firm would make house calls.

"Marie and Amos are old friends," Father Dowling said.

"Oh, not old," Maurice said. Such a lovely boy.

THE DOCUMENT THAT MAURICE Cassidy had found in the second file cabinet, bottom drawer, was signed by August Devere and Father Rusher, the then pastor of St. Hilary's. Amos nodded as he read it. "Richard Sullivan drew this up," he murmured. "He was a legend in the local bar when I arrived in Fox River."

The agreement specified that members of the Devere family would have first option to be buried in the little chapel, as long as there was room for them. The graves were considered permanent. Amos frowned. "As long as the church shall stand."

The graves in the side chapel did not quite provide the impediment Amos had hoped for. Nonetheless, he considered the document important. He could argue that the phrase "as long as the church shall stand" had the force of "until the end of time."

"Here's an odd thing, Father. Angelo Menotti is also mentioned as having the right to be buried in the chapel."

FIVE

HAVING FILED AN INJUNCTION against the archdiocese to stop the closing of St. Hilary's and the tearing down of its church, Amos Cadbury busied himself with other Devere family business.

Of course, he had no compunction about keeping James Devere au courant on his mother's generosity. As a member of the board of the Devere Foundation, James would have learned it all eventually, but Jane had gone to the limit of the discretionary amount she could award in her capacity as director. Like most family foundations, the Devere Foundation was a cozy arrangement, all members of the board related by blood or marriage, but the Deveres had taken Amos's advice not to have any member of the family benefit financially from the foundation. Amos was responsible for the reports to the Illinois attorney general, an office that had been filled over the years by friends of his, and Amos had heard stories. Some family foundations were merely devices to sequester money from taxation and make it available by way of contingency funds to members of the family. Even in Illinois such sharp practice was frowned upon. Of course, there was no need for him to give lessons in ethics to the Deveres.

"If you okay it, Amos, I suppose it's all right," Jim Devere said with reluctance. "You know what Susan says about Borloff."

They were in the smoking room of the country club, for years a quaint anachronism but in these last days earning its name once more as newer members objected to the aroma of tobacco. Jim, like all Deveres except Jane, was an ardent cigarette smoker who delighted in producing series of smoke rings that he mentally counted as they formed before him. "Seven," he said with pride.

"What is your record, Jim?"

"Nine. I could have claimed ten, but the last one was scarcely visible."

"Perhaps it will become an Olympic event."

"In this day and age?"

Amos veered away from the topic. If he wanted an apocalyptic account of the times he could go to Jim's sister, Margaret, the darling of what her niece, Susan, called the moulting right wing. How tempted Amos was to talk to Jim about a recent session he had had with Susan.

She had returned after a period of reflection that Amos had urged on her when she told him she wanted to divest herself of all the money that had come her way from the family, her trust fund, her claim on any further inheritance. "The whole shebang, Mr. Cadbury." In political and social views, Susan was the polar opposite of Margaret Ward, but her expression as she spoke was identical to that of her ideological aunt.

"A trust fund is a rather difficult thing to undo, Susan. It represents the decision of others, not your own."

"Isn't it mine?"

He explained patiently her limited control over the base amount. Susan received the income, but the endowment was encumbered for many years in a number of ways.

"My grandmother is giving away money hand over fist," Susan said. "It's true about the fortune she has turned over to Carl Borloff, isn't it?"

Amos gently amended her language. The grant to the art historian came from the family foundation, and the amount involved could scarcely be called a fortune. Moreover, it had been given for a quite specific purpose, the progress of which would be carefully monitored.

"We didn't vote on it."

"Do you plan to attend board meetings, Susan?"

"I read the minutes."

Amos was on the board and knew that Susan had seldom come to any of its meetings, somewhat to his relief and, he supposed, that of her father and aunt, as well. From time to time, she sent in suggestions for grants, most of them involving indigent artists of uncertain future.

"Your grandmother, as director, can award grants of a certain amount at her discretion, independently of the board. Of course, the board must give its approval at the next meeting."

"What's her limit?"

"Two hundred thousand."

"That's what she did for Carl Borloff?"

"Do you know him?"

"He's one of the parasites of the arts world, a step below gallery owners and dealers. Do you realize how many talentless oddballs make a cushy living off the work of others while real artists starve?"

"Like oddball lawyers?"

The passion left Susan, and she was full of apologies. "You know I would never think such a thing of you, Uncle Amos."

He had been a little put off by her earlier "Mr. Cadbury," so this reversion to honorary membership in the family was welcome. "I should hope not."

She sprang to her feet and came around his desk and kissed his cheek. Amos felt a blush suffuse his face. "Now, now."

She went back to her chair. "Did you ever read about St. Francis?" she asked.

"I recently read an interesting account of his life by Julian Green."

"What a man! When I think of him just getting rid of ev-

erything, living in rags, trusting in God, talking to birds…"
She ran out of breath. Once more her eyes sparkled with
youthful enthusiasm.

"Are you thinking of becoming a Franciscan?"

"A nun?"

"I don't think you're eligible to become a brother."

"I wonder if St. Francis would join the Franciscans if he
were alive today."

"Our Lord might have similar misgivings about Christianity, Susan."

"I'm sure he would. Not that I'm much of a Catholic."

"None of us is all he should be."

She fell back in her chair, smiling. "What a diplomat you
are."

"Just a lawyer."

She sat forward. "Right. So you'll figure out a way for me
to get rid of that money, won't you?"

"Most of my clients are concerned to hang on to theirs."

"Well, I'm not one of them."

Amos steepled his fingers and brought their tips to his
mustached lips. "What you seek to do will seem like a re-
buke to your family."

Susan made a face. "They already think I'm a fruitcake."

"Have you talked this over with your grandmother?"

"I didn't dare."

"Why don't we make that the next step?"

"Meanwhile I get richer and richer."

"You can give away your income, Susan. There are no restrictions there."

Again she sat back. "You think I'm a phony, don't you,
Uncle Amos?"

"My dear, I don't even think you're a fruitcake."

What a lovely laugh she had. Amos felt in proximate danger of receiving another kiss.

"How is your own work going, Susan?"

She let her head nod from side to side. "I'm still little more than an illustrator."

"The house working out well?"

Amos had been involved in her buying the house in Barrington. It had seemed a more wholesome environment in which to pursue her art than others she might have chosen. Amos had gotten a fairly detailed account from Captain Keegan of the neighborhood in which local artists worked. Apparently not the most edifying area in Fox River.

"I have half a mind to share Bobby's studio."

"Bobby?"

"Roberta Newman. We gave her a Devere grant."

The studio was in the district Amos wanted to keep Susan out of. "I am glad you didn't do that."

"Guess who I've met, Uncle Amos."

Amos waited.

"A grandson of Angelo Menotti!"

SUSAN'S DESIRE TO RID HERSELF of Devere money had made
Amos uneasy for several reasons. Was it possible that Jane
had said something to her granddaughter about her origins?
God knows, she had been dishing out hints and enigmatic
remarks for years. The interest in Angelo Menotti had grown
into something like an obsession, and the seeming signif-
icance of Jane's imaginary legal problems involving heirs
had been impossible to ignore. Had it been a breach of confidence to tell Father Dowling about her speculations? She
had engaged in similar imaginary problems with the priest.
It was all Amos could do not to go over the matter with Father Dowling. Surely the priest must have made the little leap
that he had, the leap that Jane seemed to be inviting him to
make. One day he went off to Peoria to visit his whilom client.

"Whilom!" Angelo roared, a hand in the collar of each of
the dogs that flanked him. Their bared teeth belied Angelo's
assurance that they were tame as rabbits. "Why have we lost
so many lovely words?"

"Perhaps so we might discover them again."

The dogs, thank God, were left outside.

In the large living room, Amos refused a drink and stood
before a portrait. "I would have come all this way just to have
another look at this."

"I'll leave it to you in my will."

"Better leave it to someone likely to survive you." Amos
had already drawn up Angelo's will. Had there been a provi-
sion for this portrait?

"Young Jane," Angelo breathed boozily beside him.

"She was a beautiful young woman," Amos murmured.

"I painted her nude. The clothes came later."

"Jane?"

Angelo gave him a sly look. "Jane Doe, Amos. No one you know." The twinkle in his eye as he spoke was the equivalent of crossed fingers.

"I didn't imagine it was Jane Devere," Amos lied.

"Of course not."

Amos followed the old man into the studio. Old man? In his nineties, Angelo was still bursting with the life force. What a satyr he must have been when he painted that picture. It was unsettling to remember that he had painted Amos's wife, as well.

Tacked to a large corkboard in the studio were dozens of photographs, Angelo's wives and progeny. Amos was almost relieved to find no Deveres among them. The photographs did not hold Angelo's attention for long. He led Amos to an easel and removed the cloth that covered it.

"Hugh Devere," Amos exclaimed.

"A fine young man. He intends to become an architect. I managed to dampen his enthusiasm for stained glass."

"So he visits?"

"Just once. I am working from these." He showed Amos some charcoal sketches of Hugh.

"What a talent you have, Angelo. Talents."

The artist shrugged. "I want to freshen this."

They returned to the huge living room, and Amos accepted the second offer of a drink. They settled down, two old men, no matter the decade or so that separated their ages.

"You don't find it lonely here all by yourself?"

"'I didn't know what loneliness was until I married.' Chekhov. No. I have my work." He sipped his lethal drink. "And my memories."

"I'm surprised you didn't marry Jane Devere when she became a widow."

"You're being crafty, Amos."

"Was there ever anything between you two?"

"A gentleman never talks. Not that an artist is a gentleman."

"She has told me that she and August monitored your work on the stained glass windows for St. Hilary's."

"I had forgotten that." Again the negating twinkle in his eye.

"Have you heard of the speculation that St. Hilary's will be closed?"

"Closed!" Angelo lurched in surprise, spilling some of his drink. He rubbed it into his sweatshirt as Amos told him what he knew. "They can't do that! I will be buried in that church."

In the little octagonal chapel Angelo had designed at Jane's request, as a resting place for her father-in-law and other Deveres.

"That was my fee. A place in the floor."

"Then you have a double grievance. Perhaps you should make a statement."

"Is that why you came?"

Amos nodded. "That, and to see Jane Doe again."

Amos took the statement back to Fox River with him. Angelo had written it out in a magnificent hand. It took persuading to keep "whilom" from the protest.

Once home, he went into his study, where he turned on the little light that illumined the portrait that Angelo had done of his late wife. After all the years of loneliness, there were moments when the pristine grief at her loss came back, and so it was now. There were tears in his eyes, but then a disturbing thought came. No, no, good God, no. Think well of the dead. This was no portrait of Jane.

SEVEN

"ALWAYS GO TO THE NONCOMS first," Tuttle said, holding the front door of the school open so Tetzel could enter ahead of him. "The generals can always wait."

The advice had a nice proletarian ring to it but sounded like bunk nonetheless. Tetzel had assumed that they would go directly to the rectory, where, Tuttle assured him, "I am both welcome and well-known." It did sound like an unlikely combination.

Once inside the school, Tuttle took Tetzel's arm and down a wide staircase they went, its granite steps chosen to endure the pounding of many feet. The banister was a little wobbly; the fixtures that anchored it to the wall needed tightening up. On the landing they turned and continued down.

"This place is in great shape," Tetzel said, shifting a plastic sack to his other hand.

"You ever want to buy a school, you could do worse than this."

"I'm more likely to buy the church."

"Keep an open mind, Tetzel. You are custodian of the public's right to know."

At the far end of the corridor they came into were closed and illumined double glass doors. Tuttle flicked a switch, and the hall was flooded with light. He immediately turned it off, then hurried down the hall. Tetzel followed the lumpy silhouette. The little lawyer obviously knew his way around St. Hilary's.

Tuttle came to a closed door on the left of the corridor,

lifted his hand as if to knock, thought better of it, and turned the knob. Locked. He tilted his tweed hat to one side and pressed an ear to the door. "Willie," he whispered. "Willie, it's Tuttle."

There was no reply. Tuttle turned and took the propitiatory six-pack from the reporter's plastic sack and tapped gently on the door. "Beer time, Willie."

After a long moment, there was the sound of a bolt sliding, and a wary face looked out at them over the guard chain. Tuttle held up the six-pack. A moment later, the chain was down, the door open, and they were inside.

"Of course you recognize the name Tetzel," Tuttle said, handing Willie a can of beer.

The little man frowned. "The Bears? No, Green Bay."

"The *Tribune*," the little lawyer said reprovingly.

"No shit."

"I wouldn't go that far."

Tetzel got a beer for himself and looked around the snug little apartment. Not a bad deal. Free room and board and a minimum of work. The television in the corner was on mute, and a large, comfortable chair was aimed at it. Magazines of an equivocal sort were scattered on the floor on either side of the chair. Against the far wall was a bed, unmade. There was a framed newspaper page above it. Tetzel went to read it. A failed bank job.

"That put me in Joliet," Willie said with something like pride in his voice.

"One of these pictures you?"

"No!"

Tetzel was sorry he had asked. Maybe wanted felons visit post offices to see if their picture is on the wall. Tetzel supposed it would be disappointing to find you hadn't made the cut. Tuttle had pulled a straight-back chair forward and gestured Tetzel toward the easy chair. Willie beat him to it. Tetzel claimed the straight-back, leaving Tuttle standing. No matter; the little lawyer began to pace, explaining the purpose of their visit.

"You know more about it than I do," Willie said after listening to Tuttle for several minutes. He had a pretty good grip on the can of beer. Tuttle had stashed the rest in a little refrigerator from which he took a soft drink for himself.

"You know more than you know," Tuttle said enigmatically. "Just give us the scuttlebutt you have picked up while going on your appointed rounds."

"You make me sound like a screw."

"You are a guard. Why else would they want you living right here in the school? It's probably a requirement of the insurance."

Tetzel broke in, convinced that this visit was a pointless detour. "I suppose people were pretty angry to hear the news that the church is coming down."

"Of course it's bugging them. You'd think they were at a wake."

"Pretty despondent?"

An opening sentence formed in the reportorial mind. *Senior members of St. Hilary's parish face eviction from the refuge which for some years has meant companionship, diversion, the opportunity to review and celebrate their long lives.* Rebecca's story of a week ago would be forgotten now, as would Angelo Menotti's statement to the *Chicago Tribune* that Amos Cadbury had released, probably to make sure that the cardinal read it.

"Well, they're in the dumps," Willie said.

"It won't hit them as hard as it does you, Willie," Tuttle said cheerfully. "What will you do when you get bounced out of this place?"

Willie sat forward, crushing the can in his hand. Tuttle took it, arced it toward the wastebasket, missed, pulled open the refrigerator, and got Willie another beer. The little man held it in both hands and stared at them. He might have been realizing for the first time that he could be out of a job. *The good thief who has found peace as the maintenance man at St. Hilary's now confronts a prospect that can scarcely please. Will eviction send him back to his old way of life, the life that led him to Joliet?*

They wasted twenty minutes proving that Willie did indeed know less than they did about the threat to St. Hilary's. "Father Dowling went downtown to talk to the bishop," he contributed.

"We'll be interviewing him," Tuttle said.

They left Willie to his worries and went down the corridor to the double glass doors.

"You'll want to talk to some of the old people," Tuttle said.

"I want to talk to the generals."

Tuttle nodded as if the suggestion were his. Through the double glass doors they went and swiftly through what had once been the gym, where their passage was followed by the suspicious glances of the old people clustered in groups.

"Just in to read the meter," Tuttle called to them.

A dapper little man hurried forward to hold the door for them and followed them outside. "I'm Massimo Bartelli, chairman of Save St. Hilary's. You're Tetzel, aren't you?"

Tetzel nodded.

"Your paper wrote us up. Any information you need, I'm at your disposal."

"Are all the old people with you on this?"

"Are you kidding?"

"How about the pastor?"

Bartelli hesitated. "We're an independent group. Father Dowling isn't likely to criticize the cardinal."

Tuttle broke in, taking Bartelli's hand and pumping it. "We may be back after we talk with Father Dowling."

"Give him a message," Bartelli said confidingly. "Solidarity."

AHEAD OF THEM WAS A WALKWAY that led to the rectory, past the occasional bench, a little shrine with kneelers in front of it, votive lamps aglow. To the left was the church, *rising majestically through the trees on the well-kept parish grounds, a place of worship for generations of parishioners, now facing the arbitrary judgment of a distant bureaucrat.*

"Let's take a look at the windows," Tetzel said.

"Good, good. We can say a prayer."

The thing about Tuttle, you never knew when his mouth was connected to his alleged mind.

Inside, the church was cool and softly lit by such daylight as got through the stained glass windows. A young woman was in the middle aisle, her camera lifted. A flash. She turned. Tetzel hurried toward her, fearful this was competition. Had the crafty Rebecca sent a photographer while she remained in the pressroom banging out the story that would scoop Tetzel?

"Who are you?" he asked the startled woman. "Who sent you?"

Her eyes went over Tetzel and turned to Tuttle. Clearly she did not regard them as worthy of her steel. "God," she whispered.

EIGHT

THE ADVICE OF A PATRON IS not to be ignored, but Carl Barloff, at the end of a lengthy conversation with Jane Devere, asked for a repetition.

"Of course I am serious," she said, annoyed. "I hope you don't think I have grown senile."

"Hardly that," Carl said, chuckling, though the thought had crossed his mind. He had come to the old woman before setting out for Peoria to meet with Angelo Menotti, a courtesy visit to inform the artist of the great project soon to be under way although Menotti had no say in the matter, despite the statement released by Amos Cadbury. Was the lawyer trying to renege on Carl's grant? He was startled to be told by Jane Devere that he must first go to South Bend and consult her grandson, Hugh.

"The architect," she explained. "Or who soon will be the architect."

There was pride in the old woman's voice, doubtless engendered by the grandson's departure from the usual practical and profitable paths trod by Deveres.

"An artist in the family," he said unctuously.

"Two."

Did she mean herself? He waited.

"Susan. Hugh's sister."

"Ah." Susan Devere. The very name made Borloff uneasy.

"You've never met her."

Carl had heard what she thought of him. "Younger or older?"

"Than Hugh? Slightly more than a year older."

"Is she married?"

"Humph. She is a liberated woman. Don't ask me from what."

"So I will go and talk with Hugh," Carl said lest she send him to Susan.

"I am putting this whole matter into his hands. He must be informed at every step of the process. At my age one must be prepared for a sudden exit or for a debilitating diminution of the faculties, something you apparently think has already begun."

"My dear lady."

"Enough of that. Off you go."

"Of course, I shall continue to report to you."

"Indeed you will."

If Carl had a forelock he would have tugged it. How annoying it was that money should be in the hands of the rich. Ah, well. He would not repine. Jane Devere's hand had opened to him and produced a sinecure indeed.

It was midmorning when Carl approached the city, and a great decision loomed. Should he continue on through the Loop or go around it on I-294? Traffic on the Kennedy Expressway was dense at the best of times, and besides that was unnervingly dangerous, hotshots darting from lane to lane, the whole six lanes of cars hurtling toward the Loop with the determination of lemmings; and it could be even worse beyond, before the sanity of Indiana was reached. He turned onto I-294 and for an hour and a half cursed the decision. ROAD WORK AHEAD. It might have been the sign over hell. Traffic was funneled into two lanes, then one, and crept along. If Carl was averaging fifteen miles an hour he would be surprised. He sought resignation; he turned on the radio and quickly turned it off again; he tried to fill his mind with pleasant thoughts. To no avail. By the time he rejoined I-94 he was a muttering maniac.

Welcome to Indiana. To Paradiso. The number of vehicles thinned. The semis seemed less intent on driving him onto the berm. His spirits rose, and he settled back. By the time he turned off for the Indiana Toll Road, he was once again the man he thought he was.

Gary prompted hellish thoughts again, but they were brief, and then on either side of him were the rolling farmlands of Indiana. He got out his cell phone and called Hugh Devere, correcting his estimated time of arrival.

"Today?" Hugh said. "I thought Grandma meant tomorrow."

Had she? She had assured him that she would forewarn her grandson, a verb Carl had not liked.

Hugh told him that lunch was out and he had a class at one. "You could come to that if you'd like."

"I only wish I could." Audit a class! No thanks. They arranged to meet at two.

"Just park across from the main gate. You could look around Cedar Grove Cemetery."

"Good idea."

Well, this was a fool's errand, so what did he expect?

He did park in the lot Hugh suggested, and he did stroll through Cedar Grove, a peaceful place as cemeteries go. When he went on into the new section he was astonished to see two huge mausoleums loom ahead. He inspected them. File away your remains until the last trump. "Bury me not on a marble shelf," he sang to the tune of the old Western. There were benches by the mausoleums where one could sit and ponder the fleetingness of life or, in the case of Carl Borloff, have a cigarette. In a cemetery everything seemed dangerous to one's health.

THE YOUNG MAN LOOKED younger than he was, and Carl felt a trace of condescension in him. How had Jane Devere described him to Hugh? An old family retainer? One of the house slaves. He made the mistake of grumbling about the mausoleums.

"They were designed by Thomas Gordon Smith!"

They went to a place called Legends near the stadium, a kind of sports bar, its walls festooned with Notre Dame sports memorabilia, televisions everywhere. A famished Carl devoured a hamburger as large as the plate it came on. Hugh had a Guinness.

"Your grandmother tells me that she has put you in charge of the Menotti project."

"Whatever that means. You don't expect any advice from me, I hope."

"I shall want you to be acquainted with each step of the process. It shouldn't take any time away from your studies."

"It's one of the best ideas she ever had."

Carl remained silent. Had Jane claimed the idea as her own? Perhaps if you financed a project, you thought that you owned it in every sense.

"She mentioned your sister, Susan."

Hugh's eyes seemed distracted by a television screen. If he had meant to say anything he changed his mind. A slight nod and that was that.

"I'll be going to Peoria to bring Angelo Menotti up-to-date on things."

This got Hugh's undivided attention. "What a man," he said.

"You've visited him?"

Hugh nodded. Carl had the sudden feeling that the Deveres were encircling his project, taking it over. Well, at least Hugh Devere didn't take the assignment his grandmother had given him seriously. The large question was, did Hugh share his sister Susan's skepticism? Carl decided that there was no need to mention that he himself had not yet made the pilgrimage to Peoria.

NINE

LADISLAW SLEDZ, PASTOR OF Our Lady of Chestokowa, called Father Dowling. His church, too, had been on the list that had appeared in the *Tribune*.

"Quinn and Perzel have agreed that we should ask for an appointment at the chancery. You're an old hand down there, Roger. We need you."

"I've already been down there, Lad."

"You have!" Sledz made it sound like a betrayal.

"I never thought of going as a group. I wonder if that's wise."

"Who did you speak to?"

"Bishop Wilenski. He assured me that there is nothing final about that list of parishes that appeared in the paper."

"You believed him?"

That a pastor should suspect the chancery of double-talk indicated the despondency into which Sledz and doubtless the others had been cast.

"I can't believe you're in any danger, Lad." Former parishioners and their families converged on Our Lady of Chestokowa from the suburbs to which they had moved, filling the huge church every Sunday.

"It's the school that's the problem," Sledz cried. "Why can't we just sell the schools to the city?"

"Have you ever thought of converting it into a parish center?"

"Roger, you could shoot a cannon through this parish any weekday and never hit a Catholic."

"No seniors still in residence?"

"No Catholics."

"Then make it ecumenical."

"Is that what's going to save St. Hilary's, the way you use your school?"

"Who knows?"

"I see in the paper that your old folks have organized."

"That was their idea, not mine, Lad."

"I could get hundreds of names, Roger, people who come here to Sunday Mass. The trouble is few of them live within the parish boundaries."

"You don't want to stir up the pastors in the parishes where they're now living. They wouldn't like the thought of all those people driving off to Our Lady of Chestokowa on Sunday."

"They're packing them in out there as it is."

"How long have you been pastor there, Lad?"

The question triggered a twenty-minute bout of reminiscence. Sledz had gone to Our Lady as an assistant and never left. His knowledge of Hungarian as well as Polish made him a natural for the place.

"You have lots of confessions?"

"They must go in the suburbs, Roger. I hope."

It was pretty clear that Our Lady was vulnerable. Roger suddenly had the thought that he and Sledz and the others were like those pathetic figures who refuse to leave their homes when a freeway is scheduled to run through it and eminent domain invoked. There was something noble in such protests, not least because they were doomed to failure.

The local story prompted by Bartelli and his group had contrasted the American situation with the European, where churches stood for centuries. A selective comparison. Many churches had been closed on the Continent. Of course the great historical cathedrals stood, but what had they become in too many instances? Cardinal Schönborn of Vienna had put it succinctly: Our churches have become museums and our museums have become churches. Of course, abbeys and convents and their churches had been knocked down under Henry and Elizabeth in England. "Bare ruined choirs where late the sweet bird sang."

"We have here no lasting city, Lad."

"Roger, if they close this place I am going to retire to Florida."

"I hope it doesn't come to that."

AGNES BROUGHT THE WOMAN to Cy's office, stood at her side and a little behind, and said, "This is Madeline Schutz, Lieutenant."

From anyone else south of the planet Pluto this would have gotten a theatrical reaction, but Cy simply looked at Agnes and at the woman. "Please sit down."

Just like that. For days they had been investigating the cruel death of Madeline Schutz, who had been cut down from a strut in Amy Gorman's garage, whose mutilated body had been clinically examined by Dr. Pippen in the morgue, and whose antecedents Agnes had been assigned to check. This should have been easy. How many Madeline Schutzes are there? Two, as it happened. An elderly woman confined to her bed in a rest home in Shakopee, Minnesota, and the victim. Agnes had actually made the trip into darkest Minnesota— well, greenest Minnesota—and looked at the old woman, who might have been in this world but certainly wasn't of it. This Madeline Schutz had spent her lifetime on a farm outside Shakopee, had buried her husband fifteen years ago, had lost both her sons in disputed foreign wars, and now sat in her bed with a vague smile as the nurse told Agnes about the bed's occupant. Madeline had a sweet smile.

The records in Shakopee were not computerized, and Agnes found checking out the woman in the rest home difficult. Harriet, an Afro-American who was really a minority in that town, came to her rescue, and between them they established that this Madeline Schutz had exhausted all her relations in this world. There were no bloodlines that had ever extended more than thirty miles in either direction from Shakopee, at least in the last hundred years. If there was any connection between this Madeline Schutz and theirs, it was known only to God. Agnes drove back to Chicago.

"You drove up there?" Captain Keegan asked.

"In my own car."

Keegan mastered his surprise and perhaps annoyance. "What did you find out?"

"Nothing."

"Well, that ought to help."

He wasn't serious—about it not helping, that is. Most investigations are a matter of canceling out possible explanations. Their Madeline Schutz had lived in an apartment in Skokie, an apartment that was found locked and, of course, unoccupied. The manager of the building, a little guy named Mintz, had trouble keeping his mouth shut. Not that he talked. He was rendered mute by Agnes's questions, and his mouth seemed arrested in the act of trying to think of something to say.

"What did she do?"

"She was a writer."

"Let me see her place."

"Let you into her apartment?"

"You can come with me."

Mintz thought about it. He didn't seem to think much of it, and Agnes had no authority in Skokie. Was she going to have to liase with the Skokie police, get a search warrant, all the rest? Apparently not. Mintz overcame his scruples.

The blinds in the apartment were tipped, and the rooms were filled with a subdued light. Everything looked neat enough in a kind of haphazard way. It was the number of books that you couldn't help but notice. Books on shelves in every room, books on the coffee table in the living room, books on the table beside the bed and on the floor, as well. More books in a bookcase in there. Then there was the other bedroom, which served as a study. A desk, a computer on a separate stand, pieces of paper pinned up on the corkboard over the desk, more books everywhere, and a neat stack of paper on the desk. Agnes bent to read the top sheet. *Aurora from Photon. The Empyrean Chronicles, Volume Six. M. X. Schutz.*

"I told you she's a writer," Mintz said.

"I know!"

In the bookshelf in the study were rows and rows of chubby paperbacks with covers to knock your eyes out, volumes in the Empyrean Chronicles. On volume five was the boast "Over a Million Copies in Print." Agnes made a note of the publisher, whose offices, surprisingly, were in Kenosha, Wisconsin. She left her card with Mintz.

It was that card that had led the woman calling herself Madeline Schutz to Agnes's office. "Mr. Mintz said that you have been making inquiries about me."

"Your name?"

"Madeline Schutz."

Agnes could never be as phlegmatic as Cy—she wouldn't want to be as phlegmatic as Cy—but she hadn't risen screaming from her chair and called a cop. "From Skokie?"

"Earl Mintz said he let you into my apartment."

Agnes took her off to the cafeteria for coffee and the reassuring presence of others. There she told the woman that they were investigating the murder of Madeline Schutz.

Madeline's head canted slightly to the right; the beginning of a smile played on her lips.

Agnes gave her a sanitized version of the condition of the body. "It's in the morgue. I can show it to you."

A shudder. "But why would you think it's me?"

It was time to take her to Cy Horvath. On the way out,

Agnes paused at Pippen's table and said, "Doctor, this is Madeline Schutz."

"Get out of here."

"The assistant coroner," Agnes explained as they left.

CY CAME ALONG WHEN THEY took Madeline Schutz to see Amy Gorman. The two women looked at each other, strangers.

Amy listened to the explanation. "Then whose body was found in my garage?"

So they were back where they had started, only now the investigation turned on a nameless victim.

ELEVEN

THERE WAS TENSION IN THE pressroom, and Tuttle became an infrequent presence. Tetzel had grown reluctant to pursue the church closings story, since this meant relinquishing the ritual killing of Madeline Schutz to Rebecca, his archrival. Menteur, good chauvinist as he normally was, favored Rebecca if only as a means of putting down Tetzel. Pure jealousy, of course. Menteur was presiding over the decline and fall of the *Tribune,* and there didn't seem to be much that he or the publisher or anyone else could do about it. Menteur had a Luddite's distrust of the paper's Web site, which was getting more hits a day than there were subscribers to the print edition. Only an idiot could ignore the implications of that, and Menteur qualified. The irony was that Tetzel half shared the attitude of his despised boss. Of course he used a computer. Typewriters were as rare as Edsels now. Tetzel had one stashed in his closet among the shoes and had recently taken it out to revive the sense of satisfaction he had felt banging away at it, but it was slow and clumsy, and manually returning the carriage at the end of each line seemed unbelievably primitive. He put it back in the closet. If he had had an Edsel, he would have hung on to it, too, as an investment.

Rebecca sauntered into the pressroom, spun her chair around by bumping it with her hip, and collapsed. "Madeline Schutz isn't Madeline Schutz."

Tetzel held up a staying hand, leaning toward the screen of his computer. His head tipped back, his eyes closed, and then, the creature of inspiration, his fingers danced on the keys for a moment and he fell back in his chair with a sigh of satisfaction. Slowly he turned to Rebecca. "Is there any pleasure keener than finishing a story?"

"Still on the endangered churches story?"

"You wouldn't believe the ramifications. How's the ritual murder going?"

Rebecca replied with words that ladies seldom use. "I told you. The body isn't the body of who they thought it was."

"It's just as dead, isn't it?"

"Yes, but whose is it?"

"You got anything here or should we go across the street?"

Rebecca got up and hipped the door shut. Returning to her desk, she withdrew a bottle of Johnny Walker Red. Tetzel produced two foam cups, shocking Rebecca. Scotch from a foam cup? She had glasses.

"You're getting fastidious."

"Even though I eat like a bird."

He let it go. Where would any of them be without Roget's *Thesaurus?* Or maybe Rebecca's hearing was going. The thought of Rebecca succumbing to the ravages of age, tottering toward the horizon, filled Tetzel with cheer, and he accepted her scotch in the spirit in which it was offered.

"Did you ever hear of the Empyrean Chronicles?"

"Sounds familiar," Tetzel lied.

"They're written by the real Madeline Schutz. Six in print, the next one already written."

"Six novels?"

Rebecca nodded while sipping, her eyes brightly on Tetzel. It had been his boast and now it was his shame that he was writing a novel. A novel! On his hard drive, filed under ULYSSES, were various bits and pieces of what he called his novel. Why had he told others about it? What might have been merely a consoling private dream had been turned into a public failure.

"Science fiction. Fantasy."

Tetzel snorted. "I can't read that sort of thing."

A sigh of disappointment from Rebecca. "I had hoped you would interview her, Tetzel. One novelist on another, rapport, special insights…"

Tetzel watched her narrowly as she spoke. She was setting him up, he was sure of it. Then he wasn't sure. Did he really have status as a novelist with Rebecca? "Tell me about her."

Listening, Tetzel felt his imagination emerging slowly from disuse. Rebecca and the police were baffled by the apparently random use of the identity of Madeline Schutz for the body hung in the garage. The woman whose house it was, Amy Gorman—Tetzel was taking notes in a casual way—had no connection with the writer in Skokie. Nor had Madeline, the science fiction factory, ever heard of Amy Gorman. There was absolutely no direct link between them.

"A dead end?"

Rebecca nodded. "The police may fiddle around with it a bit longer, but they're going nowhere."

"They've looked into religious sects?"

Rebecca frowned, then laughed. "Do you know what I thought you asked?"

"Menteur will keep you on it."

"You're wrong."

"So why should I interview a novelist who has nothing to do with the story you're dropping?"

"That's your hook, Tetzel."

Well, they had both been drinking. Rebecca certainly wasn't stingy with her scotch, but maybe she thought offering Tetzel more justified herself having another. He shrugged noncommittally and lifted his glass. "Here's to crime."

"To hell with crime."

Tuttle breezed in but at the sight of Rebecca came to a stop. He adjusted his tweed hat. "I got your call," he said to Tetzel.

"What call?"

"The one you promised to make. You said you'd keep me posted. Hazel is frantic."

"Who's Hazel?" Rebecca asked.

"Tuttle's mistress."

There are many kinds of laughter, but Rebecca's disdainful cackle was the only kind she had. She rose, bumped Tuttle aside, and went off down the hall to the ladies' room.

"What's wrong with her?"

"Don't get me started."

"Ah, the course of true love. Tetzel, a thought. Do a feature on Angelo Menotti, the artist who designed the stained glass windows at St. Hilary's. It turns out the guy's famous. He has a studio in Peoria; we could go together. He has issued a statement."

"I'm on a special assignment."

Tuttle took a chair. "Tell me about it."

Tetzel rose, steadied himself, and assumed a mysterious air. "I wish I could."

He passed the returning Rebecca in the hallway and gave her a salute.

"Is he still in there?"

"He wants to talk to you."

Lurching groundward in the elevator, Tetzel coaxed from secrecy the inspiration he had had listening to Rebecca. She and apparently the police were stymied because there was no relation between Madeline Schutz and Amy Gorman. No direct relation. The solution seemed simple to Tetzel and would have, he was sure, even if his mind had been clear. There had to be a tertium quid, a third person who linked the two. Find that link and voilà!

Meanwhile he would interview the prolific science fiction writer.

TWELVE

PHIL KEEGAN'S CONDO overlooked an artificial lake in the middle of which a fountain sent up a silvery umbrella-shaped spray of water. There were ducks on the lake that residents were warned not to feed, a prohibition surreptitiously ignored. It was the Canada geese that were the problem, wandering along the walks; their strangely designed bodies were not adapted to easy terrestrial travel, yet they were seldom in the water and used their wings infrequently. Phil had been prepared to admire the awkward birds until the management identified them as nuisances. The nature of the nuisance was delicately hinted at, but those who used the walks understood. From time to time a couple with a brace of dogs was called in to scatter the geese, but after a week, they always returned.

Phil sat at the table in his combination kitchen/dining room, holding a mug of coffee with both hands, and thanked God he was not retired. All around him were oldsters, living on pensions and Social Security and whatever else, shuffling along the walks, going nowhere. He almost thanked God that he was not like the rest of men, but the Gospel scene expelled the thought. Not even Father Dowling had seen how shaken he had been by the threat to close St. Hilary's. If that happened, Roger Dowling would go, and with him one of the mainstays in Phil's life.

It had been ten years since he had sold the house in which he and his wife had raised their two daughters, now living on opposite coasts. As captain of detectives, he worked himself harder than anyone, almost dreading going home. What in

God's name would he do if he retired, sit here looking out at the ducks and geese? The pastor of St. Hilary's had become a close friend during these lonely years. Roger had been a couple of classes ahead of him in Quigley, where the then mandatory Latin undid Phil. Eventually, he went into the army, became an MP and, when he got out, went into police work. Several evenings a week he would drop by the St. Hilary's rectory to visit with Roger, watch a game on TV, talk about the crime of the day.

"Hung in a garage?" Father Dowling exclaimed when Phil told him of the murder Cy Horvath and Agnes were investigating.

"Not even her own garage. Nor was she the Madeline Schutz we thought she was."

Roger liked to be informed of the department's work, although Phil knew they looked on things differently. As a cop, his aim was justice, an arrest, indictment, conviction, and then a long spell in Joliet. Roger Dowling understood that, but his interest was mercy. What for Phil was a crime was a sin for the pastor of St. Hilary's, and his concern was for the soul of the wrongdoer. Not wholly incompatible points of view, of course.

"Who was she?"

"God knows."

The familiar, comfortable exchange went on, but now there was the disturbing undertow that St. Hilary's might be closed and Roger Dowling reassigned. Phil didn't want to dwell on what this would mean for him, but neither could he rid himself of the thought.

"I told Massimo Bartelli to add my name to the list."

"I wish he hadn't formed that group, Phil."

"Do you just want to wait and see what happens?"

"Not quite. But the Church doesn't make her decision on the basis of protests."

"I hope the cardinal listens to them."

"We'll see."

Phil tried to understand Roger's resignation. He would do what the cardinal asked him to do; that was what motivated Roger. Phil agreed that a priest ought to be a good soldier, but still…

"You think it's going to happen, don't you?"

"Actually, I doubt it."

"Have you heard from Bishop Wilenski?"

"Two things impressed him when we talked. That the Deveres are parishioners here and that we have Angelo Menotti stained glass windows in the church."

"They are nice windows."

The Deveres. Of course, they were an affluent family, and generous. It turned out that they had donated the Menotti windows, years ago.

"Funny thing, Roger. The woman in whose garage the body was found is staying with Susan Devere."

"What's the connection?"

Phil thought a moment. "I'd have to ask Cy."

THIRTEEN

YEARS AGO WHEN FATHER Dowling had been taken to the third floor of the Devere mansion for the first time, he had assumed he was bringing the Eucharist to an invalid, but the woman who greeted him with a reverent nod toward the burden he bore looked spry and agile. Jane Devere was neatly dressed, she had a mantilla over her silver-gray hair, and, as Father Dowling approached, she dropped to her knees in a single motion. She received the host devoutly and then withdrew to a prie-dieu under a magnificent picture of the Blessed Virgin, having first waved Father Dowling into the adjoining sunny room, where coffee and rolls awaited him.

A few minutes later, folding her mantilla and setting it aside, she joined him. "I hope you won't think it presumptuous if I welcome you to St. Hilary's, Father."

"Your family must have been among the original parishioners."

"I believe we were."

Once a month or so after that, he brought her communion and they had a little chat over coffee and rolls afterward, but the years passed and Father Dowling did not feel he knew her any better than he had the first time. Until he asked about the picture. "I have always wanted to ask you about the Madonna over your prie-dieu."

She actually glowed. "Isn't it beautiful?"

"I don't recognize it."

Her chin dropped to her starched white collar. "You don't think it's a copy, I hope."

He went closer to examine the canvas. "I can't read the signature."

"Angelo Menotti."

With time, Father Dowling's monthly visits to Jane Devere grew, if not lengthy, longer, but their conversations were quite impersonal, even theoretical. She had a keen interest in Marian apparitions and was angry to hear that there were some in the Church who questioned the fact of purgatory.

"Nonsense, Father. Haven't they heard of Fatima?"

"Or Dante?"

Her expression changed. "You're teasing me."

Amos had prepared Father Dowling for the old woman's interest in the law. "I think she could pass the bar, Father. How she picks up the lore I do not know. Understandably, I suppose, she is particularly interested in trusts and wills and inheritance and all the rest, but I once had an extended conversation with her on the law of copyright, and another on benefactions. She showed me an extraordinary document that had been drawn up when August commissioned the stained glass windows for the church. That was before my time, of course. I mean as the family lawyer. What a sense of contingency that old man had."

"How so?"

"You will be interested to learn that ownership of those windows reverts to the Deveres in case of, well, there must have been half a dozen possibilities. Jane told me that she herself had insisted on those."

"Extraordinary."

"Oh, the conversations I have had with Jane Devere," Amos said with a dreamy smile.

Father Dowling often envied the old lawyer until he had the uneasy feeling that he might be on the brink of a roman-

tic revelation. After all, both Jane and Amos had lost their
spouses.

"I'll give you one example. 'Take a case,' she said to me.
She always began that way. Well, I was to take the case of a
family in which a husband fathered a child by a servant girl,
a child whose origins were kept a firm secret. It was adopted
into the family, not in any legal sense, but under the pretense
that it was the betrayed wife's child. The years pass, and that
child has children of its own. They bear the family name, but
hovering over them is the shadow of the bar sinister; they
derive from a parent who was born on the wrong side of the
blanket. Very well, time passes, and somehow the secret is
learned. Members of the family whose origins are without
blemish take action to disinherit the children of that unfor-
tunate child. What did I think would be the outcome?"

"What an imagination she has. What answer did you give
her?"

"As we say at my alma mater, I punted. She continued to
press me, and I continued to avoid the question. Thank God
I have never been confronted with such a problem."

Eventually, Jane had put a similar case to Father Dowling
as a matter of canon law. Amos had told her of her pastor's
doctorate in that subject. This time it was the case of a wife
who concealed from her husband the fact that the baby she
bore was not his. The secret was retained throughout their
marriage; the husband died; children were born of the child
that was the wife's but not the husband's. Was illegitimacy
transitive? Were the issue of that child conceived in sin tainted
with illegitimacy?

"But the child was hers."

"Granted. She marries into a family and of course bears her
husband's name. Her son, too, bears his name. What would
be their status, Father?"

He promised to do research on the subject if she really wanted to know.

"I do. I do. Some old women knit or do crossword puzzles or simply say their prayers. Conundra like that are my hobby."

"I SUPPOSE YOU HEAR HER confession," Marie said. The housekeeper was resentful of the claim the Deveres had on the pastor, particularly Jane, whom she had never met. The whole Devere family was a kind of blank in Marie's knowledge of the parish.

"What if she asked me if I heard yours?"

Marie became indignant. "What housekeeper would confess to her own pastor? You know I have a Carmelite confessor."

"I didn't know."

"Well, now you do."

The next time he visited Jane he asked her about confession. "Oh, Father Felix takes care of that."

"Father Felix."

"A Franciscan. He was an assistant here before you came and has continued to serve as my confessor. Surely you didn't think I would receive communion without being in the state of grace."

"You'll forgive my asking, but it is the kind of thing pastors should know."

"I am surprised you didn't ask me earlier. What is the latest news from Bishop Wilenski?"

"He tells me that the latest list he has prepared for the cardinal does not include St. Hilary's."

"I'm almost disappointed."

"You are?"

"I was looking forward to a court battle."

FOURTEEN

AMY GORMAN WAS DARNED IF she was going to play the role of duenna, but the constant presence of Fulvio in the house made her feel like a beady-eyed middle-aged woman. It didn't help that she had often thought how nice it would be if something developed between her Paul and Susan. It had been through Paul that she had met Susan, but soon it seemed to be the mother rather than the son that interested the aspiring young artist of such interesting genealogy. Susan had become a constant visitor after Paul went off to war again.

"I'm an orphan, you know," she told Amy.

Amy had laughed. The famous Devere family made such a claim silly. Even so, not having a mother doubtless did affect Susan, and the girl's affection was welcome to Amy. God knows she saw little enough of Paul, off in Iraq on a second tour. Did he have a death wish? She was proud of him, though. He was so like his father, who had fallen in an earlier war.

Fulvio Menotti looked like Michelangelo's *David* with clothes on. When Susan told Amy that Fulvio was sitting for her as an artist's model, doubts had arisen. What a narcissistic occupation. What had happened to the boy who posed for Michelangelo? Amy had rather pointedly remarked that her son was fighting in Iraq.

"Good for him," Fulvio said. "I figure that my time in the merchant marine counts."

"Merchant marine."

"For four years. It's as bad as being in the navy, but I loved it."

What a smile. What a charmer. And a sailor besides. It was on a freighter that made half a dozen unscheduled ports of call and carried a few passengers that he had met Margaret Ward.

"On a freighter!"

"Don't kid yourself. There's only one class on a freighter, first class."

"How long did that trip last?"

Fulvio thought, working his lips. Amy wanted to reach out and touch them. "Two and a half months."

"Margaret Ward was stuck on board that long?"

"She could have left the ship any number of times if she had wanted to. She said she was on a kind of retreat."

"How did you get to know her?"

"I tripped over her deck chair. She had set it up where she shouldn't, and I didn't see it. I helped her get it out of there. She seemed to enjoy being chewed out."

"I don't suppose she gets much of that."

"I had no idea who she was until afterward. All we talked about was fiction. She had a suitcase full of New American Library editions. She put me on to *The Rise of Silas Lapham*. Do you know it?"

Amy didn't know the novel. Susan didn't, either.

"It's by William Dean Howells."

Amy and Susan just looked at him. Then Susan said, "Some kind of right-wing stuff, I suppose."

Fulvio laughed. Susan could never prod him into controversy.

"I'm surprised you haven't thought of becoming a writer," Amy said.

Instead it was sculpture at which Fulvio worked in a corner of Susan's studio. Amy found herself fascinated by the way he fashioned clay, often not even looking at what he was doing, as if his mind's eye were on what he intended to shape. When Amy came from the office, Fulvio often joined them for supper, which was junk food sent in if she didn't get there in time to make a decent meal. It was usually about nine that Fulvio left.

"Where does he live?" Amy asked Susan.

"I don't know. Not with his father. Oil and water. I may offer him your room when you leave."

"I wouldn't do that."

"Leave?"

"Susan, I know I am taking advantage of your hospitality, but I can't go back to that house."

Susan threw her arms around her. "Stay here, Amy. Sell the darned house. You can never go back there. You shouldn't."

"Would you buy a house that had a murdered woman hanging in its garage?"

"Who knows what went on in this house before I bought it."

"You BACK IN YOUR HOUSE yet?" Emil asked. He moved around the office in his chair, since getting all of himself into or out of it was a task.

"I may sell it."

Emil looked at her. "In this market?"

It had taken all the nerve Amy had to drive her car out of the garage, wondering whose hands had been on the wheel. Why had he left the motor running?

"Maybe he thought his victim was still alive," Agnes Lamb had said.

"What a monster. How I wish you would find him."

"So do I."

So she remained with Susan, wondering about her relationship with Fulvio.

Margaret had told Fulvio about her niece and urged him to look up Susan, whom she had described as politically illiterate.

"I told her we'd make a good pair," Fulvio said.

Amy looked at Susan to see what effect this had on her. Apparently none. Maybe with a father as handsome as hers, Susan had gotten used to male beauty. Even so, offering a room to such an Apollo would be the height of imprudence. Not that she could put it that way to Susan. It would have provided motivation.

"Do you see your grandfather often?" Amy asked him.

"He told me I should have stayed in the merchant marine."

"He disapproves of your becoming a sculptor?"

"You wouldn't want to hear him on what has become of the arts."

Susan said, "I think my grandmother Jane had a crush on him."

Fulvio grinned. "I think it was mutual."

Fulvio's father was a nature nut who lived in Jackson Hole, Wyoming. He had been an instructor in economics at the University of Chicago, a Milton Friedman fan. Susan groaned.

"I don't know anything about economics," Fulvio said.

"Neither do I."

"Why should you? You're loaded."

"This is my first glass of wine," Susan protested.

"You know what I mean."

"Don't rub it in."

Susan had told Amy of her Franciscan dream, to give it all away and embrace poverty. Did that include the house in Barrington?

"I have to have a studio."

"Of course you do."

Susan was determined that she would make it as an artist. If not, she would take up—maybe economics. "I certainly wouldn't want to just hang around and make a business of the work of others."

As it had before, that led to talk about Susan's bête noire, Carl Borloff, the affected parasite, the alleged expert on religious art. "Everything about religion interests him except faith. The whole thing is aesthetic with him."

"You don't know that."

Amy had been edified by Susan's Sunday Mass going. It shamed her back on track herself.

"Photographs of stained glass windows! Anyone can do it."

"Have you tried?"

For answer, Susan got out her camera and showed the shots she had taken of the windows at St. Hilary's.

FIFTEEN

CARL BORLOFF WAS BROWSING in the Barnes & Noble bookstore on Dirksen Boulevard, checking to see how many of the ten copies of *Sacred Art* he had on display there were sold. He closed his eyes and prayed as he let his fingers move over the shrink-wrapped copies. Ten! The giant of despair had its feet on his shoulders and was pressing him down. How in the name of heaven could customers resist the magazine? Seen from several paces back, it leapt to Carl's eye, easily the most aesthetically designed and striking of any of its companions in the rack. Perhaps if he ran naked through the store flourishing a copy, attention would be paid. Undeniably, simply having something available for readers, even in such a much visited bookstore as this, was not enough.

He took a deep breath, suppressing a sigh. Just think of what his depression would be if it were not for the book of Angelo Menotti's windows. Then, before his spirits could rise, he had a terrible vision. A magnificent book, a superlative book, a book that any knowledgeable person would praise, and there it languished on the shelf like these copies of *Sacred Art*.

Someone beside him reached out and took a copy of *Sacred Art*. Carl was frozen in place, scarcely breathing. Would the same hand return the copy to its nine companions? There was the sound of tearing, and Carl turned. The man was removing the shrink-wrap from the magazine.

"Now you'll have to buy it," Carl said, hardly recognizing his own voice.

"I intend to." The man was turning the pages. "I've never seen this before. It seems excellent all around."

"I am the editor," Carl said. At least he formed the words, but they issued silently from his constricted throat. "And publisher." These words were audible.

"I beg your pardon?"

The young man seemed more amused than put off by Carl's incomplete sentence.

"I said I am the editor and publisher."

"Here to monitor sales?" An engaging smile. The young man reminded Carl of a Leonardo sketch.

Carl laughed. "That's right, and yours is the first."

"Let me pay for this and give you a cup of coffee."

Watching the man hand over his credit card, then sign the slip and take the magazine, Carl's spirits rose.

The young man put Carl at a table and then went to fetch the coffee. He had left the issue of *Sacred Art* on the table. Carl turned it so passersby could see it. The man returned with their coffee.

"I am Carl Borloff." He held out his hand.

Before taking it, the man sat, opened the cover of the magazine, and checked. "How do I know you are Carl Borloff? Perhaps you lurk here impersonating editors." He said it so gently, it would have been impossible to take offense.

Carl got out his driver's license and handed it to the man. After a moment, they were shaking hands.

"And you are?" Carl asked.

"You can call me Charles Ruskin. Actually, I am here on the same mission as you."

"How is that?"

"I am a publisher, and I'm gratified to say that our entire allotment has been sold."

"Congratulations."

Charles Ruskin picked up the copy of Carl's magazine

and might have been weighing it in his hand. "This excellent publication represents perhaps ten percent of the task. Warehouses are full of wonderful books, books that will never have readers. At least the copies in the warehouse won't. Other books, books of far less ambition and accomplishment, fly off the shelves, in the phrase. What is the difference?"

"Luck?"

Ruskin nodded. "Of course luck is a factor, it always is. There is good and bad luck, though. It is unwise to trust to luck in either of its forms. The artist will find it vulgar, the poet winces, but novelists as a rule are less likely to fight the truth that ninety percent of their success is due to salesmanship. Hustling, as they say, to save their pride. A small example. Your magazine sits on a shelf among how many other competing publications? Only a discerning eye would notice it." He smiled away the autobiographical implication. "My books are in display cases in the aisle, impossible not to notice and, as I have just gratefully learned, and not for the first time, impossible not to buy."

"Are you located in the Chicago area?"

"In the area, yes."

"What is the name of your firm?"

"Argyle House." He studied Carl, his blue eyes twinkling. "Don't say you've heard of it."

"I'm afraid I haven't."

"That is because there is no need to know the publisher. The publisher is selling not himself but his authors. Perhaps you find all this irrelevant to your own efforts?"

Carl thought for a moment. What harm could there be in telling this man? He was a publisher; he seemed to be immersed in the world of books. "I am preparing a book myself."

If he had expected surprise, if he had imagined delight, if he had sought for interest, he would have been sorely disappointed. Ruskin looked away. "I suspect that every other customer in this store has a similar project."

"Mine is subsidized. It will be done and it will be published."

Ruskin sat back with a pensive expression. He turned over the copy of *Sacred Art*. Then he smiled. "The Devere Foundation!"

"How did you know?"

"I make it a practice to study the reports from foundations. Yes, yes, I remember the item. I thought your name was familiar. Tell me about it."

Carl hunched over the table, and words poured from him. Suddenly he was eloquent, authoritative, a man who knew exactly what he was talking about. He had Ruskin's undivided interest now. No need to conceal the amount of the grant that Jane Devere had given him. This man would already know. Carl spoke of his interviews with possible photographers, his visits to pastors in whose churches Menotti windows were to be found.

"I hope you don't intend to publish it yourself."

"I haven't gotten that far yet."

"A self-published book, even if the self is an entity such as this." Again he lifted the copy of *Sacred Art* from the table. "A self-published book is like a letter to oneself. Even so special a publication as you no doubt plan becomes, when you are done, a commodity. Then other skills and expertise must be called into play. Let me recommend an exercise. Go to the section of remaindered books and look at all the art books there. You will find many excellently done, yet there they are, discounted, humbly asking to be taken for a pittance. That need not have been."

"Has Argyle House ever published art books?"

"If we had, I can assure you they would not end up as remaindered books." He sipped his coffee. "Each of our products—no, that is an exaggeration. Put it this way, the majority of our products represent ventures into territory we have never before occupied. The correct answer to your question as to whether we have published art books would be, not yet."

A silence fell over the table. The conversation had reached a critical point. Ruskin took out his billfold and extracted a card, which he handed to Carl, rising as he did so. "I am so delighted to have met you."

Carl half rose, but Ruskin had turned and started away. "Wait. You forgot this," Carl said urgently.

"Good heavens!" Ruskin cried, taking the copy of *Sacred Art*. "Our conversation has distracted me."

FIFTEEN MINUTES LATER, Carl still sat at the table, holding Ruskin's card. Kenosha? Well, what difference did that make, he chided himself. Once publishers had clustered in New York or elsewhere on the East Coast. Now they were scattered across the country. What a tremendous piece of luck. Of course, Ruskin had not made any overt remark, but it seemed clear that he could become interested in the Menotti book.

His coffee had cooled. He put down the container. Then dark thoughts came. How accidental had his meeting with Ruskin been? The man had known of the Devere grant. Had he read it with the eye of a predator? Even to formulate the thought was sufficient to dismiss it. So far as Ruskin knew they might never meet again.

THE NEXT TIME THEY MET was in Kenosha. "Welcome to Argyle House," Charles said. "You see, it actually is a house. Unlike Random House."

They went around a corner of the porch to another entrance. The interior was humble, but there were books everywhere and piles of what must be manuscripts that would compete for the interest of the publisher. Charles led him to a desk where a woman sat. A nameplate before her read J. J. RUDOLPH. She smiled away apparent annoyance at being interrupted. Charles said, "And this is Jo Jo. Jo Jo, did I mention running into Carl Borloff in a Chicago bookstore?"

"The art book?" She was perhaps fifty years of age, heavyset, her hair cut closely to her head. Large liquid eyes looked up at him over her half-glasses. "I have yet to do an art book."

SIXTEEN

Only Madeline Schutz knew how anonymous a bestselling author could be. Her novels with their shiny, glitzy covers beckoned to travelers in every airport of the nation, they were a staple of the book displays in supermarkets, she herself had seem them, dog-eared and supple as an evangelist's Bible, in the hands of dreamy-eyed youths of all ages, but no one made a connection between her and the M. X. Schutz on those covers. They were paperback originals, published by a small firm in Kenosha that decided to take a plunge into science fiction. They had yet to get more than a perfunctory notice in *Publishers Weekly.* The longest review she had ever had, of the third of the Empyrean Chronicles, *Miranda and the Moonlet,* had been in a Nashville paper, and the reviewer spent most of the time discussing an alternative plot. Perhaps if her high sales had spelled wealth, Madeline could have been more philosophical about this, but the contract she had signed with Argyle House—for ten books—had been carefully drawn, and Madeline received only a small share of what must be the enormous profits.

At the time, she had been so eager to get into print, to be a published author, that she had hardly glanced at the contract before signing and sending it back to Kenosha lest the publisher change his mind. It had been a sacred moment when she held a copy of the first chronicle in her hand and felt that her dreams had at last been realized. A year later, after she had sent in the second chronicle, she had yet to receive a royalty report. She wrote a timid letter of inquiry and received a phone call in return. J. J. Rudolph turned out to be a woman, and she was effusive with her praise. Madeline was assured that her series had surpassed all the expectations of the house. She asked when she would receive her royalties. There was a long pause.

"Do you have a copy of your contract there, Madeline?"

"Should I get it?"

"No need for that if you can remember the main points. Your royalties will be based on the second and later printings."

"Not on the first?"

Ms. Rudolph was patient. She outlined for Madeline the risks a publisher took in launching a series aimed eventually at ten volumes. Placing titles with the distributors who alone could make or break a book was not the work of a summer day. "You realize that your books are available everywhere."

"Yes, I know that."

"You will be delighted to learn that arrangements are being made for second printings of both the first and second chronicles."

"How many copies are there in the first printings?"

"Three hundred thousand! You can imagine what that costs us."

"I don't seem to be on Amazon.com or the other online book sites."

"We have had our disagreements. Our board has voted not to do business with them."

"Will the second printings be as large?"

"One hundred thousand copies each."

Later Madeline could not remember how the conversation had ended. After hanging up, she had got out her contract with Argyle House and for the first time read it carefully. She could not believe she had signed such an agreement. No, that wasn't true. She could very easily believe it. At that point in her career, she would have *paid* to get her book in print. A week after her phone call, she received a check for twenty thousand dollars, which was described as an advance against royalties for the second and later printings of the first two chronicles. Madeline doodled on a pad trying to establish what her royalty on one hundred thousand copies would be. Her royalty was 10 percent but, she noticed, not of the cover price of the novel but of the net earnings of Argyle House. J. J. Rudolph responded to her next letter promptly and briefly. There was a 60 percent markup on her titles. Madeline joined the Authors Guild and immediately sought their advice on her arrangements with Argyle House. The answer was not comforting.

She was assured that most contracts were eminently fair to authors, but there were rare exceptions, and, alas, Argyle House was one of them. Hers was not the first complaint they had received. If she had sought advice before signing the contract, she would have been advised to take her work to another publisher.

Another publisher! How many had turned her down before that bright day when Argyle House had expressed interest in her work. The tragic truth was that even now, knowing what she did, having received the letter from the guild, she would have gone ahead and signed the contract.

She had always written quickly. Now her pace became quicker still. Her only hope of release from the servitude of the contract was to finish the ten chronicles and then hope to find an honest publisher.

Then the body had been found hanging in a garage in Fox River and identified as hers. One of her purses was missing and some clothing.

Her first crazy thought was that it was a warning from Argyle House. They had somehow learned of her inquiries at the Authors Guild. Perhaps the guild had contacted them.

Madeline left her apartment and drove to Elmhurst and took a motel room using her mother's maiden name, paying cash to avoid any question about her credit card. For several days she cowered in dread. She had not even brought her computer. She never traveled without a computer, but she would have been incapable of rocketing off into outer space in her present mood. She watched the news; she read the newspapers. On the fourth day she became angry. She would go to the police and explain that that was not her body they had found hanging in the garage.

What a relief it had been to pour out her story to Agnes Lamb. The interview with Tetzel the reporter not so much, since he seemed to resent most of what she told him.

"The Empyrean Chronicles?" Agnes had cried. "I have them all. I love them."

"Thank you."

"I've never met a real live author before." Agnes reached out to touch Madeline's arm as if to see if she was real. "You know what I kept thinking when Mr. Mintz let me into your apartment and I saw the manuscript on your desk? I thought, that is the last chronicle."

"I wish it were."

"You don't mean that."

"Sometime I'll tell you all about being a famous author."

She did tell her, later, all of it, feeling like a fool as she described it all. Agnes listened to her with a stern expression. Then she began to take notes.

"Agnes, what if there is some connection between Argyle House and the woman found hanging in the garage?"

"The thought is bound to occur," Agnes said.

SEVENTEEN

CY HAD PIPPEN READ HIM her complete report on the woman found hanging in the garage of Amy Gorman's apartment, as much for the information as for the pleasure of the company of the lovely and inaccessible assistant coroner. That she was a strikingly beautiful woman would have been obvious to anyone with eyes to see; that she was inaccessible, at least to Cy, stemmed from the fact that she had a husband—the ob-gyn man, or Ojibwa, as Cy thought of him—and that there was a Mrs. Horvath, the love of his youth and middle age, till death do them part and all the rest. Still, in the case of Pippen, Cy was incapable of custody of the eyes.

"I miss the phrase 'ritual killing.'"

"I looked it up. It doesn't apply. Unless Elizabethan practices were ritual killings."

Cy waited. Pippen loved to explain. When Henry VIII or Elizabeth hanged someone, the victim was cut down while still alive, then drawn and quartered. This victim, no longer Madeline Schutz, had been mutilated while she still hung.

"Probably after she was dead. Have you identified her yet?"

"Agnes is working on it."

They were seated in the cafeteria on a middle floor of the courthouse, accessible to cops, coroners, and clerks of court. Pippen wore her lab coat over a black turtleneck with a medallion adorning her bosom. From time to time, she tossed her head and her ponytail responded.

"Did you find a knife?"

"No."

"It probably wasn't a knife. Do you know that instrument that looks all handle with a razor blade that can be released by pressing a button? I don't know what they're called."

"Why not a knife?"

"These were incisions, not cuts."

"A deranged surgeon?"

Pippen shrugged. Cy drove from his mind the instruments that Pippen used on bodies when performing an autopsy. "How will Agnes go about making an identification?"

"She's open to suggestions."

"There was paint under the fingernails."

"Under?"

"Oil paint. Maybe she was an artist."

"Not a housepainter?"

"You could have it analyzed."

Pippen closed the report and laid a long-fingered hand upon it. She might have been displaying her rings, except that Cy was certain that she had no idea of the moral war that raged within him whenever they were together. No one knew but his confessor, who was puzzled by Cy's story.

"Impure desires?"

"Not really."

"What, then?"

"Carelessness about the occasion of sin?"

"I think you're being scrupulous."

"I hope so."

Temporary relief came with absolution and lasted until the next time he saw Pippen.

When they left the cafeteria, they descended in the elevator to Pippen's refrigerated quarters in the basement of the building. Her ostensible boss, Lubins, a political hack, was seldom there. Cy collected a specimen of the paint from beneath the fingernails. The clothing that had been found in the trash can in the garage was already in the lab, along with the purse. All that had been stolen from the real Madeline Schutz. The paint beneath the fingernails would not give them an identification, only an occupation or maybe a hobby.

Agnes was waiting for Cy when he got to his office. She rattled off an account of her visit with Madeline Schutz. "Should I look into Argyle House?"

"Isn't that pretty far-fetched?"

"Yes, but what's near-fetched?"

"Remember when the lawyer suggested to Amy Gorman that she shouldn't go home? Who did she stay with?"

Agnes consulted her notes. "Susan Devere."

"Of the Devere family?"

"Hence the name."

"What does she do?"

"Let's find out."

BARRINGTON, ILLINOIS, HAS become a large area of new homes surrounding the town of that name. Susan Devere lived in the town, in a modest trilevel, the upper level of which had been converted into a studio. She came to the door in a smock, her hair pulled back on her head, a look of annoyance on her face. They showed her their ID.

Agnes said, "We're looking into the body found in your friend's garage."

A mouth opened in surprise is seldom attractive, but in Susan's case it erased the annoyance and made her look beautiful. She fiddled with the lock and opened the door.

"She still staying with you?" Agnes asked as they went in.

"Would you want to go back to that house?"

"You're a painter," Cy said.

She made a face. "You're a detective." Her tone was somewhere between sarcasm and teasing. Her smock was smeared with paint; there was a daub on the side of her nose.

"Where do you work?"

"Come on."

She led them upstairs into a large room lighted by sky-lights. It was a mess. An easel stood at an angle to catch the light; there were little tables around it covered with tubes and bottles, and brushes galore standing handles down in what looked like a Ball canning jar. Rags. A plume of smoke rose from a huge ashtray. Along the walls several pictures in various stages of completion were propped. The canvas on the easel was a portrait.

Cy studied it. "Amy Gorman?"

"You are a detective."

"And you're quite an artist."

"That, unfortunately, is still a minority opinion."

"What made you an artist?"

"Affluence. My family has more money than any family ought to have. But I was damned if I was going to become a patron of this or that."

"Like your grandmother?"

"Our tainted family's solitary boast. Is that sacrilegious?"

"Why would it be?"

"Wordsworth was referring to the Blessed Virgin. Our tainted nature's, etc., etc."

Neither Agnes nor Cy had anything to say to that.

Cy said, "The murdered woman was a painter, too."

"How do you know that?"

"There was paint under her fingernails."

Susan examined her own nails, then nodded. "It's hard to get out. Hence the nail polish."

"Has Amy Gorman any idea why her garage was selected?"

"We never talk about it. What's there to say?"

"How did you come to know her?"

"Through her son, the one now in Iraq."

"Do artists ever get together?"

"How do you mean?"

"Meetings, whatever."

"There are clubs. Those who work in pastels sometimes meet together to criticize one another. So do watercolor people. Oils? We're a pretty solitary group. About the only time we meet is for art shows."

Cy said, "I wonder if you would do us a favor. The paint under the fingernails is about all we have to go on. Would you take a look at the body and see if it's anyone you ever saw?"

"A dead body!"

"It is pretty gruesome," Agnes said. "Think of it as a favor to Amy Gorman."

"I'm already providing her with a hideout."

"Isn't she back at work?"

"Yes. I couldn't do what you ask."

It took fifteen minutes to convince her that if Agnes could stand a visit to the morgue, so could Susan Devere. "The coroner is a woman," Agnes added. "A very pretty woman."

Cy glanced at Agnes as if she had revealed his secret.

Pippen met them as if she were a hostess, and in her presence Susan Devere relaxed.

"I've never been in a morgue before."

"Most are here on a first visit," Pippen said cheerily. "Let's go. If 'twere done well 'twere done quickly. Is that right?"

"Close," Susan said.

Down some steps and into a storage room, where Pippen went humming to a drawer, grabbed the handle, and slid the body out. Head first. Agnes wheeled Susan around to the side.

"My God, it's Bobby!"

"I've never fainted before in my life," Susan said when they got her to Pippen's office and a cup of coffee was put in her hands. "Can I smoke here?"

"It's not going to harm any of my customers."

Susan lit up. "Bobby who?" Agnes asked.

Her name was Roberta Newman. That was enough to get Agnes going, and soon they had not only a name but an address, a list of traffic violations, an application for a fishing license, and the tag number of her automobile.

Meanwhile, Cy took the still shaken Susan back to Barrington. "How well did you know her? Bobby?"

"I didn't know her at all. I knew who she was. Our family foundation gave her a grant. She kept winning prizes."

"You've been a great help."

"Don't ever ask again."

EIGHTEEN

ROBERTA NEWMAN HAD LIVED, apparently alone, in a loft a block off Dirksen Boulevard in downtown Fox River, and it was there she produced the pictures that, as Susan had said, kept winning prizes, even if these had been awarded from the lower rungs of the ladder of success. On the wall that seemed to prevent the skylight from falling into the loft was one of her awards, a plaque whose metal legend had been removed, making for a much more usable dartboard. Below it, also the recipient of darts, was a photo cut from the paper, Bobby flanked by the sponsors of the Fox River Art Show, 2007. Well, success hadn't gone to her head.

The first time Agnes saw the loft, it was with Cy Horvath and the lab crew, searching the studio for some clue as to why Bobby had been found hanging in Amy Gorman's garage. No one seemed to expect to find anything, and that is what they found. Nothing that could help.

"That was just routine, Cy," Agnes complained as they drove away. "Can't you make them go at it again?"

"Would you like someone telling you you don't know your job?"

"Is that what you're telling me?"

How could you pick a fight with the Rock of Gibraltar? Cy just didn't react the way other people did.

"You keep at it, Agnes."

"You mean that?" She could have hugged him. "Of course you mean that. Thank you, I will."

"No need to tell Keegan."

"Who's Keegan?"

Was that the first time she had ever heard Cy laugh?

Before going back to the loft, Agnes had a long talk with Pippen, tugging her sweater close around her to fend off the chill of the morgue. How in God's name did Pippen stand her job? "You going for the pension or what?"

Pippen laughed. "I think of it as a public service."

"If I was a doctor…"

"You'd be worried about malpractice suits." Pippen told her about her husband, who was being sued by a patient who'd been shown the wrong pictures by his nurse and was furious when she didn't have twins.

"She'll be laughed out of court."

"We'll see. So what about Roberta Newman?"

"Susan Devere keeps asking when we will know who killed her fellow artist."

"Tell her about unsolved crimes."

"I keep thinking, what if she had been a friend of mine?" Agnes inhaled. "Can you give me any idea what I should be looking for?"

Dr. Pippen got out her autopsy report and flipped through the pages. After a minute, she looked at Agnes. "What I think was used to cut her? I think artists use them." She paused and frowned. "And terrorists. A half razor blade in a holder. I don't know what they're called. You find that and something might be done."

On her visit to the studio, Agnes did find a couple of safety razor blades, apparently used to cut art board, but there was nothing like the box cutter Pippen had described. She sat in a chair and stared at the tilted drafting board before her on which a number of sketches were pinned. The easel was just a few steps away flanked by little tables filled with paint and bottles and brushes and rags. Agnes rolled the chair over to them and inspected them. Nothing. She got up and went to the canvases propped against the wall. One was of a nude black woman, standing, skinny, her right hip angled as she demurely crossed her legs, the expression on the face making her look like someone out of hell.

There was a tap on the door, and Agnes sprang to her feet. She had her weapon in her hand and stood next to the door. "Who is it?"

"It's Louellen, Bobby."

Agnes opened the door, keeping out of sight. A woman looked in. When she turned her head and saw Agnes, she jumped, but Agnes caught her wrist before she could head for the stairs. "Come on in, Louellen."

"Who the hell are you?"

"A friend of Bobby's."

Even clothed, miniskirt, scooped blouse, a huge bag over her shoulder, the woman had the expression in the painting.

"I never saw you before."

"Well, I never saw you, either."

"I have a room downstairs."

Louellen entered and pushed the door shut. She stood and looked around. "How about this place?"

"How well did you know Bobby?"

The woman's eyes narrowed. "What you getting at?"

Agnes felt she owed it to Louellen to show her ID. The woman let out a yip. "Don't tell me Russell missed a payment again."

"Don't worry about Russell."

"Humph. I'll worry about him when he starts worrying about me."

Louellen glided across the studio, glanced at the canvas Agnes had been struck by, and shook her head. "If I looked that bad I'd go broke."

"I asked you how well you knew Bobby."

Louellen dipped her head and made a face. "Nothing like that. She had her man."

"I'm going to make coffee."

"I'm going to help you drink it."

Louellen got her bag off her shoulder and dropped it on the floor, where it gaped and then sagged into itself. Agnes didn't want to know what Louellen carried around in her bag, but before turning away she saw it. She reached in and pulled it out. She pressed the release, revealing the blade. She looked at Louellen. "Where did you get this?"

"It's for protection. In case anyone gets rough."

Agnes took it with her when she put water in the pot and put in coffee. She longed to tell the woman that she was on the sure path to hell but wasn't lost yet. *Come on down to the tabernacle and listen to Preacher Lester and feel your heart move. Get saved, girl, while there is yet time.* That's what she would have liked to say, but she was here in another capacity, and that had to come first. "You want to put this on the stove, Louellen?"

There was a hot plate in the part of the studio where there was a table and chairs. There was a huge bed, too, hardly a foot off the floor. Having put on the coffee, Louellen came and placed her pointed shoe on the edge of the bed and jiggled. They waited until the coffee was done, and then they sat at the little table and stared across at one another.

"Bobby give you this?" Agnes held up the blade.

She shook her head.

"Who?"

"How'd you come to be a cop?"

"How did you come to be…" She couldn't say it. At the tabernacle, they had lots of ways of saying it, Jezebels, lost women, sisters of Satan, others.

"Not becoming it would have been hard."

"Tell me how you got this."

"You gonna tell Bobby?"

"When was the last time you saw her?"

"I don't keep a calendar."

"Guess."

"A week. More. I don't know."

"So you took this before then?"

Louellen lit up, and Agnes was relieved that it was a cigarette. The girl tipped back her head and blew smoke upward. She looked at Agnes and then around the studio. "It was seeing me when she painted me that turned him on. I wasn't surprised when he started dropping by. Couldn't bring himself to just say it, you know? His story was he was worried about me. Did I realize what a dangerous life I led. I needed him to tell me that? So he gave me that."

"And then?"

Louellen smiled. "You want the details?"

"He was Bobby's boyfriend?"

"While she had him."

"What do you mean?"

"He came and went."

"What's his name?"

"Ask Bobby if you're so interested."

"Louellen, Bobby is dead. Why do you think I'm looking around here? We're trying to find who did it."

"Dead!"

"She was found hanging in a garage, and someone had cut her open. I think with this. Or one just like it."

"Jesus Christ!"

"Invoke his name, girl. That's the first step."

Louellen laughed a frightened laugh. "You think Charles did it."

"Do you know how I could find him?"

"How would I know a thing like that? He came to my place."

"What did he look like?"

"You'll find a picture of him over against the wall."

"Show me!"

Louellen searched for ten minutes before giving up. "It was here."

"Now it's gone. Describe him for me."

"I'll draw you a picture."

"You're an artist?"

"Well, I can draw a picture. Bobby said I could be an artist myself." Louellen pulled the little wheeled chair up to the drafting board and tacked a piece of paper to it.

Before she began, Agnes asked her what the sketches pinned to the board were.

"For a book. She did pictures for books, too," Louellen replied. While Louellen with a frown began to move the pencil across the paper, Agnes went to the two-drawer file cabinet, on whose top more art paraphernalia lay. She opened the top drawer. A series of lettered tabs on folders, all of them full of papers, letters, whatnot. She ran her fingers along them from back to front, but found nothing. When she got to A. Argyle House. The folder was empty.

"This is pretty close, I think," Louellen said. She untacked the sheet and held it out to Agnes.

"This is good!"

"How can you tell if you never saw him?"

Agnes looked at the sketch. The face was almost cherubic, the eyes rounded in innocent surprise, a beatific smile on his full lips. "He looks like an angel."

Louellen lit another cigarette. "Oh, he has a lot of devil in him, too."

NINETEEN

FATHER LADISLAW SLEDZ could hardly contain himself when he called Father Dowling. "Did you get a letter, Roger?"

"I never even made the team."

"From the chancery! Our Lady of Chestokowa is spared. Wilenski called first, and I asked for it in writing. Now the letter is here."

"Good for you, Lad."

"I didn't do a thing. All those Poles who moved to the suburbs got through to Wilenski. What could he do? He's related to half of them. It turns out he's some sort of cousin of mine, however removed. Well, he's not going to remove Our Lady of Chestokowa."

It would have been churlish to begrudge Sledz his good news, but of course it implied bad news for St. Hilary's. No call or letter from Bishop Wilenski had been received by Father Dowling, and he rather doubted now that the threat to the parish could be lifted.

The following morning, Amos called, excited by a story in the *Chicago Tribune* about the sparing of Our Lady of Chestokowa. Roger Dowling tried to make light of the fact that he himself had had no further word from the chancery office.

"I will call on the cardinal myself."

"I wouldn't do that, Amos."

How could Father Dowling not think that the formation of Save St. Hilary's and the injunction Amos had filed against the archdiocese had worsened matters? The injunction now lay in some legal limbo, waiting for there to be an overt threat to St. Hilary's for an injunction to stop. Newspaper stories apparently did not provide a sufficient basis for an injunction. Still, the proposed injunction became an item of local news.

"Let me know as soon as you hear, Father." Amos paused. "Good news or bad."

WHEN FATHER DOWLING returned to the rectory after saying his noon Mass, he was surprised to find Bishop Wilenski waiting in the front parlor. Marie told him of his guest, her eyes wide with hope.

"I wanted to see the parish, Father. I should have warned you I was coming."

"Warned me?"

"Let you know in advance." The bishop seemed to regret his choice of words. "Is this a bad time?"

"Lunchtime? It's perfect. Come, let's see what Mrs. Murkin has prepared for us."

Anyone who drops by in midday can scarcely be surprised to be asked to stay for lunch.

"I don't know when we last had a bishop at this table," Marie said.

"Have you been here long, Mrs. Murkin?"

"Since the glacier."

"Marie had been here for years before I came, Bishop."

"There were Franciscans…" Marie began, but decided not to call up those awful memories. "It was so good to have a diocesan priest assigned here again."

Off she went to the kitchen to fetch the tuna casserole that had filled the house with a delicious aroma.

"Would you like some wine, Bishop?" she asked when she had filled his plate.

"Do you have beer, Mrs. Murkin?"

Bishop Wilenski opened his napkin and draped it over his episcopal tummy. What was it that was said of a man when he became a bishop? He would never again have a bad meal or have the truth spoken to him. Wilenski put his hands on the table and looked around benevolently. "What a wonderful place you have here, Father. No wonder you like it. I'm looking forward to being shown around."

Marie, having heard this, became ever more unctuous. Surely the bishop had come with good news.

After lunch, Roger took the bishop first to the senior center, where Edna Hospers explained her operation. The seniors seemed intent on showing the bishop what a good time they were all having. On to the church, then; Roger first showed Bishop Wilenski the side chapel, and then they moved slowly down the main aisle, studying the stained glass windows. It was impossible to read Wilenski's expression. Finally they were settled in the pastor's study.

"I wish I had good news for you, Father. I'm afraid that the protest of the old people and the threat of an injunction have displeased the cardinal."

Roger waited.

"I have sent out a few letters of reprieve."

"Father Sledz called me."

"The cardinal told me to wait when I suggested sending one to you."

"Then nothing is settled?"

"Father, if it were my decision alone…" He stopped himself. "What I would suggest, and I've given some thought to this, is that you make an appointment with the cardinal. No one could make a case for the parish better than you."

"Did you mention this to him?"

"I did."

"And?"

"He said it couldn't do any harm."

"Could it do any good?"

"I have long since given up trying to read the cardinal's mind."

TWO DAYS LATER, ROGER Dowling was admitted to the cardinal's residence and put in a room to wait for him. In a few minutes, he heard the heavy step of the cardinal, who in a moment was in the room. He held out his hand but prevented Roger from kissing his ring, and they simply shook hands.

"Be seated, Father. Be seated."

The domed, hairless head of the cardinal, the object of jocular remarks from the clergy, seemed oddly shaped. Youthful polio had affected the cardinal's gait, but the smile on his smooth, unlined face was beatific. He was a native of Chicago, as he reminded Father Dowling, and had come by what seemed an inevitable if circuitous route to his present post. His smile faded slowly as he looked at Father Dowling.

"You certainly have loyal parishioners, Father."

"It is the parish they're loyal to."

"Of course. You have no idea how I envy pastors. My life has been largely academic and administrative. Of course, I am myself a pastor now." A pastor who had taken part in the conclave that had elected the present pope, the cardinal having been assigned to Chicago by John Paul II. "It still pains me that any decision I make must anger as many people as it pleases."

"Whatever you decide, Your Eminence, will not displease me."

The cardinal looked at him, as if to see whether this was merely the pro forma remark of one whose obedience he could claim. He joined his hands, elbows on the arms of his chair. He studied the ring on his right hand that the late pope had put there. "In any case, your anger or pleasure will have to

wait. I am still undecided about St. Hilary's. Bishop Wilenski
gave an excellent account of your parish."

"I have enjoyed being there."

A cardinalatial smile. "You are careful with your tenses,
Father. How long have you been there?"

Roger told him. "I was in Yakima then."

Was he suggesting that he had had to move more than once
at the pleasure of his superiors?

"Tell me about the Devere family. Some of them have
been buried in your church?" The little side chapel did not
seem much of an impediment to whatever the cardinal might
decide. He was interested in the Menotti stained glass windows. "Some beautiful windows from older parishes have
been relocated in new churches in the suburbs." He paused.
"Not always with aesthetic effect. Still, it is a solution." He
paused again. "One that would prompt another public letter
from the artist."

Roger said nothing.

"He was certainly eloquent. I had no idea he was still alive.
Have you met him, Father?"

"No." He seemed to be exonerating himself from prompt-
ing Angelo Menotti's letter.

"But we cannot be as temperamental as artists."

For ten minutes, the cardinal reviewed for Father Dowling
the pressing economic reasons for retrenchment. Churches
could not be retained as museums. Roger found himself sym-
pathizing with the problems this frail-looking man faced. A
prince of the Church. There must be times when that exalted
title seemed ironic to him.

A young priest appeared in the doorway and gave a nod.
Time for the next appointment. The demanding schedule must
go on. Roger knelt for the cardinal's blessing.

"God bless you, Father."

The remark might have been addressed to a condemned man.

TWENTY

Menteur called the pressroom, and Tetzel answered. "Did you like my latest piece on St. Hilary's, Lyle?"

Menteur asked, "Is Rebecca there?"

"I haven't seen her in days."

"I'm not surprised."

"Is she on leave?"

"Tetzel, that woman is a bundle of energy, a model for us all."

"Rebecca?" Was Menteur talking of the overweight, chain-smoking, man-hating bimbo who occupied the desk next to Tetzel's?

"Check out her story on Menotti. It's already on the Web site."

"Menotti! But he's part of my assignment."

"How so?"

"He designed and installed the windows in St. Hilary's, for Christ's sake."

"Let's not get into motives. The church closing story is dead, Tetzel. Have you seen the new list?"

Tetzel had his own list, but Menteur was already on it. Rebecca came into the pressroom then, and Tetzel said, "I'll pass on your message." He hung up.

Rebecca was whistling tunelessly as she collapsed into her chair and turned first east, then west. "Any good news about St. Hilary's?"

Tetzel tried to smile knowingly. Was she referring to the list Menteur had mentioned?

"Your stories probably will have a lot to do with getting St. Hilary's off the chopping block."

Tetzel was astounded. Was Rebecca actually praising him? The woman had been in the grips of professional jealousy since being assigned to the pressroom, eclipsed by the presence of a seasoned and renowned reporter. She knew of the novel he wasn't writing, too, and there was nothing more likely to anger a colleague than the suggestion that one of their own was at work on a novel. Novel. Madeline Schutz. My God, he had to write that up before Rebecca decided to go back to it. From now on he would concentrate on the woman found hanging in Amy Gorman's garage. Rebecca avoided violence, except of the verbal kind.

Tetzel turned and tapped a key, bringing up the *Tribune*'s Web site. Rebecca smiled at him from the screen. He turned the monitor so she couldn't see herself.

Rebecca seemed able to see around corners, though. "Is my interview with Angelo Menotti already on the Web site?"

"It's a slack news day."

Rebecca took umbrage at that, doubtless because she expected him to reciprocate her praise.

He took a deep breath. "Great story."

"Thank you. I would have thought Menotti would be happy about the project to make a book of all the stained glass windows he designed."

"He isn't?"

"He says over his dead body."

"How old is he?"

"Ancient. You may be right. As long as he's alive the project is dead."

There was no reason not to read her story about Angelo Menotti, and he did. It was largely big gobs of quotations from the artist, Rebecca confining herself to crisp questions that got the old man going. She should have given him co-billing. My life, as told to Rebecca Farmer. Maybe he would try that technique in his account of his interview with Madeline Schutz. He should have brought a camera with him. Well, maybe not. He wanted to portray her as a phenomenally successful writer, and the setting told against that. Her account of how she had been jobbed out of royalties on the first three hundred thousand—three hundred thousand!— copies of each of her chronicles should be shouted from the rooftops.

"Good idea," Rebecca said when he told her he intended to go on with that story.

Tetzel could reconcile himself to the prolific author because of the way her publisher was shafting her.

"Want to go over to the Jury Room?" Rebecca asked.

"Maybe I'll meet you there later."

"What are you working on?"

"This last chapter has been giving me trouble."

"Chapter!"

"Sometimes I wish I had never begun the damned thing, but I'm in the homestretch now." He sighed a creative sigh. Rebecca muttered something and lumbered from the pressroom, wearing her laurels. Featured on the paper's Web site. He groaned. Scooped by Rebecca! What now seemed to Tetzel the heart of the series he had been doing on St. Hilary's had been purloined by a crafty colleague. If she hadn't been put up to it by the loathsome Menteur. The editor brooded in his smoke-free office knowing that the courthouse had been exempted from the draconian antismoking ordinance that had been patched together in a smoke-filled room and rushed to a vote when there was a bare quorum in the city council. It would be like Menteur, his mouth full of chewing gum, to send Rebecca down to Peoria to interview the great artist Angelo Menotti. Spite, pure spite. Well, he would show them what real reporting was.

"WHAT DO YOU KNOW ABOUT publishers, Tuttle?"

"What's your next question?"

"Argyle House, ever hear of it?"

"Why would I?"

"I want you to go there with me, as my counsel. There are legal sides to this."

"Can you afford me?"

"Take it!" came from the outer office. Hazel.

Tuttle shouted back, "Run a Google on Argyle House."

"I already am."

A minute later there was the racket of the printer in Hazel's office, and then she bustled in. She was about to toss it on the desk when she was given pause by the mountain of books, papers, briefs, foam containers from Chinese restaurants. She handed the printout to Tetzel.

"I'll read this to you on the drive, Tuttle."

"Where is it?"

"Wisconsin."

"Wisconsin!"

"Just across the state line. We'll leave Hazel here if you're worried about the Mann Act."

Hazel took a playful swing at Tetzel and went rhythmically from the room.

TWENTY-ONE

FLYING BACK TO CHICAGO from a lecture in Tucson, Margaret Ward sipped her sorry excuse for a drink and wished she had flown first class. On domestic flights, that hardly seemed worth it, but you did get a decent drink. Drinks, if you wanted them, and after some lecture crowds the plural seemed called for. Good heavens, what was known as the conservative movement! All those complacent people she had just left, residing in the very state Barry Goldwater had represented, yet who seemed to think it was just a matter of hanging on to their money. Not that she herself had the least qualms about prudently increasing the amount that was hers as a Devere. She had been a conservative, a philosophical conservative, an Edmund Burke conservative, long before she gave a thought to money. At first she had fought the love she felt for her husband, Bernard. He had been more of a Devere than she was, of an artistic temperament. All they'd had was five childless years. Only her brother, James, seemed to realize that what August Devere had amassed had to be managed and multiplied, and not just by investment. Devere Inc. had made its money from the coal mines of southern Illinois and was now into various sources of power, the proud owner of several nuclear power plants. How long had it been since a new such plant had been built? Devere platforms rose above the angry waters of the Gulf, pumping oil from the depths below. Thanks to James, Devere was in the front ranks of those who scoffed at the folly of ethanol, wasting all that corn to produce a fuel that cost more than gasoline. Only in America, America as she had become.

Margaret put her head back, closed her eyes, and thought about Margaret Devere Ward. Know thyself. That sounds so easy, but what is more difficult, really? She knew a priest in New Orleans who always greeted her with "What's it all mean?" Father Boileau seemed to be kidding; you had to know him to know what a serious man he was. Never be serious about serious things? That wasn't it. Has anyone ever become what he set out to be? Until she met Bernard, Margaret had thought seriously about becoming a nun. The only one she had ever told this to was her grandmother.

The old woman, not so old then, had nodded. "It is a temptation."

"Temptation?"

"Unless you become a Carmelite. Or better still a Carthusian."

There were no Carthusian convents in the United States. Margaret had visited one, nestled in the foothills of the French Alps, but she had been unable to imagine herself a member of that community. It would have been like emigrating. As for the Carmelites, well, it turned out there were Carmelites and there were Carmelites, and she had met some bad apples. Bad Carmelite apples. It was then that she became aware of what was happening in the Church. It proved to be a detour of more than a decade. She had given up then, referring it all to the Holy Spirit, and had broadened her horizon, encouraged by Michael, who really hadn't the least interest in any of it. Was that why she had loved him?

What an odd thought. Of late, she had been reading a lot about *acedia*—a neglected capital sin. Translating it as sloth didn't begin to capture it. Distaste for spiritual things? Too often now she thought of her enthusiasms as trivial. Was that a temptation? Finally, at Jane's urging she had gone to Father Dowling.

"DO YOU EVER GET BORED, Father?"

"Not when I have visitors like you."

Margaret smiled. "I'm growing tired of doing what I know are good things to do."

"Take a vacation."

"I recently spent months on a freighter. Once I thought I had a religious vocation."

"Tell me about it."

She told him about it, she mentioned what her grandmother had said, and she spoke of her books and lectures, and while she did she began to feel ashamed, coming here to whine. She fell silent. "I sound pretty silly, don't I?"

"Your grandmother is a wise woman."

"All this is a temptation?"

"The slough of despond."

"Where does that phrase come from?"

"Bunyan."

"Paul?"

Had she ever seen a priest laugh so heartily?

"Your family may very well save this parish, you know. Bishop Wilenski was quite interested to know that you live in the parish and that August Devere commissioned the stained glass windows by Angelo Menotti."

"A funny thing. His grandson was a sailor on that freighter I was on."

"His grandson."

Margaret smiled. "Our family seems haunted by Angelo Menotti. My mother insists on helping a third-rate art historian just because he professes an interest in Menotti." She stood. "I've wasted enough of your time."

"I'm glad you stopped by."

He came with her to the door, and when she got into her car and looked back he was still standing there. What a fool he must think she was.

TWENTY-TWO

TUTTLE SUGGESTED TAKING Peanuts Pianone along, just for the ride, hardly for company.

"Is this his day off?"

"A day like any other."

As Tuttle had hoped, Peanuts offered to take them in a police cruiser, and he tanked up in the departmental garage before coming for them. He was wearing a uniform. "My suit is at the cleaners."

Tetzel groaned and got in the backseat, which was separated from the front by wire mesh. Thank God Peanuts hadn't brought a dog. Tuttle almost got the passenger door closed before Peanuts took off. For the first several miles, he used the siren, zipping along, changing lanes, leaning over the wheel, a manic smile on his face. Once he got that out of his system, he turned the siren off and settled into a steady eighty miles an hour. They had turned onto I-94, headed north, before Tuttle solved the mystery of his seat belt.

"Keep your eye out for a McDonald's," Peanuts told Tuttle.

"I don't suppose there's any Chinese on the highway."

"South of Beijing," Tetzel said. It occurred to him that he had fallen in with fools. What after all was the reason for this trip? The suggestion had been his; he had to take the blame. J. J. Rudolph was Madeline Schutz's editor at Argyle House, and Tetzel had wanted to interview her before running the risk of libel in his story about the exploited author. Imagine showing up with this menagerie. His idea had been to call ahead when they were on the way. Now he just hoped the editor would not be in her office and he could rely on his imagination and the legal department in writing about her.

Before they left Illinois, Peanuts swung off when he saw a McDonald's sign. The drive-through? No way. Tuttle and Peanuts wanted the comfort of the plastic seats that accommodated the average American rear end. Tetzel had often wondered if they sold beer at McDonald's. Now he knew the sorry truth. He settled for a small order of french fries and munched them while his companions did away with several Big Macs and slurped soft drinks from quart-sized containers.

"Want to take something along, Peanuts?" Tuttle asked.

"We'll probably find another."

"Another?"

Tuttle smiled at Tetzel. "It's his car."

Well, the taxpayers', anyway.

With the help of the map on Tetzel's iPhone, Peanuts found Argyle House. It turned out to be an old three-story dwelling looking lonely on a large lot that was mainly ground cover, hostas, out of which a tall elm with a narrow yellowing trunk rose and seemed to hold its parasol of yellowing leaves over the roof of the house. The driveway was cracked, and out of the cracks grew dandelions and other hardy weeds. There was no car in evidence, no sign of life anywhere. Peanuts turned into the driveway and advanced slowly toward the garage, which was located at the back of the lot.

"You sure this is it?" he asked, coming to a stop.

Tetzel opened the door and got out, glad to be able to stretch his limbs. He had been prepared for something modest, but this house made dreams of authorship and publishing seem indictable crimes. Peanuts stayed behind the wheel, but Tuttle scooted around the hood and came up beside Tetzel as he went up the porch steps and creaked his way to the door. A storm door. The blinds on the door and in all the windows were closed. The doorbell did not encourage the thought that it would work. It seemed to have been painted over long ago, when the house was last painted. He tried the knob of the storm door; it turned, he pulled. The inner door was locked.

"It doesn't look like they use the front door much," Tuttle said, and there was a hint in his voice that Tetzel had taken them a long way to not much.

Tetzel let the storm door bang shut, then followed the porch around the corner of the building where he came in sight of a side door. There was a sign jutting from the wall. ARGYLE HOUSE. Reassured, Tetzel headed for it.

There was a bulging screen door here, a bulb burning dimly in the fixture beside it. The inner door was ajar. When is a door not a door? When it's ajar. Tetzel leaned in. "Hello, hello."

He followed his voice inside to a small hallway and then up a flight of three stairs leading to the main floor. The one-time dining room of the house was an office of sorts. The woman seated at the desk did not look up.

"I'm Tetzel of the *Fox River Tribune,*" he began, advancing on the desk, then stopped both speaking and moving. He flexed his knees and lowered his body as if to capture the woman's attention. Her eyes were wide open, and she seemed to be staring at something. What an ugly complexion. "Ma'am?"

Tuttle put a hand on his arm. "Tetzel, she's dead."

The little lawyer circled the desk and lifted the end of the rope that had been used to ship J. J. Rudolph off to the department of unsolicited bodies.

"Call the police," Tetzel said as if he had a rope around his throat, too.

"Peanuts?"

Tetzel had his iPhone in his hand, not knowing how it had got there. With an effort he called 911. Ringing and then a mechanical voice. "You must first dial the area code when calling this number."

"Come on," Tuttle said. "Let's get out of here."

Tetzel was on his heels, unthinking, and soon they were on the porch. He looked at Tuttle.

"Did you touch anything else?" Tuttle was asking, rubbing the door handle vigorously with his handkerchief.

"The front doorknob."

They were cleaning it of telltale prints when the police car turned into the driveway. The two men, one an officer of the court, the other a defender of the people's right to know, froze. They exchanged a look. Tuttle, after a moment, adjusted his tweed hat, bounced down the steps, and hurried off to where Peanuts was talking to a local cop who wondered what a patrol car from Fox River, Illinois, was doing in Kenosha. Composure of a sort returned to Tetzel. He called out, "Officer."

The cop, who seemed to be enjoying his exchange with Peanuts, turned. Was obesity a requirement for the Kenosha police? The inner man was visible in ripples and rolls all over his uniform.

Tetzel came up to him. "I wasn't sure my call went through. Officer, there is a body in this house."

The fat little lips seemed to be seeking the right expression. Reflections of Tetzel looked back at him from the sunglasses the officer wore.

"Come on, I'll show you."

On the way to the house he began writing in his head. *Your reporter is not often the first on the scene of the crime, but today in Kenosha, Wisconsin...*

PART THREE

ONE

EVERY JURISDICTION HAS A sense of turf, but their colleagues in Kenosha were unusually reluctant to include Fox River homicide in a joint investigation of the death of J. J. Rudolph. Cy Horvath went up there with Agnes to see what the problem was. It turned out that there were three problems, Tetzel, Tuttle, and Peanuts, and not necessarily in that order.

"They did report the crime," Agnes said.

The murder investigation is now in the all too fallible hands of the Kenosha police, the Keystone Kops of the area... The chief was quoting from Tetzel's story, which had achieved wide circulation. In it Tetzel's role in discovering the murder was featured, with strong supporting roles given to Tuttle and Peanuts.

"Can you control your local press, Chief?"

"The mayor is the publisher." Chief Sweeney said it with one hand covering his mouth. Cy didn't pursue it. Sweeney might know of the influence of the Pianones in Fox River. Ah.

"As for Officer Pianone..." How to put this? "He is on the force as a favor, Chief."

The eyes above the hand darted away. Let him who is without sin throw the first stone.

"And Tuttle is a lawyer. You know lawyers."

The hand dropped, and the chief sat forward. "Lieutenant, you're welcome to take part in the investigation."

"Thank you, Chief. Detective Lamb will be our principal liaison."

On their feet then, handshakes all around, and off to the

homicide bureau where Brady, Cy's counterpart, assured him that the reluctance had been all on the chief's part. "He's scared to death of his father-in-law."

"Who's he?"

"The mayor."

With Brady they went out to Argyle House. They found the officer assigned to guard the scene asleep in the chair in which J. J. Rudolph died. He was unapologetic when awakened.

"I've been trying to make contact." He looked eagerly at them, concentrating finally on Agnes. "If I could channel her thoughts…"

"Get out of here, Sweeney. Check out the library lot for overparking."

"I don't have to be here to make contact."

"Sweeney?" Cy asked after the metaphysical cop was gone.

"Nephew."

From that point, things began to move. Agnes had full access to the crime scene report, the coroner's report, and something of the history of Argyle House. And who was J. J. Rudolph? Jo Jo Rudolph, as she was called, the attempt at pronouncing her initials perhaps preferable to calling someone of her build Johanna Josephine.

"An odd name," Agnes suggested to the research librarian in the Kenosha Public Library.

"I knew her before she went away," Miss Pageant said.

"Away?"

"She was on the school paper, not in editorial but in makeup and readying copy and all the stuff kids don't care to do. She loved it. After graduation, she got an internship with a paper in Peoria. It was just ten years later that she came back, bought that old house that should have been condemned long ago, and paid too much for it. Maybe she thought it would give her an in with the mayor."

"He owned it?"

"He has a habit of gobbling up property like that. For the land maybe. Or maybe he wants to own the town literally. Anyway, she got going. Argyle House was successful, I suppose. Not the kind of books we'd want here."

"What's wrong with them?"

"They appeal to the baser instincts. Some of the science fiction is all right."

"She published M. X. Shutz."

Miss Pageant made a face.

"You don't like science fiction?"

"My problem is I love the English language. We do have the Empyrean Chronicles on our shelves, however. Readers like them."

"Did you see much of Rudolph after her return?"

A thoughtful pause. "I tried to. Jo Jo seemed to have developed selective amnesia about the past. Not that we were ever close. The only time I went to Argyle House, there was a man there who looked me up afterward. Very inquisitive. He called himself a silent partner. He never shut up. He actually flirted with *me!*"

Agnes let it go. Miss Pageant was pressing fifty, but she looked as if she had passed it years ago. "What was his name?"

"Charles something. Much younger than Jo Jo."

Jo Jo's father, it emerged, had been the village atheist, always available for comments on organized religion. "He made it sound like organized crime. Poor Jo Jo absorbed all that. Has it ever occurred to you that science fiction series tend to invent their own religions?"

"I never thought of that."

Agnes decided not to tell the research librarian about the body they had been led to believe was that of M. X. Schutz. No need to trouble Miss Pageant about Bobby, either. Miss Pageant's description of Charles was close to Louellen's description. Agnes showed Miss Pageant the fallen woman's sketch of Charles. The research librarian nodded. "That is he," she said. She went on loving the English language even as she frowned at the sketch.

Captain Brady followed Agnes's account, rocking in his squeaky chair, which needed lubrication. "It looks as if Fox River is deeper in this than we are."

"Well, at least as deep."

Agnes spent a full day in the offices of Argyle House, sitting in the chair in which Jo Jo had been found dead and in which Officer Sweeney had been trying to contact her in the next world. On the desk before Agnes were stacks of files. There was no mention of Charles in the papers of incorporation, but then he had told Miss Pageant he was a silent partner. The silent partner who never shut up, according to Miss Pageant. The correspondence was also devoid of any reference to Charles. Agnes told herself she would have had to be an idiot or a relative of Mayor Sweeney not to see that Charles was her target. He was connected with Bobby Newman, and he called himself the silent partner of J. J. Rudolph, both of whom had met their deaths by violence. Then she found a file labeled NEWMAN, ROBERTA.

There were sketches of the kind that Agnes had seen on Bobby's drafting board, and the correspondence made it clear that she was illustrating a book for Argyle House. It didn't sound like one Miss Pageant would want on the shelves of the Kenosha Public Library. *Planning the Same-Sex Wedding.* Agnes glanced at the pictures, put them back in the folder, and sat back. A minute later, remembering Officer Sweeney, she grabbed another folder. Twenty minutes later, she found the

Borloff/Devere file. She looked over the agreement that had
been drawn up between Carl Borloff and the Devere Foundation. Argyle House had been promised an initial payment
of one hundred thousand dollars by Carl Borloff.

TWO

CARL BORLOFF WOULD NOT have found Angelo Menotti's studio if he hadn't rented a car with an electronic map. Flying to Peoria rather than driving amounted to a little statement as to the altered financial standing of Carl and his various undertakings. *Sacred Art* was modestly established, but the grant to prepare and publish the book of Menotti stained glass windows made flying feasible. Before he left the rental car lot, he punched in the address of the studio, something he had obtained through Hugh Devere; no need to remind Jane Devere that Carl had not yet met the artist whose work had suddenly propelled him into affluence.

"Count on having a real experience," Hugh said.

"You've been there?"

Hugh had gone at the urging of his mentors in the Notre Dame School of Architecture but also because of a surprising thought of his own. All the talk of the Menotti windows and his family's connection to them led Hugh to look into the techniques of stained glass, and he had become fascinated. He had been surprised by the artist's dismissal of the thought that Hugh might be diverted into the genre that had made Menotti famous.

"Do you know the kind of churches that are being built now?" the old man had roared, and nothing Hugh could say about new developments in church architecture made a dent.

"He's been out of the picture so long he really doesn't know what he's talking about," Hugh told Carl.

"Well, my interest is in stained glass that has already been done."

"Lots of luck."

Carl had smiled when Hugh had said this, and he smiled again as he remembered, directing his car to an area of the city where the Kickapoo River branched off from the Illinois. He followed a two-lane county highway to the point where the imperious voice on the electronic map told him he was about to turn right. "Turn right," she said iambically again, and he did, entering an unpaved road that wound through old trees that seemed to be fighting among themselves to hold their places. The woods ended, and he came into an open area and saw the one-story building sheltered by enormous weeping willows. Carl came to a stop and savored the scene. It might have been a symbol of peace and isolation.

Then there was the sound of barking as Carl approached the dwelling, and he froze. He was terrified of dogs. He had always been terrified of dogs. The barking did not diminish. If he had dared, he would have turned and dashed for his car, but for all he knew those beasts would take this as provocation. He took his cell phone from his pocket with a minimum of movement and punched Angelo Menotti's number. As on the previous occasion, he had to wait through a dozen rings before a melodious voice said, "Hello."

"Carl Borloff. I am just outside."

"Yes, I see you. Why are you hesitating?"

"The dogs."

"Good grief, they're the most gentle dogs in the world. Come ahead."

Carl moved gingerly toward the house, and as he did the barking stopped. A door opened, and the mythical figure of Angelo Menotti was framed in it. The dogs on either side of him were subdued, but Carl found their look menacing. Menotti insisted on introducing these beasts to Carl, and they sniffled and pressed against him and seemed to drop their objections. Menotti addressed them as Gladys and Jo Jo. Carl's surprise at these names must have shown.

"A little sentimentality. If I knew you better I would explain."

To Carl's relief, Menotti shooed the dogs outside after admitting his visitor. It took an act of faith to think he was facing a man in his nineties. The old man was clean shaven; his hair was still thick and wreathed his head with silver waves. The eyebrows might have been filters through which he viewed the world. "So you are an art historian." There was an edgy amusement in the deep bass voice.

Carl had brought the latest issue of *Sacred Art* as well as an earlier one in which several Menotti windows had been featured. He had sent the artist that issue and others but received no acknowledgment. He asked Menotti if he had received them.

"I considered suing you."

"Suing me!"

"One doesn't like people trafficking in his work without authorization."

He had turned to lead them into a large room with an enormous fireplace, the walls full of paintings, the mantel crowded with art objects. Through open glass double doors a studio was visible. Menotti noticed Carl's interest. "Come."

The studio was not the workplace of an artist who had retired. There were several easels with canvases in various stages of completion; along one wall of the studio was a chest-high bench on which shrouded clay studies sat. The far end of the studio was apparently where Menotti worked on stained glass, or had worked.

"Not for forty years," he boomed.

"That's a shame."

"The shame is not mine, young man. Blame the architects."

Carl let it go. This was Hugh Devere's problem, not his.

Menotti moved about in the studio, glaring at a canvas, removing a moist cloth to frown at the molded clay beneath it.

"Work in progress," Carl breathed, intending it as a compliment.

"I suppose you drink."

"Thank you." It was now midmorning.

"I'll take that for yes."

They returned to the adjoining room, where Menotti busied himself at a bar. His suntan pants hung baggily to his sandaled feet, and the sweatshirt bore traces, front and back, of his work in the studio. He came to Carl and handed him a short, heavy glass full of brown liquid. Menotti lifted the one in his other hand. "To the ladies."

He took a healthy swallow from his glass, and Carl followed suit. This brought on a fit of helpless choking. My God, it was straight whiskey. Menotti watched as Carl gained control of himself.

"I thought you were objecting to my toast."

"This is pure whiskey."

"Well, it's bourbon. Are you married?"

"No."

"Why not?"

"No one ever asked me."

Menotti roared. "Never asked you to marry them or never asked if you were married?"

"Neither one."

"I am ninety-four years old."

"I wouldn't believe it."

"It is not a matter of belief. I meant it when I said I thought of suing you."

"I had permission of the pastor in whose church the windows are."

"What difference does that make?"

Carl drank again, managing it better now that he knew what it was. Bourbon had a fine bouquet undiluted. "I'm glad you didn't sue me."

"Don't provoke me again. Tell me about yourself."

"I'd rather hear about you."

"Ninety-four years of mischief. Religious art is a powerful aphrodisiac. You must already have learned that. Would you have imagined that stained glass windows are a way to a woman's heart?"

Through the next several hours, Carl was confronted by dozens of remarks to which he had no reply and on which he could not comment. Menotti replenished their bourbons, announcing that he had not eaten a noonday meal in decades, and talked on. The old man might have been trying to shock him away from admiration for his art, speaking of it as a means of seduction. He couldn't possibly mean that. As for his threat to sue, there was no need to respond to that. Even less need to remind Menotti that he had no authority over his stained glass windows. Let old Mrs. Devere explain that to him if he raised objections later.

"Such beautiful things you have hanging here."

Menotti glanced around. "Some are better than others."

"That portrait fascinates me."

"It is not for sale." His tone was playful.

"I could never afford it if it were." He rose and stood before the painting. It was a young woman, standing, hands joined in a way that seemed to draw her shoulders down, and great eyes that looked directly at Carl. He had never seen such a painting described in any Menotti catalog.

"I call it *Young Jane*. I painted her nude and then clothed her later, on request."

The flight home was uneventful, but on the drive from the airport Carl heard on WBBM of the murder in Kenosha, Wisconsin.

THREE

TUTTLE HAD TOLD HAZEL TO keep on the phone until she contacted Carl Borloff. When finally he had the art historian on the line, Tuttle explained that he had been on the scene when the body of J. J. Rudolph was found in her office at Argyle House. "Sources tell me that you had entered into an agreement with Rudolph."

Tuttle held the phone away from his ear while Carl Borloff sputtered in response. He seemed to be denying that he had dealt with J. J. Rudolph. "The police have found the file in her office, Mr. Borloff."

"What happened up there?"

"It would be easier to discuss this face-to-face."

A long silence. Thus Napoleon must have pondered after Borodino. Borloff, too, decided to push on to Moscow. "Where?"

Tuttle was about to give the location of his office, but he didn't like the thought of all the intervening time when the fish might get away.

"I'll come for you, and then we can decide where to talk."

Borloff agreed.

When Tuttle came out of the inner office, Hazel indicated her approval of the way he had handled it. "Bring him here."

"We'll see."

"You will want a witness."

"My dear woman, have you ever heard of the sanctity of lawyer-client communications?"

"I'll be here."

Tuttle skipped down the four flights to his car. Never had the nonfunctioning of the elevator seemed less of an annoyance. He held in his hand the slip of paper on which Hazel had written Borloff's name and address. Printed, actually. Strange woman.

The address turned out to be an apartment building, and the figure huddled in the shadows Carl Borloff. Tuttle switched his headlights on and off, not an effective maneuver in the afternoon sunlight. He tapped on the horn. The figure jumped. Tuttle opened the driver's door, got half out of the car, and waved his tweed hat. "Borloff! Tuttle."

The figure emerged from hiding and hurried to the car. Tuttle was back behind the wheel when Borloff slipped into the passenger seat. Immediately he put the car in motion.

"You're a lawyer?"

"That's right."

"You have to help me."

"Mr. Borloff, that is why I am here."

Borloff's manner relieved Tuttle of any residual sense of shame that he had because he had pursued the client rather than vice versa. Every lawyer pursues clients. The argument is over method. Given the nervous anxiety of his passenger, Tuttle dismissed the Jury Room as a place where they might consult. The Great Wall of China? This restaurant was the scene of many happy moments for Tuttle, but somehow it seemed inappropriate.

"Unfortunately, the elevator is temporarily out of order," he said when he had swung into the caretaker's parking space behind his building.

He hopped out and rounded the car to release Borloff, who was struggling with the seat belt. Tuttle had meant to warn him about that belt.

They mounted the four flights to Tuttle & Tuttle in silence. Pausing outside the door to get his breathing under control,

Tuttle reached for the knob, opened the door, and gently pushed Borloff inside. He followed with an expectant smile. Hazel wasn't there.

"She must have left a message on my desk," Tuttle said.

Borloff came to a stop after going into the inner office. Tuttle tried to see it with a stranger's eye. He hoped that the disarray suggested a busy man. He got the foam containers from the Great Wall into the wastebasket, making room for them by putting his foot on top of the cornucopia of refuse and stepping down. His foot stuck in the basket. He hobbled around to his chair, waving Borloff to a seat. "Just put those things anywhere. On the floor."

Borloff's mental state made him unaware of these details. Once seated, he began almost immediately to speak, a veritable volcanic flow of words. "I have been robbed," he cried. "You have to get that money back for me."

No need to prod this fellow with questions. Tuttle, working the basket off one foot with the other, listened in fascination. Borloff wanted to begin from the beginning, to tell Tuttle of first coming to the Chicago area, how he had acquainted himself with the sacred art of the city and then the great decision to launch *Sacred Art*. No parent could have spoken more proudly of its child. The mention of the Devere Foundation caught Tuttle's ear.

"They are your patrons?"

"I have others, of course. Small benefactors. Without the Deveres, though, nothing would have happened."

He looked almost wild-eyed at Tuttle. "I did not tell them about Argyle House."

Tuttle nodded noncommittally. He was still in the learning stage. Borloff had taken a document from his inner pocket and was caressing it. After hesitating, he extended it to Tuttle.

"What is that?" Tuttle asked, not moving.

"I suppose a copy was found at Argyle House. Like a fool I made them a copy."

Tuttle took the document, flipping rapidly through it, from the letterhead of Amos Cadbury down to the signatures of Jane Devere and Carl Borloff at the end. On the way he had seen the amount the Devere Foundation was turning over to Borloff. Unless he was mistaken, the sum would be repeated indefinitely.

"Until I complete the project."

"Is it described here?" Again Tuttle fluttered the pages, imagining Amos Cadbury composing the agreement.

"Only by name. The Angelo Menotti Project."

Tuttle listened in disbelief. The money pipeline had been opened to Carl Borloff to produce a book of photographs of stained glass windows. The little lawyer's mind reeled. Was it for this that early generations of the Devere family had labored and amassed wealth? Had Jane Devere ever taken a good look at the beneficiary of her largesse? Tuttle could see Borloff in a lineup. He might have been one of the furtive figures emerging from equivocal movie theaters of old. He did not instill confidence in the Tuttle breast.

"All that will come out, I'm afraid."

"I gave him a check for one hundred thousand dollars." Borloff's whisper would have been appropriate in the confessional.

Tuttle wanted to tip his tweed hat in reverent respect for such a sum. "Him?"

"Argyle House! I tried to stop payment on the check, but it has already been cashed."

"You said him. Argyle House is, or was, a woman. J. J. Rudolph."

"He worked with her. He took me there."

"Where you wrote the check?"

"That was later."

Tuttle paused. "Made out to whom?"

"To Charles!"

"Charles?"

"I met him in Barnes & Noble!"

Then came the incredible tale of how Borloff had fallen in with a hitherto complete stranger, been dazzled by the man's apparent expertise in publishing, been taken to Kenosha to meet J. J. Rudolph. Once back in Chicago, Charles had given Borloff a first-class dinner. It was in the glow of brandies afterward that Carl had made out a check for one hundred thousand dollars payable to Charles. Tuttle's hands were gripping the arms of his chair. Whatever the fate of that one hundred thousand dollars, there was more where that had come from.

"Charles what?"

"I don't know!" Borloff got out his checkbook and held it up for Tuttle to see. In recording the check he had written simply Charles.

"You must have written more than Charles on the check."

"Of course I did."

"Well?"

"I don't remember! You must think me mad. What will the Deveres say?"

Tuttle sat forward. "Give me a dollar."

"A dollar. What for?"

"A retainer. Thereby you become my client. I intend to get onto this as quickly as possible."

Borloff eagerly got out a dollar.

Tuttle took it, rising. "For the nonce, I would recommend that you go into seclusion."

FOUR

"KENOSHA?" REBECCA ASKED, contempt in her voice. "Why run a story that length on Kenosha? What's it got to do with Fox River?"

Tetzel kept his counsel. When Menteur made the same comment, doubtless prompted by Rebecca, his only reply was "I was surprised when you ran the whole thing, Lyle."

"It was a slow day."

"I'm back on the murder of the artist, Bobby Newman." Tetzel held his breath. It would be like Menteur to assign that to Rebecca, the fink. That fear was allayed by both Menteur's silence and Rebecca's crowing. Her piece on the women attendants in European men's rooms had drawn a lot of comment on the *Tribune* blog, much of it scatalogical. Now Menteur wanted her to do a series on her European trip.

"Good idea," Tetzel said.

"Did I ever tell you how the men in Naples treat women?" Rebecca asked.

"Several times." Female tourists complained of having their bottoms pinched in crowds. Rebecca had probably backed through Naples without result.

An hour before, Tetzel had found a pensive Tuttle in the Jury Room, nursing a soft drink. He looked vaguely at Tetzel when he sat across from him. "This is more complicated than we thought, Gerry."

"Nothing is more complicated than I thought."

"What do you know about the Devere Foundation?"

"Look it up."

"I have." Tuttle paused. An ethical war seemed to be raging in the little lawyer's unethical heart.

"Tell me about it."

"I have a client."

"That is news? It's me, isn't it?"

Tuttle was puzzled.

"We went to Kenosha as lawyer and client."

This seemed to decide Tuttle. He sat forward. "Listen."

Tetzel listened. His drink arrived, and he sipped it, following Tuttle's story. Think of it as a confidential conversation between lawyer and client. The client Tuttle spoke of, however, was Carl Borloff.

"Agnes Lamb is on it, Tetzel. She was on the Bobby Newman murder. She is liaison with the Kenosha police. The tertium quid, the missing link, is Charles. She is bound to see that."

"Who's Charles?"

"That, my dear fellow, is precisely the question."

Tuttle laid it out. His new client, Borloff, had turned over one hundred thousand dollars of the pile he had been granted by the Devere Foundation to produce a book of photographs of Angelo Menotti's stained glass windows. Bobby Newman had been preparing illustrations for an Argyle House book. Tuttle had learned from Peanuts Pianone that a hooker who worked out of a room in the building where Newman's loft was had spoken of a man in the case. Tuttle was assuming that that man and the man who had wheedled the money from Borloff were the same man.

"Borloff?"

"Borloff. Tetzel, put your investigative reporting skills to work on this." He laid a piece of paper on the table. "That's a photocopy Peanuts got for me. An artist's sketch of Charles."

Tetzel picked up the photocopy. The man looked like a choirboy, maybe because he wore his hair long, over his ears.

Whoever had made the sketch had been fascinated by the cleft chin. Tetzel put it into his pocket, finished his drink, and stood. The two men looked at one another. An alliance had been cemented.

TETZEL WENT BACK ACROSS the street and up to police headquarters. Captain Keegan was at his desk, a half-eaten sandwich in one hand, papers in the other. He looked at Tetzel over the tops of his glasses.

"Good story on Kenosha."

"I understand Officer Lamb is working with the Kenosha police."

Keegan grunted.

"What have you learned about Charles?"

"Who's Charles?"

"I asked you first."

"Ask Cy or Agnes."

"They in?"

"Do you want an escort?"

Cy wasn't in his office, and Agnes was in Kenosha. On the way down in the elevator, Tetzel studied the photocopied sketch Tuttle had given him. Before getting into his car, he lit a cigarette. Traffic went east and west; pedestrians hurried along, oblivious of their surroundings. The sun glanced off plate glass, hurtful to the eyes. Tetzel's heart went out to the scene. He might very well recall this moment and this scene when he wrote his memoirs. *Little did I expect as I set off for Bobby Newman's studio...*

The blighted area off Dirksen was an unsavory area that Tetzel had seldom visited while sober. Vague memories of moral lapses disturbed the feeling that had been gathering in his breast for the past hours. He was onto something. There was a link between the studio loft at the top of the building he stood before and a brutal murder in Kenosha. Kenosha.

Argyle House. Then, with a rush that made him catch his breath, he remembered. Argyle House was Madeline Schutz's publisher. He turned on his heel and hurried back to his car.

Mintz was seated on the lawn in an old chair with a rifle over his knees. He scowled at Tetzel. "Rabbits."

"What kind of gun is that?"

"An air gun." Mintz lifted the rifle and cocked it.

Tetzel danced away from the wavering barrel. "Put that damned thing down."

"I wish rabbits scared so easily."

There was a *pffft* and then a *ping.* Mintz had shot at the birdbath and hit it. The old guy was elated. "I didn't even aim."

"Maybe that's the secret. Miss Schutz doesn't answer her bell."

"It's disconnected. These are her writing hours. I hook it up again when she's done."

"When's that?"

The watch he reeled out of his pocket must have been the one he had used when he worked for the railroad. "Now."

Tetzel waited while Mintz rewired the doorbell. Then he gave it a push and immediately started up the stairs.

"Better hurry. She takes a nap after her writing."

"She tell you all her secrets?"

"Don't be a smart-ass. She is a real lady. She gave me some of her books."

Tetzel turned at the landing, and the old voice fell away. A door opened, and Madeline looked out. "Did you ring the bell?"

"I waited until you'd finished writing."

"I don't have anything but ice water," she said as they went inside.

"My favorite drink." While she took ice from the refrigerator, Tetzel got out the photocopy. He fought the impulse

to show it to her at once. He did not want her to be distracted
by other things. Too much rode on her reaction to the sketch.
Tetzel imagined himself passing on the crucial discovery to
Cy Horvath and Agnes Lamb.

"What's that?" she asked, handing him a glass of ice water.

Ice water! She wasn't kidding. He sipped it, grateful that
there were no witnesses. "This is a sketch of the man who is
very likely a murderer."

She took it and glanced at it. "I've already seen this. Agnes
Lamb showed it to me."

Tetzel had often felt like this when an opponent turned
over his hole card. He put the ice water angrily away. "What
did you tell her?"

"That I had never seen anyone that looked like this picture."

"I'll bet she was disappointed." The way he was now.

"I suppose. I *have* seen someone since who looks like that."

"Where? When?"

"At Barnes & Noble." She smiled and dipped her head. "I
was checking sales."

"The bookstore on Dirksen?"

"Yes."

"Madeline, you have to get out of here. You're in danger.
That man is a killer."

"Why does that put me in danger?"

"He's connected to Argyle House."

Sometimes a simple declarative sentence contains a chapter of warnings, inferences, reasons. He helped her pack up
her computer. He asked Mintz to come up.

"Look, Earl. Madeline is coming with me. I'll go out to
my car and drive away. In a few minutes I'll be coming down
the alley. Madeline will sprint out and hop in—"

Mintz looked devastated. "You're eloping?"

Madeline assured him that her heart still belonged to him.

"You might keep that rifle handy, Earl," Tetzel suggested.

Going out to his car, he had the creepy feeling that he was being watched. He got in, started the motor, and shifted into Drive. Before he got to the corner, he had the sinking certitude that he had left Madeline unprotected. He should have called Keegan. He should have…

Two blocks away he turned, then soon turned again, entering an alley and bumping along it to the block where Madeline lived. He slowed, trying to identify the right garage. A figure arose from behind a trash container. Tetzel got the passenger door open, Madeline slid in, and they were off.

"See if you can get hold of Agnes," he said.

"She gave me her cell phone number."

"Call it."

FIVE

EDNA WAS CHARMED BY THE young man who knocked on her office door and smiled in greeting.

"Am I interrupting?"

"Come in, come in." She actually felt her heart flutter.

He strode toward her and extended his hand across the desk. "Charles Ruskin."

He took the chair she indicated and looked around the office. "It still looks like the principal's office."

"Don't tell me you were a pupil here." He would not be the first former student of the school who had come back for a nostalgic visit and sat across from her like this. She had almost come to enjoy their reminiscing.

"Would that surprise you?"

Edna studied his face. Can a man be beautiful and still a man? Charles Ruskin could only be described as beautiful, and he was indeed a man. Not many men could wear their hair long and not recall the scruffy sixties, but his had a natural curl. And that cleft in his chin!

"I am trying to think how many years ago it was that the school closed."

"It was long closed when I took this job. I can't believe you go back that far." She sounded like a gushy girl and didn't mind it a bit.

He laughed. "I have a portrait in my attic that shows the ravages of time."

"So you were a member of the parish?"

"In a sense I still am."

"Your parents still live in the parish?"

"Oh, no. They have both gone to God, and I have been out and about in the world."

"Oh?"

"I attended college in California."

"Now you're back."

"Business has brought me back."

"Business."

"Willie Lohman is employed in the center, I understand."

Willie! Edna became apprehensive. Willie had spent time in Joliet, as had her husband, and while Edna did not like to think of him and Willie in the same thought, the years when she had been alone with the children, waiting, waiting, came rushing back, and with them the resentment, however irrational, she had felt toward those who had been responsible for Earl's prison term. She still felt edgy around Captain Keegan and Lieutenant Horvath. Was Ruskin a member of the enemy camp?

Of course, she said none of this. "He has an apartment in the basement of the building."

"I'll want to talk to him."

"About what?"

"I wonder what contacts he has had with other graduates of Joliet."

Edna grew aloof. "You'll have to ask him."

"Have you yourself..."

"No."

She would give anything if she could rush downstairs and talk to Willie before Ruskin got to him. Had there been visitors of the kind he meant? Edna had noticed nothing, but Willie was a furtive fellow, still distrustful of the world into which he had been released.

"I have been reading about the stained glass windows in the church."

"The stained glass windows?"

"They were designed by Angelo Menotti. I suppose they attract many visitors."

"You would have to ask Marie Murkin about that."

"Who is Marie Murkin?"

"The housekeeper at the rectory. She has been here forever. I'm surprised you don't know her."

"I don't think I was ever in the rectory."

"Ask her." For once Marie's crusty manner seemed a blessing. She would know how to handle this young man. Or would she, too, be undone by his handsome face? There is no statute of limitations on female folly. Edna did not feel disloyal to her sex in thinking this, but then there was enmity between her and the housekeeper, who persisted in trying to treat the center as part of her domain. Only Father Dowling had prevented open hostilities from breaking out. "Marie Murkin is just the one to see."

"After I talk to Willie." He stood. He seemed about to extend his hand across the desk once more, but he must have noticed the change in her attitude. "In the basement, you say?"

"Down two flights."

"You've been very helpful."

He was gone. Edna slumped in her chair. Had she been helpful? She couldn't see how. She sat there thinking of that impossibly handsome man confronting Willie. The little maintenance man would tell him nothing, she was sure of that, and she was glad. No matter how many of Willie's old companions might have dropped by to see him, Edna felt protective of them all. Of Willie, too. If only she had directed the man to Marie Murkin first.

She got up and went to the window and looked down at the walk that led to the church and rectory. There was no sign of Ruskin. How long had he been gone? Was it possible that he had hurried over to the rectory to see Marie? Back at her desk, Edna looked at her phone. She could call Marie. She could call Willie. Oh, why hadn't she called Willie as soon as Ruskin left and told him to go into hiding?

The next hour passed with glacial slowness. Was he talking with Willie? Would he learn things that would bring back all those lost years when Earl was in Joliet? Of course, Earl was not at all like Willie; there was no comparison. Any sensible person would know that Earl had been innocent of the crime for which he had spent all those years away from her and the children. Earl had insisted on his own guilt, wanting a punishment he did not deserve. There had been something noble in that. Father Dowling himself had said so. There were tears in Edna's eyes now, and anger in her heart. Why, oh, why had Charles Ruskin come to spoil an otherwise perfect day?

When finally she did go downstairs, Edna looked into the former gym, where seniors were occupying themselves in various ways, bridge, shuffleboard, television, knitting, talking. She had learned that it was best not to try organizing things for them. They did not want to be treated like children who must be amused. They did very well by themselves. When she left the gym she went down the hall to Willie's room.

She knocked on the door, her heart in her throat. What if Ruskin was still there? Surely he would wonder why she was checking on Willie. She never checked on Willie. It was silly that she should let some stranger affect her comings and goings. She knocked on the door again, harder. Still no answer. She turned the knob and pushed, but the door was locked.

Her spirits soared. Willie must have disappeared before Ruskin came down. She turned and went with a light step toward the stairs, until she thought of Marie. Marie! She went up the stairs two at a time, as if she were ten years younger, and hurried into the office. She snatched up the phone and called the rectory.

"St. Hilary's rectory," an unmistakable voice said.

"Marie, this is Edna. Did a man named Ruskin come see you?"

"See me?"

"Apparently a former student here. He was curious about the stained glass windows in the church."

"What was his name?"

"Then he hasn't come."

"Edna, you're not making much sense."

"I know. Marie, I'll be over in a jiff, okay?"

"Edna, you are welcome in my kitchen anytime you like."

Having hung up, Edna enjoyed the sense of relief she felt. Ruskin had not found Willie, and he had not gone to the rectory. She took the steps one at a time going down.

At the first floor, she stopped. The hallway here was lined with pictures of graduating classes. She went to the first on the right, the last class to graduate, and studied the faces of the boys and girls. None of the boys looked at all like Charles Ruskin. She went on to the next class, and the next. She examined all the pictures on the right-hand wall, beyond those that could even plausibly contain Charles Ruskin, no matter how untouched by age. Dorian Gray indeed. Who was he?

SIX

MARIE MURKIN WELCOMED James Devere to the rectory almost with the degree of unction with which she admitted Amos Cadbury, but the confident man of business, scion of what amounted to the leading family in the parish, seemed to Father Dowling just a son concerned about his parent.

"Father Dowling, I want to talk to you about my mother."

In answer, the pastor busied himself with his pipe, an operation that for the moment seemed to relax his guest.

"A pipe," he said wondrously.

"Do you smoke one?"

"I did. Margaret mocks me for surrendering to the zeitgeist. She dedicates every cigarette she lights to the surgeon general."

"Why did you quit?"

"It's a long story."

Father Dowling wondered if James's wife hadn't represented the voice of the zeitgeist for Margaret. That formidable woman had been unsparing in talking of her sister-in-law.

"To think that I brought them together! When we were young together, Diane was a sensible woman. Oh, the ravages this culture has made on so many." Margaret slid a bracelet halfway to her elbow and then brought it down again. It might have been the blade of the guillotine. "Susan is her mother's daughter." Diane had had her consciousness raised, in the phrase, and seemed to devote herself to every cause that Margaret considered antithetical to pure reason as well as to the tradition of the Deveres.

It was his mother, not his late wife, that had brought James Devere to the St. Hilary's rectory. "You see Mother regularly, I know. She thinks the world of you." He paused. "Father, does she strike you as…" He stopped, trying to find the right words. "She is very old."

"Yes."

"What do you know of the Devere Foundation?"

"Why don't you tell me what you think I should know."

Speaking of the details of the family foundation enabled James Devere to regain his practical authority. He outlined the formation of the foundation and explained the original endowment, the amount of which surprised Father Dowling.

"The board is made up of members of the family. We meet regularly and have the usual disagreements as to people and projects worth backing. My mother is the director. This is not quite an honorary position. She has the discretion to make awards up to a certain amount on her own sole judgment. In principle, the board can veto these at the next meeting, but, of course, that is both unlikely and impracticable. Money once given is difficult to retrieve. Are you aware of the project to produce reproductions of Angelo Menotti's stained glass windows?"

"Amos Cadbury has mentioned it."

"Amos!" James Devere threw himself back in his chair. "He drew up this absurd agreement with Carl Borloff."

"Absurd?"

"Unwise. Borloff is at best a minor figure in local art circles. I rely on my daughter for this assessment. I have no independent views, but I have asked around, and I find that Susan is right."

"You have spoken to Amos?"

"Of course. His argument is that he is our lawyer; he facilitates and does not make our decisions. That is disingenuous. He is himself a member of the board. It was one thing for my mother to support Borloff's little magazine, a magazine nobody reads, but to place a sizable sum in his hands and to promise subsequent funding into some indefinite future goes over the line. Of course, it is the connection with Angelo Menotti that explains her weakness."

"The board will discuss that further agreement?"

"It must come to a vote, but rescinding it would mean war. Father, what is your impression of my mother's clarity of mind? You realize how old she is."

"Ninety-two?"

"Ninety-two."

"I know you do not expect any clinical judgment on your mother's mind from me."

"No, of course not. A pastoral judgment."

"I have always found her alert and quick-minded."

James Devere nodded vigorously. "On most things, yes. On most things. On anything concerning Angelo Menotti she takes leave of her senses."

"I know how impressed she is by his work. The Menotti Madonna in her apartment is marvelous."

"The man is a great artist. At least he was. My grandfather was his first patron. The Deveres have been generous to Menotti over the years. But, Father Dowling, Carl Borloff is not Angelo Menotti. The sum promised to him rivals the total we have given Menotti himself. And for what? A book of photographs. A book to be prepared by a man whose track record amounts to a few issues of an amateurish little art magazine."

"I'm not sure why you're telling me this."

James Devere stared at the priest. After a moment, he said, "Neither am I. Maybe I expected you to talk some sense into her about this project. All I have to do is say it out loud to know how ridiculous that is. No, I can't put the burden on anyone else. The only way to stop this folly is by a vote of the board."

"Did Amos look into Carl Borloff's ability to carry out the project?"

"Father, he is putty in my mother's hands."

"You seem to have a sense of Borloff's abilities."

"We looked into it as soon as we heard of the discretionary grant. My daughter and I. She knows a good deal more of the art world than I do, of course. A good deal more than my mother, since that world has changed so much in recent years. Nothing Susan told me about this man suggests that he is worthy of such confidence."

"I wonder what Hugh thinks of him."

"I haven't discussed it with him. He is away at school, you know."

"Is he a member of the board?"

"Of course, but, like Susan, a rather infrequent presence. Of course, he was away in California for years, at college there."

"Thomas Aquinas College?"

"Do you know it?"

"Indeed."

James sat forward. "I myself like the place." As opposed to whom? "How much better to give them money rather than Borloff."

On the whole, it was a confusing visit, but at the end of it James had made a decision. "I am going to have a talk with Borloff. I have never met the man. Perhaps I am being unjust to him. Everything I've said about him is at secondhand." They had risen and gone down the hall to the front door. "Yes, I'll talk to Borloff."

SEVEN

Cy Horvath and Agnes Lamb sat in a back booth in the Jury Room reviewing developments.

"You're sure, Agnes?"

"He hasn't been home in three days."

"You got someone watching the place?"

"I've been spelling them. I want to talk to that man."

Carl Borloff might not have disappeared from the face of the earth, but he had been keeping clear of his apartment. Agnes connected this with what she had turned up in investigating the murder of J. J. Rudolph in her office at Argyle House. "He was scheduled to turn over one hundred thousand dollars to her, Cy."

"He didn't?"

"There is no record of receipt."

"You think he absconded with the money."

"I don't want to think. You always tell me not to think."

"It's no effort for me."

What a sweetheart he was. For a Hungarian. Too bad his lack of facial expressions suggested a man still under the effects of Novocain.

"Cy, let me tell you why that would be a stupid thing to think."

They were investigating the murder of J. J. Rudolph. Borloff had come into a pile of money from the Devere Foundation and had entered into an agreement with Argyle House to publish the book he was planning on the Menotti stained glass windows. The agreement involved an initial payment of one hundred thousand dollars, which apparently had not been made. Someone had done away with J. J. Rudolph. End of agreement. Argyle House and J. J. Rudolph were the same thing.

"No employees?"

"She farmed everything out. I don't know anything about publishing, but the only things done in-house were done by J. J. Rudolph. Among those things was working with authors. The overall design of the books, too. She hired artists, copy editors, printers as needed. She apparently had acted as her own secretary."

"Did she make any money?"

"Pots. Did you ever hear of the Empyrean Chronicles?"

Cy just looked at her.

"A series of science fiction books by our old friend Madeline Schutz."

"Schutz!"

"The one we thought got murdered. The one who actually was murdered, Bobby Newman, did some illustrations for Argyle House."

Of course, Cy already knew how the Kenosha publisher connected with Bobby Newman. Schutz? He might not have heard of the Empyrean Chronicles but he knew of the writer and her publisher. "Lots of connections," Cy said.

"If only we knew what they mean."

"Did you ever track down Bobby Newman's boyfriend?"

"Other people besides Louellen saw him around there, but nobody knows where he came from or where he went. I think he's our murderer, Cy."

"What's his connection with Argyle House?"

"You would have to start thinking, wouldn't you?"

AFTER SHE LEFT CY, AGNES drove to Madeline's place. Mintz, the building manager, didn't recognize her out of uniform. She reminded him of her previous visits.

"She ain't home."

Agnes already knew that Madeline hadn't answered her phone. "I don't suppose you know when she'll be back."

The little man rose suddenly, snatched up his rifle, and fired. The rabbit who was munching on plants near the garage didn't even move.

"Give me a try," Agnes said.

She took the air gun, cocked it several times, and sighted in on Bunny Rabbit. What harm could a BB do? Even so, she aimed at his rear end. *Pft.* The rabbit lifted off the ground and took off.

"Lucky shot," Agnes said, handing Mintz his rifle.

He was impressed. "Think you could do it again?"

"Got any more rabbits?"

"How about the weather vane on top of the garage?"

She cocked the rifle twice more than she had before. There was a slight southerly wind. The BB she had just shot had dropped a foot on its way to the rabbit's hind end. Agnes took all this into account and brought the weather vane into the rifle's sight. *Pft. Bam.*

"By God, you're good," Mintz cried. "Where'd you learn to shoot like that?"

"Hey, I'm a cop."

"Madeline went away."

"Went away?"

"Cleared out with some guy." Mintz looked jilted.

Agnes stared at him, then dug Louellen's sketch out of her purse. "This guy?"

"Naaw. He was middle-aged, smelled of booze. I was surprised she even talked with him."

"You should have asked his name."

"I did."

"Well?"

"Nutzell, Zittle, something like that."

Breaking the rules, Agnes thought. "Tetzel?"

"That's it."

"Let me take another shot with your rifle."

"I ought to give you the damned thing. I can't hit the side of the garage."

Agnes lowered the rifle to her hip and squeezed the trigger, and a pellet bounced off the side of the garage. "That's easy."

THE PRESSROOM IN THE courthouse was empty except for Rebecca Farmer.

Agnes dropped into Tetzel's chair. "How are things going in men's restrooms?"

"Don't laugh. It's become a series. Read the one about Naples."

"I don't have to go to Italy to be pinched."

"Lucky you."

"Where's your partner?"

"Partner! Did you check across the street?"

"He's not there. I understand he's writing about Madeline Schutz."

Rebecca needed help remembering who Madeline was. She didn't know what Tetzel was working on. "He spends most of his time on his novel."

"His novel."

"No one's ever seen it, of course."

"He and Madeline have a lot in common."

"How so?"

"Two novelists."

"Make it one."

"Is Tetzel married?"

"Married! Have you taken a good look at him?"

"You have?"

"How can I help it, sharing this office with him?"

"I hope he hasn't tried any Neapolitan stunts."

"I'd break his arm."

"Apparently he's eloped with Madeline."

"That's impossible."

"I have it from an eyewitness."

"To what?"

"Now, be nice. Where do people elope to nowadays?"

Rebecca picked up the phone and punched numbers angrily.

"Who are you calling?"

"His cell phone."

Rebecca scowled into the middle distance and then came alive. "Tetzel! The cops are after you."

Pause.

"They think you eloped with Madeline Schutz."

A frown. She slammed down the phone.

"I hope I wasn't interrupting anything."

EIGHT

WILLIE HAD WET-MOPPED THE center aisle of the church and was now balanced precariously on a stepladder dusting the tops of the stations that stood out from the wall. Jesus falls the third time. Willie was trying to avoid falling the first time. Above him, the stained glass windows were alive from the sunlight outside. They were daytime objects. Once the sun went down they weren't much to talk about. Willie was talking to himself. He considered it a kind of prayer. He always felt out of place in church, given his checkered history. On the other hand, he liked to think of God as an accomplice. He heard a door open and close, and he shut up, looking busy. Probably Marie Murkin come to call instructions to him. Footsteps approached.

"Willie?"

He turned carefully and looked down. A once familiar face looked up at him. Holloway! Willie nearly lost his balance. Holloway grabbed the ladder and kept it steady. If there were any more rungs, Willie would have climbed higher. As it was, he went slowly down to the now grinning Holloway.

"Still reading the Bible, Willie?"

They had all kidded him in the place when he got interested in the Bible. Who would have thought it would be so interesting? After a while he had given up trying to convince them that he was into it for the story.

Holloway had been his cellmate at the end. He stood now gaping at the stained glass windows. "The chaplain told me you was working here."

"Let's go outside." His earlier thought that Marie Murkin might drop in had returned. He took Holloway's arm and hurried him toward the main door. In the little alcove, Holloway wanted to examine the pamphlets, but Willie kept him going.

"You don't seem glad to see me, Willie."

"You don't want to meet the housekeeper."

"Afraid of competition?"

Willie laughed. "Maybe you should meet her. Ever work in a church?"

"Funny you should ask."

They sat on the front steps and lit cigarettes, and Holloway spoke of the first time he'd gotten into trouble. Prying open the poor box in his parish church. "I told the priest I thought the money was meant for me. I didn't have a dime. So he gave me a couple bucks." Holloway might have been giving the explanation of his life of crime.

"How long you been out?"

"Doesn't the suit tell you?"

"I got rid of mine in days."

"I've been reading about this place, Willie."

Willie was trying to figure out a way to get rid of him. He had too good a thing going here to have it screwed up by Holloway. He could imagine Marie Murkin's reaction if she found he was being visited by former companions in Joliet.

"Is it true you live in the basement of the church?"

"Come on. I'll show you my place."

He took Holloway along the sidewalk on the far side of the church, away from the rectory, and to what had once been the main entrance of the school. Holloway was impressed when Willie whipped out his keys and let them in. Willie put a finger to his lips as they went down a flight. In a moment they were at his door and then safely inside.

Holloway stood where he stopped, turning slowly around, his mouth open, his eyes alight. "This is yours?"

"I thought of renting an apartment somewhere, but this is gratis."

Holloway took off his cap and slapped it against his leg. "It's enough to make a man go straight."

Now that he could, in the privacy of his own quarters, enjoy Holloway's envy, Willie waved him to the chair. "No, no. The easy chair." He went to the little fridge and got out two cans of beer, tossing one to Holloway, who caught it in his lap.

"Ouch." Holloway quaffed the beer with closed eyes. He kept them closed as he rested the can on his belly and gave out a long sigh. He opened his eyes. "Remember dreaming of moments like this?"

It would have been easy to fall in with Holloway's mood, to recall their daydreams about the outside when they returned to it. The main element of those dreams was that no one would be directing your life, telling you what to do, counting you off, looking in at you sleeping. Marie Murkin aside, Willie had it all right here, and Holloway's envy became menacing.

"Who's your parole officer?" Willie asked.

"Please. Not while I'm drinking."

"Have him get you a job."

"It's a her. Phyllis. I think she loves me."

"How could she help it?"

"I said I'd been reading about this place. Those stained glass windows. Tell me about them."

"The stained glass windows?"

"Phyllis says they are priceless." Holloway dipped his head and looked at Willie. "I told her nothing is priceless. Except her, of course."

"Be careful. She'll steal your heart away."

"How are they anchored, Willie? Up on that ladder, you must get a good look. Are they cemented in or what?"

"What are you getting at?"

Holloway crushed his empty beer can and waited for another. Willie brought it to him. He felt like bringing it down on his head.

"Just one of them, Willie. Depending on how they're set in, it would be a quick job."

Willie snatched the second can from Holloway's hand and bent over him, furious. "Cut that out! Don't even think it. You pull a stunt like that and we're both back where we belong." He stood. "Besides, what would you do with a stained glass window if you had one?"

"You want to hear the plan?"

"No! There is no plan. Holloway, it's been good seeing you, but you are as much trouble as you ever were. What have you been out, days, weeks, and you're this anxious to go back? Grow up, for God's sake."

Holloway looked up at him like a naughty dog, then began to nod his head. "You're right, Willie. You're right. It was just a crazy dream. Give me the beer."

There was a knock on the door, and the two men froze. Willie saw that he hadn't thrown the latch when they came in. He split his lips with a finger, pulled Holloway from the chair, and led him to the john. Once he had him out of the way, he went to the door. It was Marie Murkin.

"You just going to leave that ladder standing like that in the church?" She was sniffing, picking up the smell of beer.

"I'm on break. I was about ready to go back."

"You can forget that for now. I put away the ladder. I put away the mop and bucket." Marie had her head inside the door, looking around. "What a sty."

"Thanks for taking care of the ladder, Mrs. Murkin. I appreciate that."

She glared at him, to see if he was smarting off, then softened. She withdrew her head. "You can finish up tomorrow."

When Willie closed the door on her, he put up the chain.

The john door opened, and Holloway looked out. "Is the coast clear?"

Willie looked at him, angry, but pitying, too, a brother under the skin. He had to get rid of Holloway before he moved in with him. Maybe he could move in with Phyllis.

NINE

SUSAN FELT THAT SHE WAS running a boarding house. First Amy Gorman, and now Madeline Schutz, who had shown up on her doorstep saying she was in danger of losing her life. The dramatic phrase lost its force because of the silly smile Madeline wore as she said it. "I quote my rescuer."

Susan looked beyond Madeline, where a car was pulling away from the curb. "Anyone I know?"

"He's a reporter. The one who did the piece on me. Tetzel?"

"He says you're in danger?"

"It's quite an exciting story."

It was mistaking Bobby's body for Madeline's that had brought first Amy and then Susan and Madeline together. So Susan took her inside, relieving her of the duffel bag as they went.

"Be careful. My computer is in there. I hope you can lend me a nightie. I left in a hurry."

Susan had to agree that it was an exciting story. Halfway through it occurred to her that it was some stunt the reporter was pulling so he could make another story of it. It seemed pretty far-fetched that a crime committed in Kenosha, Wisconsin, could involve Madeline, even if the crime had been committed at the house that published her books.

"Argyle House itself is a crime." Susan had heard the saga of Madeline's witless agreement. Only an aspiring artist could understand her vulnerability when the chance for publication was dangled in front of her. Susan knew all kinds of artists who would sell their souls in order to get into a gallery. Well, their bodies, anyway—and galleries that were probably less impressive than Argyle House. "Maybe this will get you out of your contract."

"I never thought of that!" Almost immediately second thoughts came. Get out of her slave contract with Argyle House and have to find another publisher?

Susan got Madeline settled with her computer in a far corner of her studio, turned the portrait of Fulvio to the wall, and tried to get back in the mood. No easy task. How could she drive from her mind all the hullabaloo about the Devere Foundation? First her father called all in a snit because Grandma Jane had made use of her discretionary powers as director and given away some money. That's what the money was for. It wasn't theirs anymore; they had to give it away. The only decision was the choice of beneficiaries. It wasn't the money but the recipient that made Susan sympathize with her father.

"Carl Borloff!"

"I know what you think of him."

"Isn't backing his stupid magazine enough?"

"You're not impressed by *Sacred Art?*"

Why go on about it? Art critics are like sportswriters, nerds who couldn't play a game to save their lives pontificating about those who can. Susan doubted that Carl Borloff could draw a straight line, not that there was much of a market for straight lines nowadays, so what qualified him to rank artists and works of art? She wondered if Angelo Menotti's reputation could survive Borloff's enthusiasm.

Her father explained that there wasn't much they could do about the money already given to Borloff, but they could certainly veto the long-term agreement that his mother and Amos Cadbury had drawn up. Amos Cadbury! Susan thought of her doomed effort to get the family lawyer to let her give away her money. So why was she complaining about Grandma giving money to Carl Borloff? Because he was a fake? Where would her own money go if she could get rid of it?

"Susan, this is one board meeting you must attend. Hugh has agreed to be there."

"Hugh? I don't believe it."

"I wish the two of you had a more robust sense of family."

"Dad, it's not the family, it's the money."

"Do you think it's tainted?"

"Of course not." It suddenly occurred to Susan that her father worked very hard and that his success had not made him remote from Hugh and herself. What a petulant spoiled brat she must sound like to him. She promised her father that she would attend the board meeting of the Devere Foundation.

"Thursday at three. At home."

"Right."

Home. The Devere Home. Grandma on the upper floor and her son in one wing and her daughter in the other. Hugh had kept his room there, but Susan had her house in Barrington. With two guests.

Amy Gorman listened while Susan explained that Madeline would be staying in the house for a while.

"Where will you put her?"

"I'll sleep on a cot in my studio. She can have my room."

"Susan, she can take my room. It's time I went home."

"Nuts. You can't go home until they lock up whoever put the body in your garage. Madeline's on the run, too. Maybe from the same man."

"I am not on the run."

"You know what I mean."

"The thought of my house gives me the creeps. I really think I must sell."

"That better wait until the body in the garage is cleared up and forgotten."

They went into the studio, where Madeline looked up from her computer. Susan mentioned what she was working on.

"The Empyrean Chronicles!" Amy exclaimed.

"You read them?" Madeline asked, coming alive.

"My son does. He's in Iraq. Paul." Amy seemed to be surveying Madeline for eligibility as a daughter-in-law.

What a matchmaker she was. She insisted that Susan and Fulvio were destined for each other. "Think of it. Your aunt meets him on a cruise where he is impersonating a sailor. He turns out to be the grandson of Angelo Menotti, the great discovery of the Deveres. Anyone in the room could see the sparks fly when you two first met," she had said.

"Amy, go make yourself a drink. Lots of ice. After that, a cold shower." Susan was glad that she had turned her portrait in progress of Fulvio to the wall.

Amy made herself a drink, and Susan popped a bottle of white wine. Madeline didn't want wine. "I still have to write a page or two in order to complete my daily stint."

"How many pages do you do a day?" Amy asked.

"As many as possible. I have three more volumes to go." She flourished an object that was attached to a cord she wore like a necklace. "My USB storage device. Everything I've ever written is on this little baby."

"What if you lost it?"

"What if a meteor four times the size of Earth slammed into Chicago?"

Susan got Madeline settled in her room and then sat down with Amy, who had made herself a second drink.

"Hard day at the office," Susan commented.

"Who's she running from?"

"A man who was a pal of Bobby Newman. Maybe the pal who killed her and hung her in your garage."

Fulvio came before they had even begun to think of dinner. With a drink and a half in her, Amy was in a beaming mood, so Susan kept her distance from Fulvio lest Amy beam them up the aisle.

"I have another houseguest, Fulvio. Someone I think you'll like."

Amy made a face. She had other plans for Madeline.

Fulvio perked up when Susan told him of the man Madeline was hiding from. A man who had been sketched by a woman who knew Bobby Newman. "As soon as Madeline recognized the man in the sketch she was packed off to me. I should let her tell her own story, though."

Susan went down the hall and called, "Madeline!" She followed her voice up the stairs. Maybe, exhausted from her daily stint, Madeline was taking a nap.

Indeed, that was what she was doing. Susan didn't have the heart to wake her. She would have to meet Fulvio some other time.

TEN

Traditionally, Amos Cadbury's role at meetings of the Devere Foundation board had been as mediator, as voice of reason when disagreements became too sharp, as both involved and an impartial spectator. On this occasion, he arrived at the Devere house with the criticisms of James heavy on his heart. It was not often that his legal work was called into question, and indeed not even James had suggested that there was anything unusual, legally, in the agreement that Amos had drawn up at Jane's request. He had drawn up an agreement in order to shield Jane's decision from the charge that it was arbitrary, even whimsical. Extending the agreement into an indefinite future had been couched in provisos that neither Jane nor Borloff seemed to notice. Those carefully inserted restraints were to ensure, among other things, that the whole board must go along with Jane, with the proviso that even her discretionary grant could be voided by the board.

Who can be his own advocate effectively? Amos had not defended his work in any detail when confronted with James's displeasure. "Your quarrel is with your mother, James. Not with me."

"You aided and abetted her."

"That is not an apt description of legal help."

"Would she have gone ahead without you?"

"James, she already had. She had written a letter to Borloff. The agreement was to supersede that letter and tighten matters up."

It was not any reluctance to explain what help he had been to Jane on the Borloff matter that weighed on Amos now. The real cloud over the board meeting was the apparent disappearance of Carl Borloff.

Jane said, "I asked him to come today and stand by for any questions you might wish to put to him."

"Did he answer?"

"He did not."

Susan chirped, "Shouldn't that be sufficient to forfeit the grant?"

"What do you mean, he disappeared?" Hugh asked. Before Jane had called them to order, by tapping on the tabletop with her pen, Hugh had expressed the hope that this wouldn't take long. "He could be on a trip. He could be taking a little vacation. He could be paying another visit to Angelo Menotti."

"Has he been there?" Jane asked.

"Getting a warm reception, in several senses of the term. Menotti thinks he can stop Borloff's project."

"I know. That isn't so." Jane seemed saddened by the realization. "He has moral rights, I suppose, but no legal ones. Amos?"

"An artifact is the property of the purchaser."

Susan professed to be shocked by this.

Margaret tut-tutted. "Photographing a window is scarcely to do violence to it."

The table at which they sat was not quite ovoid; its curved sides were joined at their ends by straight edges. Amos sat at one of these, Jane at the other, and facing one another across the middle were James and his sister, Margaret. Susan sat next to her father, Hugh next to his aunt.

"Who is Carl Borloff anyway?" James demanded.

Amos intervened. "I take it that your question is the be-

ginning of our discussion of the arrangement entered into by
the foundation and Carl Borloff."

Jane nodded. "So ordered." She had once glanced through
Robert's Rules of Order and from time to time employed a
phrase from it.

Susan provided a very negative account of Carl Borloff,
her language judged tendentious by Amos.

Jane slapped a hand on the table. "This foundation has
been supporting the work of Carl Borloff for some years. We
provide an annual subvention to keep his journal *Sacred Art*
afloat."

"It would sink without it, Grandma."

"That may or may not be true. My point is that it is ridiculous to refer to Carl Borloff as someone hitherto unheard of
around this table."

"We're not discussing the subvention to his magazine,"
James said.

"We are, however, referring to an individual to whose magazine we have given a subvention at least three times. He is
not a stranger."

"He couldn't be any stranger."

"Now, Susan."

In the manner of such meetings, the discussion was a
scarcely coherent flow of remarks, short speeches, crisp re-
actions, interventions by Jane, inquiries put to Amos, with
repetitions frequent. Susan was sketching on a pad. Hugh
looked frequently at his watch. James had all the ardor of
someone fighting what he himself considered a lost battle.
Margaret, seated very erect in her chair, might have been an
observer. She might have been gathering herself to speak,
and finally she did.

"The underlying problem is this family's long attachment
to the work of Angelo Menotti. I do not question, of course,

the soundness of that attachment, but perhaps it makes us vulnerable to such proposals as that before us. Is there any pressing need of or demand for a collection of photographs of Menotti's windows?"

"Margaret, all you have to do is look at them."

"In church. Where they have their native habitat. Those churches are all accessible. Anyone with the least bit of interest could easily visit them all in a matter of days."

"Are you against reproductions of great works of art?"

"In this case, the artist apparently is. You say he has no legal right, Mother, but you added that he has a moral right to say what is done with his work. You say Borloff visited Menotti. Did he receive permission to proceed?"

"Menotti told him he would sue him if he did," Hugh said, smiling. "He is quite a character."

"Then you've made the pilgrimage, too?"

"I have."

"Hugh," Jane cried. "You must tell me about it. Not now, of course."

Margaret said, "I have told some of you that I met a grandson of Menotti's on a freighter."

"A grandson!"

"Yes, Jane. Susan has met him since."

"You have!"

"Would you like to meet him, Grandma? I'll bring him here."

It was Amos who tapped the table with his pen. "I fear we are wandering rather far afield. Let me propose that the board confirm the discretionary grant made by our chairman, after which I will draw attention to features of the agreement with Borloff that will remove any suspicion you may have that this is carte blanche."

"He has probably made off with the money already given him."

Amos brought his long fingers down across his mouth and stroked his chin. "I am afraid he has squandered a good portion of it already, James. At the time we discussed his project, he had made no arrangements with a publisher, and he had yet to interview possible photographers. The discretionary grant was meant to cover any number of start-up costs. It seems that Borloff made arrangements with a publisher whose president was recently found murdered in her office."

"You mean Argyle House," Susan said.

"I do. It seems to be a very unusual publishing house."

"Tell it to Madeline Schutz."

"What do you mean?"

"They're robbing her blind. Her books sell like crazy, but her royalties only start after the first zillion copies, and she's committed to writing ten novels."

"Good Lord," Margaret murmured. "Argyle House? I never heard of it."

"It's been in the news."

"I wonder if Borloff turned over any money to them?"

At that moment Mrs. O'Grady came to the doorway and beckoned Margaret, mouthing, "Phone."

Margaret rose. "I'm sorry, but I have been expecting this call. I thought we would be done by now."

Margaret's question was answered after she left the room.

"A check for one hundred thousand dollars signed by Borloff has already been cashed," Amos said. "I am a joint holder of the account, another precaution of the agreement, James."

"A check made out to Argyle House?"

"To Charles Ruskin."

"Who is Charles Ruskin?"

Susan said, "No doubt an accomplice."

"It sounds more like an alias, Susan. Ruskin?"

After it was over, James suggested to Amos that they should hire an investigator to locate Borloff.

"I shall aid and abet you," Amos said.

James laid a hand on the lawyer's arm. "Uncle Amos, I think you're as suspicious of that fellow as I am."

Uncle Amos. How long had it been since James had called him that? It warmed his heart.

ELEVEN

EDNA SPOKE WITH OBVIOUS reluctance, and Father Dowling understood why. Any reference to Willie could create the impression that he and Edna's Earl were similar cases. Of course, that was absurd.

"Have you yourself seen any of his old associates here?"

"No. But that doesn't mean they haven't been here."

"That's true. Of course, Willie can have visitors. I never told him otherwise. Would you want me to tell him that now?"

She looked at him with anguish. "Oh, this is awful. I know it is because I couldn't possibly mention it to Earl. How is anyone to be rehabilitated if they're treated as if they can't be?"

"Tell me about the man who asked about Willie."

Edna seemed happy for the slight change of topic. "He was very handsome. He used his looks, too, if you know what I mean. He could wrap anyone around his little finger. He had me chattering away like an idiot, and I had never seen him before in my life."

"Did he say why he was interested in Willie's visitors?"

"As soon as he mentioned that, I got him out of here. I sent him down to Willie if he wanted to know such things."

"What did Willie say to you about that?"

"He's never mentioned it. I don't blame him."

Father Dowling thought he might ask Willie that when he talked with him.

"Oh, another thing. He said he had gone to school here—at least he gave that impression—but he didn't."

"Did you ask Marie?"

An unwise question. He was kept busy trying to keep relations between Marie Murkin and Edna civil.

"I looked at all the class photographs downstairs, at least all of them in which he might have appeared. He wasn't in any of them."

"He would have changed since eighth grade."

"Not him. I am sure he was as pretty a boy as he is a man."

"I'm glad you told me this, Edna."

"It must sound silly to you."

"Not at all."

When Father Dowling left, he went down the stairs. At the bottom he hesitated. He felt drawn to those rows of photographs of St. Hilary's graduates, but what would he be looking for? A pretty boy? That was so vague as to be useless.

He continued down to the lowest floor and tapped on Willie's door. Silence. Then movement within. The door opened slowly, and Willie looked out. "Father Dowling. Come in, come in."

In a corner was a television set with a muted ball game on. Portrait of a maintenance man at work.

"Marie tells me you do a good job in the church, Willie."

"What did she say?" Willie asked, his voice rising.

"Well, she did say she had to put away your ladder and mop and things."

"Oh, she told me that. Is she my boss, Father?"

"I wouldn't say that."

"I wish you'd tell her."

Father Dowling took the straight-back chair, facing Willie, who had collapsed into a very comfortable-looking recliner. He seemed to shrink in its embrace.

"This must be a lonely life for you, Willie."

"Father, for years I dreamt of living alone."

Father Dowling smiled. "I'm sure you did. Do you ever see any of your old friends?"

"Old friends."

"From Joliet."

Willie banged the arms of his chair. "She saw him, didn't she?"

"I don't understand."

"Marie. She saw Holloway. I knew it. I was dusting the stations and suddenly he was there, at the foot of the ladder. I brought him over here right away. I was sure no one had seen him."

"Holloway is someone from Joliet?"

Willie nodded. "The way he talks, he'll be there again."

Purists would say that parolees getting together were breaking the rules. Father Dowling asked Willie if that was what he meant.

"Father, if I were you, I would get one of those security outfits to look after the parish."

"What in the world for?"

"Do you know what Holloway wanted to do? He wanted to lift one of the stained glass windows from the church, one of those everyone seems interested in now."

"Good grief. Wouldn't that be difficult?"

"I told him it would be impossible. I did everything but tell him I'd snitch to his parole officer."

Ah. "I think he was talking to Edna, Willie."

"He? No, Holloway's parole officer is a woman. He claims she's nuts about him. She'd have to be."

"Willie, the next time Holloway, or any of your old friends, shows up, bring him to the rectory. I'd like to meet him."

Willie smiled a grudging smile. "He is a character."

When he got back to the rectory, Marie told him he'd had a call from Amos Cadbury.

"Is he in his office?"

"I suppose. He didn't say."

Amos was in his office. "Father Dowling, can I give you dinner tonight?"

"I'm afraid not, Amos. I'm giving you dinner."

So it was arranged that Amos Cadbury would dine with the pastor of St. Hilary's that night, in the rectory.

After dinner, with Marie fussing around the table, looking in from the kitchen at regular intervals, her antennae eager to pick up praise from Amos, praise that unfailingly came, Father Dowling and Amos adjourned to the study, the lawyer with a glass of Courvoisier, the pastor with his umpteenth cup of coffee for the day. The conversation turned to the Devere family, and Amos gave an account of the recent board meeting of the Devere Foundation. "I can speak freely because, of course, the minutes can become a public record."

"What was on the agenda?"

"Support for the project of photographing Angelo Menotti's stained glass windows."

"They'd better hurry. Willie is afraid one of the alumni from Joliet would like to steal one."

"What on earth would one do with a stained glass window?"

"I hope that's a problem I will never face."

"No word from the cardinal?"

"No." He was tempted to go on, but that would only prompt grousing about being in such suspense. "I suppose there must be a market for one of Menotti's."

"Father, there are times when I wish I had never heard of Angelo Menotti. His presence broods over that family. Jane Devere is excessively devoted to the man. Of course, she knew him well, long ago. He is a difficult fellow. I suppose it is the artistic temperament. Jane urged me to draw up his will, and I did. It gave him a chance to review his accomplishments, and his checkered life."

"Has he children?"

"Children? The man is excessively philoprogenitive. At least he was."

"How many?"

"I don't think he is sure himself."

"How could he get them all into his will?"

"Exactly. The one he omitted was furious. Angelo offered him a bust of his mother."

"That must be worth something."

"It is worth a great deal, but it was not the boy's mother. His fury only increased."

"He is ninety-something?"

"Ninety-four. A man my age should not begrudge longevity in others, but there are times…" Amos waved the thought away and drew on his cigar. "Back to the board meeting. The recipient of Jane's generosity, Carl Borloff, is nowhere to be found. Of course, it is imagined that he took the money and ran. I doubt that. He very imprudently turned over a good part of the discretionary grant to a man who does seem to have debouched. James Devere has conceived a great resentment against Carl Borloff. He asked me to hire an investigator to find him."

"Have you done so?"

"A strange thing. Margaret drew me aside after James's suggestion. 'Don't bother,' she said. 'I have already hired someone.'"

TWELVE

AFTER INCREASINGLY ANXIOUS days in which he had not heard from his client, Tuttle blamed only himself. Had he not told Borloff to get out of sight? Of course he had. Wasn't that good advice? Of course it was. He should have specified that Borloff was to let his lawyer know where the hell he was.

"I hope you got a hefty retainer," Hazel said. For a while there she had been a regular cheerleader, but now she was slowly reverting to her virago vices.

"Are you kidding?"

"Better let me bank it."

"I'm using it for expenses."

"Remember to keep records."

Tuttle escaped his office and went slowly and meditatively down the four flights to his car. Retainer. He pulled out the single he'd asked Borloff for, to seal their bargain, lawyer and client. For all he knew, Borloff was at the bottom of the Fox River. This cheerless prospect turned his mind to Peanuts Pianone. He called Peanuts from his car. "I'll pick you up in front of the courthouse."

"What's the deal?"

"Are you in uniform?"

A pause. "I can change."

From what to what?

Peanuts was in uniform. Tuttle rolled down the window. "I'll put this in the garage. We'll need a cruiser."

Peanuts actually saluted. Uniforms do that to people. Tuttle slid down the ramp into the basement garage, putting his

car in Chief Robertson's spot. Tuttle got out of the car and
stretched, trying not to think. He was better when he was
spontaneous. How can your conscience bother you if you
don't let it know what you're planning? Peanuts rolled up in
a gleaming cruiser, and Tuttle got in. "This car makes getting arrested almost attractive."

Peanuts said nothing, but Tuttle had not expected to engage his old friend in lively repartee. "Why the uniform?"

"My suit that was at the cleaners? They lost it."

"Sue them." A Pianone for a client? Whoa.

"That takes too long. You should have heard my brother."

"I hope the cleaners are insured."

Peanuts grinned as if he were modeling for jack-o'-lanterns.
"They better have fire insurance. They had a fire last night."

"I hadn't heard." Tuttle did not want to hear more. The
Pianone family's activities were at once notorious and unnoticed, officially. An idea came. "The Pianones got connections
in Kenosha, Wisconsin?"

"Where we were?"

"Yes."

"Maybe."

Tuttle let it go. His friendship with Peanuts, the white sheep
of the Pianone family, was based on the fiction that Peanuts
was just another cop rather than an affirmative-action hire
on behalf of the Pianones.

He gave Peanuts directions to the building in which Borloff
lived. Maybe the guy was dumb enough not to follow his
lawyer's advice. Peanuts squeezed into a space at the curb,
easing the vehicle ahead of him forward, despite the protest
of its brakes.

"You'll never get out of here, Peanuts."

Again the jack-o'-lantern grin. Tuttle had a sudden image
of a cleaner's establishment in flames. He erased it and followed the uniformed representative of law and order to the

entrance of the building. Peanuts pulled open the door and hurried in as if he were making a raid.

Inside there was a long hallway dwindling into darkness like an illustration of perspective and, to the right, a door marked STAIRS.

"He's on the second floor."

"Who?"

"My client."

Peanuts held the door open for him, and Tuttle huffed and puffed his way upward. It was the first door on the right on which there was a sign. SACRED ART.

"Funny name," Peanuts said.

Two pushes on the bell got no response. Tuttle stepped aside, and Peanuts went to work. In a minute, the door was open.

"How do you do that?"

Peanuts shrugged. Tuttle stepped into the apartment. There were lights on.

"Borloff? It's Tuttle."

Tuttle went through the living room toward the light. On the threshold he looked in at the desk, computer, bookshelves. Peanuts was crowding next to him.

"He's not here," a voice behind them said.

Tuttle looked at Peanuts, and Peanuts looked at him. They turned. The man was seated in a chair in the living room. He reached up and turned on the light beside the chair.

"Who the hell are you?"

The man rose in a supple motion and extended his hand to Tuttle. Unable to think of an alternative, Tuttle took it. Peanuts was trying to free his pistol from its holster. Tuttle put a staying hand on Peanuts's arm.

"I am a private investigator." The man pulled out his wallet and flicked it open.

"I won't ask how you got in."

"I understand you are Borloff's lawyer. Surely you know where he is."

"Are you looking for him?"

Was this the danger Tuttle's instinct had suggested, leading to his advice to Borloff to get lost?

"My client would like to speak to Borloff."

"Who is your client?"

"Margaret Ward."

Tuttle sank into a chair. The Deveres must think that Borloff had taken a powder with their money. Dreams of making a bundle from Borloff drifted away. "Let me know when you find the son of a bitch."

"He appears to have left in a hurry."

"That was on my advice."

"Ah. Where did you send him?"

"That's privileged information."

"Meaning he isn't there? Perhaps we should combine forces. How much do you know of his arrangements with Argyle House in Kenosha?"

"Tell me what you know."

"Homicide is out of my line, of course."

"Homicide?"

"Come, come, you were there when the body was found."

Good grief, was he suggesting that Borloff had done away with J. J. Rudolph? Even to admit the thought was to see its plausibility. Borloff felt he had been robbed. He wanted his money back. In a rage, he strangled Rudolph. Did the sequence of events make that possible?

The man extracted a card from his wallet and handed it to Tuttle. "I'll leave you now. I know you'll want to look around this place. I hope you are more successful than I." In a gliding motion, he was at the door. Before closing it, he called, "Arrivederci."

"Ciao," said Peanuts.

THIRTEEN

THE PRESSROOM HAD BECOME intolerable to Tetzel. Rebecca's stupid series about her European trip was the talk of the town. Well, of the pressroom. Rebecca couldn't shut up about it.

"What's next?" Tetzel asked, getting out of his chair with the help of leverage gained by a hand on his desk.

"Have you ever heard of the *Mannequin Pis* in Brussels?"

Rebecca was describing the little statue in the Grande Place as Tetzel headed for the door. "I look forward to reading about it."

"I'll e-mail the draft to you so you won't have to wait."

Jeez. How the hell could he eclipse his rival? When he had asked for an assignment, Menteur had told him to show a little initiative. "Look at Rebecca."

It was because he couldn't stand looking at her, or listening to her, that Tetzel was fleeing for the elevator, destination unknown. The Jury Room? What good was sitting in a bar when you weren't avoiding work? Outside, Tetzel wandered up the street, crossed, realized he was on the way to Tuttle's office, and thought, well, why not?

By the time he got there and had climbed the four flights of stairs, Tetzel felt ready to collapse, which he did when he stumbled into the office. Hazel looked at him with concern. "You all right?"

He was too bushed to reply. Hazel rose and went into Tuttle's office; in a minute she was back with a bottle. She poured a generous belt for Tetzel and laced her own coffee. "He thinks I don't know where he hides it."

"Tuttle doesn't drink liquor."

"Then there's more for us." A toothy smile, a glint in her eye. Tetzel lifted his glass. Hazel lifted her cup. "To the ladies." Hazel, having sipped, laughed. "Do you know, I really believed you when you said you were going to write about secretaries."

"I meant it," Tetzel said, suddenly meaning it. Was this the idea he sought? He could encroach on Rebecca's supposed lock on women's news. "Where's Perry Mason?"

"Aren't you going to interview me?" Hazel asked coyly.

Jeez. "Let me get my breath."

"Did you ever consider getting in shape?"

Hazel's shape, he realized, was formidable. She was definitely a lot of woman. The thought made Tetzel uneasy. "Did he tell you all about our visit to Kenosha?"

"It got him a client. If he can find him."

A client? Never show ignorance. "I thought it might."

"Not what you would call prepossessing."

Tetzel liked the thought that he was a walking Roget's *Thesaurus.* "You weren't impressed?"

"What is an art historian anyway?"

Carl Borloff! "Whatever he says he is."

"Well, he is one dumb bunny, I can tell you that. I suppose writing a check that large seemed like Monopoly money."

"How large?"

"One hundred thousand dollars." She pronounced each syllable separately. The reportorial mind began to function. Borloff had been given a bundle by the Devere Foundation. Hazel, when encouraged, said that the big check had gone to Argyle House. Which then went bust. She drew back her shoulders as she said this. Tetzel looked away, feeling like a voyeur. In celebration of their camaraderie, he accepted another dollop, if three ounces counts as a dollop. Was Hazel trying to weaken his defenses? Sentences were forming in

Tetzel's head. *Local foundation bilked of large amount by missing art historian.*

"Why do you say missing?"

"Our mutual friend can't find him."

Did that count as being missing?

"Meanwhile, you can interview me." She rolled her chair closer to Tetzel.

He rose. "As soon as I complete the story I'm on."

Her face showed disappointment. "What is it?"

"Do you know the *Mannequin Pis?*"

"I didn't know they could."

She laughed a nasty laugh. It was pretty clear Hazel shouldn't drink on the job. Still, it must get lonely working for Tuttle. A couple more drinks and Hazel might start looking pretty good. Bah. Even Rebecca Farmer looked good through an alcoholic fog.

Tetzel had opened the door. "You should make them fix that elevator, Hazel."

"I think of the stairs as exercise. Still, I'm glad the ladies' and mannequins' are on this floor." Again the nasty laugh.

THE STAIRS WERE LESS exercise going down, thank God. On the street, Tetzel considered going back to the courthouse for his car. As he stood there, a police cruiser rolled to the curb. Tuttle hopped out, looked in to thank Peanuts, and turned to Tetzel. The cruiser took off with a squeal of taxpayers' tires.

"Coming up?"

"I just came down."

"Hazel there?"

"We had a nice talk. How about the Jury Room?"

Ten minutes later, they were in a booth. The walk had brought back Tetzel's shortness of breath. Maybe he would get in shape, join a health club, cut down on booze, get more sleep, eat sensibly. He sipped his drink as these salutary thoughts slid by his mind.

"Did you find Borloff?"

"Don't worry about Borloff."

"Of course I won't. If I had a wad like that I'd head for Vegas."

"How much did Hazel tell you?"

"I'd rather get it from the horse's whatever."

The more he listened, the surer Tetzel became that a great story had just dropped in his lap. The mention of the private investigator added to Tetzel's speculation about what the Deveres' reaction to Borloff's absconding must be.

"The Deveres hired him?"

"Who else would?"

Tuttle described again the effect of hearing that voice behind them when he and Tuttle were looking into Borloff's workroom.

"He's lucky Peanuts didn't shoot him."

"Peanuts would be lucky to hit him. What was his name?" Tuttle stared at him, sorting through possible lies.

"You didn't ask."

Tuttle looked offended. "He gave me a card. It was one of Margaret Ward's."

"You'd starve as a reporter, Tuttle."

"Just what Rebecca said about you."

TWENTY MINUTES LATER, Tetzel was at his computer in the pressroom, slurping coffee, trying to get his mind clear. His exposé of Carl Borloff would write itself. Absconded. Debouched. He pushed away Roget. Why not simply *stole?*

FOURTEEN

W HEN A MOS C ADBURY ASKED Margaret what had prompted her
to engage the services of a private investigator, she expressed
surprise. "Amos, Susan has been warning us about this man
for months. What she had to say at the board meeting merely
summarized long-held views. Some weeks ago, I decided to
find out whether what she said was true."

"May I ask who your private investigator is?"

"He's not a professional investigator, Amos."

"An amateur?"

"I met him on a recent cruise I took on a freighter." She
hesitated. There seemed no reason to say that he was a grandson of Angelo Menotti. "I have confidence in him. If my confidence is misplaced, what has been lost?"

"What's his name?"

"He will use the name Charles Ruskin."

Amos was silent, doubtless expecting her to say more.

"I needn't tell you, Amos, that I very much sympathize
with Menotti's objection to such exploitation of his work.
Particularly by such a man as Borloff."

"That seems to have become a majority opinion on the
board."

"Amos, Charles Ruskin, as we shall call him, is the grandson of Angelo Menotti."

"His grandson!" Amos seemed stunned by this information.

"Given the way Angelo Menotti haunts our family, I suppose that it is not too surprising that I should meet one."

"And given the number of his offspring."

"How many grandchildren does Menotti have?"

"I don't think he himself is sure. He kept a fairly accurate account of his children, however. Legitimate and illegitimate, as he hastened to add. As for grandchildren and now great-grandchildren, he just throws up his hands—and puffs out his chest."

"He is a lovely boy."

"If this man isn't a professional investigator, what is his profession?"

"He was in the merchant marine."

After speaking with Margaret, Amos sat for a long time in silent meditation. As he made his decision, he considered it from various angles. He would be second-guessing Margaret, but then James had urged him to engage a private investigator. That advice still stood, despite Margaret's revelation. He decided that he could proceed in good faith. He had a call put through to Maxwell, a trustworthy man who had often done investigative work for the firm. Maxwell was in Amos's office within hours.

Amos provided Maxwell with a succinct account of the misgivings of the board about Carl Borloff. "These misgivings were strengthened by the fact that Borloff seems to have disappeared."

"So the first task is to find him."

"That appears to be the case. There is something else you should know."

Maxwell waited, expressionless.

"Margaret Ward decided, on her own, to enlist the help of someone she calls a private investigator. He is not a professional. He calls himself Charles Ruskin."

"I never heard of him."

"I am not surprised. You might make Ruskin a secondary target of your investigation."

Maxwell nodded.

"Margaret tells me that Ruskin is a grandson of Angelo Menotti. One of many. I suppose he shares his grandfather's, and Margaret's, belief that the Devere Foundation does not have any right to finance such a project as Borloff proposed. From a strictly legal standpoint, they are wrong. The stained glass windows are the property of the parish churches in which they are found."

"Not the property of the Deveres?"

"Oh, my, no."

"If there is such opposition to Borloff on the board, how in the world has he managed to receive so much Devere money?"

"That, I am afraid, is a rather long story."

He made it short, feeling almost disloyal to Jane in even saying so little as he did. How could he convey the interest of Jane Devere in the artistic reputation of Angelo Menotti? It was almost an obsession. If it weren't for Jane, it was doubtful Borloff would have been supported by the Deveres even in putting out *Sacred Art*. There was little doubt in Amos's mind that Susan had avoided board meetings lest she be forced into open opposition to her grandmother.

Did Maxwell find any of this relevant to his task? He absorbed the information given him, even asked a few questions, but when he stood and summarized his commission he was terse. "Find Carl Borloff and find out just what Charles Ruskin may be up to."

That was that.

The decision left Amos uneasy. James had overstated the case, but Amos *had* colluded with Jane in her efforts to fund Borloff's project. The fact that he had wrapped her generosity in legal provisos ensuring that the art historian would not have carte blanche with a considerable amount of money had been his defense against James's accusation. Should he have, could he have, opposed Jane and persuaded her that she was embarking on a risky venture? James apparently thought so. Amos rather doubted it. His course had been that of the cautious facilitator of Jane's wishes.

LATER THAT SAME DAY, having dined at the country club, Amos betook himself to the St. Hilary's rectory. His mood, he reflected, was that of a sinner going to see his confessor.

FIFTEEN

FOLLOWING TUTTLE'S ADVICE, Carl Borloff stuffed toilet articles
and some clothes into a sports bag, grabbed his briefcase,
and took the stairs down to the basement garage to get his
car. How easy it was to imagine Charles in pursuit, Charles
who had deceived him into writing a check for one hundred
thousand dollars! Zeros seemed to trail away from that
innocent 1 as he emerged from the garage and got into the
traffic. Where was he going? Into seclusion. For how long?
Block after block he drove, and as he did the sense of urgency
drained from him. Was Tuttle any more trustworthy than
Charles? Why didn't he go to Amos Cadbury? Cadbury and
Jane Devere had underwritten his great project, although Carl
had felt the lawyer's skepticism as the terms of the agreement
were drawn up. At the time, he had dismissed it as a lawyer's
caution. What would be Cadbury's reaction when he heard
of Argyle House and that damnable check for a good portion
of the money granted the project? He couldn't go to Amos
Cadbury. If only he had more confidence in Tuttle.

When he got onto the Northwestern Tollway, he headed
toward Rockford, why he didn't know. He settled into the
right-hand lane and let other cars zoom past him, their driv-
ers having a destination. If not Amos Cadbury, why not Jane
Devere? He could tell her everything, bring her the bad news
himself, throw himself on her mercy. No, he couldn't. He had
been robbed, and yet he felt like a thief.

Approaching an off-ramp, he saw signs indicating motels.
He turned off, paid his toll, and went on to a stop sign. Most

of the motels here were reached by a road arching over the tollway. To his right was a Red Roof Inn. Carl went to the right.

He pulled into a parking place and looked indecisively at the motel. There was a porch running along the upper story, and there were men with beards and ponytails and tattooed arms with their backs against the railing. Loud voices, crude voices. The proletariat. Members of the underclass. He couldn't stay here. Then the very negative features of the motel commended themselves. Who would imagine Carl Borloff staying in such a place? He got out of the car and went into the office.

The middle-aged woman behind the counter had a crew cut and a T-shirt with the message TRY ME rippling over her apparently braless breasts. A cigarette in her ashtray sent up a plume of smoke. Carl asked if she had a room. She had a room. How much? She squinted at him and pointed at a chart behind her.

"I'll pay cash."

She watched him count it out, then scooped it up, bouncing her breasts. "I'll need a credit card, too."

"I'm paying cash."

"For incidentals. There's a bar in your room."

The point of paying cash was anonymity. He might just as well have used his credit card to pay for the room. Try Me took his card, made an impression of it, then slapped it and a key on the counter. "Checkout time is noon."

He got his sports bag from the car, leaving the briefcase for now, and climbed the stairs to the second floor. He had to run the gamut of the beer-drinking crowd in order to get to his room. They fell silent as he approached, did not move to make his passage easier, and began to snicker as he went by.

"Nice suit," someone said.

Carl pretended he hadn't heard. He did not look back when he got to his door and needed several tries to get the key into the lock. Inside with the door locked and bolted, he felt in prison rather than seclusion. Everything in the room offended his aesthetic sensibilities, the bedspread, the furniture, the lamps, and, dear God, the pictures. He went to one and studied it. There was nothing technically wrong with it despite the garish colors. Flowers in a vase, but what still-life subject is not a cliché? Whoever had painted this dreadful thing had learned the basic skills, had doubtless one day dreamt of... Of what? Were all artists ambitious? Imagine someone who had aspired to nothing higher than this. He turned and threw his sports bag on the bed. Then he threw himself beside it and, embracing it, fell asleep.

He wakened to a darkened room, immediately shut his eyes against the dark, and remembered where he was. A party seemed to be raging outside his room. He sat up and spent minutes trying to turn on the bedside lamp, hunting around the bulb for the switch. The switch was in the base of the lamp. A very low–wattage bulb that created shadows in the room. He twisted his watch into view. He had been asleep three hours. He could fall asleep again, but he was hungry. He swung his feet off the bed, listening to the hoots and shouts outside. In order to get something to eat, he would have to run the gamut of those yokels. He couldn't do it.

The small refrigerator held little bottles of wine, liquor, soft drinks, junk food, chips, peanuts, candy bars. His stomach rumbled. He snatched a bottle of wine and a bag of chips.

With a struggle he freed a plastic cup from its plastic container. Wine gurgled into the cup. He tore open a bag of chips and began to thrust them into his mouth to quiet his stomach. Washing them down with wine, he remembered Angelo Menotti serving him a glass of bourbon. He thought of the artist's house, secluded, safe. Who would look for him there?

If those barbarians ever got off the porch, he would get out of this place and head for Peoria.

Cheered by the thought, he sat on the bed and took up the television controls. The set leapt into life. News. An earnest couple trading inane remarks, shuffling papers as they read from the teleprompters. Then, incredibly, his own face appeared on the screen. He turned up the sound and learned that Carl Borloff, art historian, was being sought by the police. The worst was yet to be. There was no mention of the money. He was being sought for the murder of Roberta Newman. Who? They were babbling about Argyle House and the murder of J. J. Rudolph. Horrified, Carl turned off the set, then immediately turned it on again. The babbling couple had given way to a weatherman. Once more he switched off the set.

He had to get out of here.

Out of there he got, passing unnoticed through the celebrating underclass. Did he dare drop by his place and get his computer? He decided to chance it.

PART FOUR

ONE

AFTER TALKING TO CHARLES Ruskin for a few minutes in the pressroom, Rebecca got him out of there. The Jury Room, she decided, was definitely not the place to talk. When they came out of the courthouse, Rebecca was still thinking. It occurred to her that the obvious place was the *Tribune* building, where Tetzel was unlikely to show up.

"You haven't spoken to anyone else?" she asked Ruskin.

"No other journalist."

"Come along."

What an impossibly good-looking man he was. So deferential, too. He insisted on calling her Miss Farmer, and she checked her impulse to correct him. How do you pronounce *Ms.,* anyway? All the way to the *Tribune,* Rebecca was fearful that they would run into someone who might carry the word to Tetzel. She had been at work on the final installment of "Rebecca's Travels," episodes in her recent trip to Europe. She still hadn't figured out a way to write up the red-light district of Amsterdam that would get by Menteur. All those hookers, sitting in windows as men shuffled by staring sheepishly at them! What had happened to the Netherlands? As a girl, Rebecca had read a little book about Dutch twins, and everything had seemed sweet and neat with lots of cheese down there below sea level.

"Have you ever been to Amsterdam?"

"What's in Amsterdam?"

"You wouldn't believe it."

She pushed through the doors of the *Tribune* building and

led Ruskin to the elevator. The car was crowded, and as they rose Rebecca noticed all the women noticing Ruskin. She sought and found his hand so she could get him safely out of the car. When they entered the city room, she led him right back to Menteur's office, past desks where envious women stared and males glared. Rebecca had her arm through Ruskin's now and smiled up at him as if she were smitten. As if she weren't. Maybe he liked older women.

"Lyle," she cried, bursting in on the editor, "this is Charles Ruskin, and I am about to write the most important story of my career."

Menteur, whose massive cynicism was both a professional hazard and an asset, looked at the hand Ruskin thrust at him. He took it, shook it, and looked at Rebecca. "This part of the Amsterdam piece?"

"This is the solution to two recent and brutal murders."

"Have a seat."

"Charles was asked by Margaret Devere Ward to check out the background of a man who has been the recipient of a massive grant from the Devere Foundation."

"Carl Borloff," Charles said. "I have indisputable evidence that he murdered Roberta Newman and a woman named Rudolph in Kenosha."

After listening for two minutes, Menteur held up a hand. "Don't talk it, write it."

"I just wanted to give you a heads-up."

"Have you spoken with the police?" Menteur seemed to find it painful to look at Ruskin.

"Not yet."

"That can wait. Get it written pronto, Rebecca. I'll run it by legal, and we'll go with it."

Rebecca commandeered a computer, sat Ruskin down, and said, "Let's start with Roberta Newman."

Ruskin had a flair for narrative, there was no doubt of that. Rebecca could almost see the studio from which the artist must have been forcibly taken to her grisly death in the garage of Amy Gorman. "Why Amy Gorman?"

"She's a friend of Susan Devere."

"Why did Borloff create the impression that the body was Madeline Schutz's?"

Ruskin sat back and passed a hand over his gorgeous face. It was all Rebecca could do not to reach out and caress it herself. "We're dealing with a pretty quirky guy here."

It was all speculation, of course, trying to figure out motive. He would rather stick to facts. "Bobby told me about him."

"Bobby?"

"Newman. Roberta."

"You knew her?"

"She asked me to sit for her."

"No wonder you know the studio so well."

"Bobby was doing some illustrating for Argyle House. Borloff was making arrangements with Argyle House to bring out an art book. The Menotti stained glass windows. The link is Devere money."

"We have to have some motive."

Ruskin studied her for a moment. "I said he was a quirky guy. Hookers ply their trade in the same building as the studio. According to Bobby, one day she came back to her studio, walked in, and…" Again he studied Rebecca. Her breath caught. This could be as lurid as Amsterdam.

"They were going at it?" she prompted.

He nodded. "Borloff had hung the girl up by her wrists and…"

Rebecca gasped. Her sense of what she could make of this was expanding. "I want to see that studio. I want to go to Kenosha. I am going to write this thing in the first person as I am guided around the scenes of the crime by Charles Ruskin."

"There's no need to mention my name."

"Not mention your name!"

"Can't I just be 'sources'?"

"Let's not decide that now. Come on."

She stopped at Menteur's office and told him how she wanted to do it. He thought about it. "He'll go around with you?"

"How else could I do it?"

Rebecca hardly noticed the effect Ruskin was having as they hurried to the elevators. She was wrestling herself back into professional mode. This hunk was a source, not just the most gorgeous man she had ever been seen in public with.

IT WAS A PART OF THE CITY Rebecca had never visited, though of course she had heard of it. It was called the Pits. In Amsterdam, she had fearlessly walked along the street where rows of windowed prostitutes refused to look at potential customers, instead preening themselves, looking alluring, sometimes with paraphernalia that suggested tastes like those Borloff apparently had. She was glad to have Charles as her escort here.

"Of course, I came to know this district well."

"As a model?"

He made a face. "I thought of it as having my portrait painted."

Rebecca hesitated when they got to the building. How much hands-on experience did she need to write the story?

A skinny girl came out just as they were about to enter. "Charlie!" The girl glanced at Rebecca, widening her eyes in disbelief. "You new?"

"Louellen," Ruskin said.

"Long time no see."

"I have been busy about my father's business."

Rebecca's Presbyterian girlhood surged up, and she thought it almost sacrilegious for him to use that phrase.

"Is he a monkey? Well, gotta go," the girl said.

"Good luck."

"Call it that if you like." Off she strutted, swinging her purse.

"Another model," Charles said.

The climb to the top floor was punishing. Rebecca found herself panting, and she got a stitch in her side. Twice she called a halt in order to rest. Finally they were at the door of the studio. Yellow tape was drawn across it. Of course, this was a crime scene. She was filled with disappointment. To her surprise, Charles detached the tape, got out a key, unlocked the door, stood aside, and bowed. She opened the door, and then they were inside. With his knuckle, he flipped a switch inside the door, and fluorescent lights blinked themselves into a steady state. She advanced slowly into the studio, already describing it in her mind's eye. Charles went to a huge bed and sat. It swayed under him. He grinned. "A water bed."

A lesser woman would have felt uneasy, alone in such a place with a man who seemed to enjoy making waves as he shifted back and forth on the sloshing bed.

"This is where she came upon Borloff and Louellen."

"The girl downstairs?"

He nodded.

"Is your portrait here?"

He hesitated, then rose. "Let's look."

He tipped back canvases tilted against the wall, one after another, then shook his head. "It's gone."

"Perhaps the police took it."

He looked at her. "I suppose so."

"That one looks like the girl downstairs."

"I believe it is."

A skinny little nude who seemed at once sad and perky.

Rebecca spent twenty minutes absorbing the atmosphere, thinking of the artist who had worked here and then met her death by violence, strung up in a garage and made to seem someone else.

When they were going down the stairs, Rebecca thought she had enough. A trip to Kenosha no longer seemed desirable. After all, Tetzel had written of that.

TWO

MAXWELL LIKED WORKING FOR Amos Cadbury. With any other lawyer, the chance of it being a divorce case was high, and Maxwell, a family man, had come to find tailing adulterers boring. Cadbury wouldn't touch a divorce with a ten-foot pole. A missing person was a welcome change.

His first stop was at police headquarters. He always liked to let the police know what he was doing, in case their paths crossed in the course of an investigation. Cy Horvath brought him up to speed on what he and Agnes Lamb were working on. Maxwell asked for a photocopy of the sketch of the mysterious Charles, and while he waited for it had a cup of coffee with Cy.

"You ever regret getting off the force, Max?"

"Every other day."

"Business good?"

"It is when I get a call from Amos Cadbury."

When the photocopy came, Maxwell folded it and put it in his pocket. "You got one of Borloff?"

"I don't draw."

"What's he look like?"

Cy's description was better than Cadbury's.

"What's Cadbury's interest?"

"He thinks he ran off with a pile of Devere money."

When he was going down in the elevator, the car stopped, and a man and a woman got in. Maxwell made way, managing not to show surprise. If that wasn't the man in the sketch Horvath had just given him, Maxwell would eat his hat, an

out-of-fashion homburg. He kept to the back of the car, ears
cocked, but the couple did not speak. On the street floor,
Maxwell followed them through the lobby and outside. The
woman looked across the street, shook her head, and kept
going. Maxwell followed. He watched them enter the *Tribune*
building, then went back for his car. Five minutes later he was
parked at the curb in front of the building, a handicapped card
in his windshield. He told himself that they might have come
out while he was away. Sitting here like this could be a big
waste of time, but wasting time was what he mainly did for
a living. He would gamble that they were still inside.

Cy had told him a bit about the man in the sketch, someone named Charles Ruskin, but Maxwell had not hung on his
every word. It had seemed just a conversation to pass the time
while he waited for the sketch. There was overlap between
Cy's job and his own. He thought of alerting Cy to the man's
presence in the *Tribune* building but decided against it. He
didn't know for sure that he was still in there.

There was a talk show on the radio when he turned it on.
He turned it off. Then he turned it on again and searched in
vain for Western music. He gave up and lapsed into silence.
He thought of having a cigar. He decided to have a cigar.
When he had unwrapped it, he left it unlit in his mouth. They
lasted longer that way.

Half an hour had gone by since he had seen the subject who
was not his subject go into the *Tribune* building. He would
give him forty-five minutes, maybe even an hour. Then they
came out, the woman going to the curb and waving for a cab.
She was lucky. One slid up, they entered, and they were off,
Maxwell following.

The cab went down Dirksen and eventually turned off. The
Pits? Well, well. This was beginning to be like a usual job. If
they wanted a room, though, why not a decent hotel? A decent
hotel. What an oxymoron. Once hotels had their own detec-

tives on duty to prevent hanky-panky on the premises. Now everyone was routinely asked how many keys they wanted. Nowadays the Pits were everywhere. Ginny, his wife, used to ask about his day, but that was long ago. She thought he was making it up.

The couple got out of the cab in front of a scroungy-looking building. Maxwell parked and put up his handicapped sign. This time he would light the damned cigar. At the door, the couple was stopped by a skinny hustler. She seemed to know Charles. Unless Maxwell couldn't read lips, she had addressed him by name. After a minute, the couple went inside, and the skinny girl pranced up the street. Maxwell got out and called to her.

She stopped and looked him over as he approached. "What can I do for *you?*" she asked in lilting tones.

Maxwell got out the sketch and unfolded it. The girl followed this with interest, maybe expecting a new approach.

"You know this guy?"

She backed away, swinging her purse. "You, too?"

"What do you mean?"

"I drew that picture."

Maxwell looked at it. "You forgot to sign it."

"Got a pen?" She scrawled a signature and handed it back to him folded.

"Was that Charles you just talked to?"

"Are you a cop?"

"The next best thing."

"I've told the cops all I know, which is nothing."

"What do you know of Carl Borloff?"

"Never heard of him."

"Okay. Thanks."

"Is that all?"

"Hey, I'm a married man."

"At least you admit it."

He watched her go off rhythmically down the walk. The poor kid. Suddenly, she wheeled, coming back in a rush, and disappeared into the building from which she had earlier emerged.

BACK IN HIS CAR, MAXWELL thought that he had had enough diversion. He called Cy and told him where he could find Charles Ruskin.

There was silence on the line. Then, "Thanks, Max."

"Sleazy-looking place."

"You know artists."

"I just met one."

"Be careful."

"She said she drew your sketch."

"Louellen."

"We didn't get on a first-name basis. If you're coming, I'll wait for you."

"Would you keep on him, Max? If he leaves."

They were just then emerging from the building, Ruskin and the woman. He told Cy.

"Don't lose him."

It seemed he already had. Ruskin was gone, and the woman was headed toward Dirksen. There was no sign of her former companion. If that was a quickie, it could make it into the *Guinness World Records.*

"Cy, he's vamoosed."

"We'll find him."

Maxwell put the handicapped sign on the seat beside him and started the car. He had Borloff's address taped to the dashboard. Fortunately he knew the city as well as a cab-driver.

There wasn't much hope of catching Borloff home, but Maxwell liked to acquaint himself with his points of reference. Twenty minutes later, he was parked in front of Borloff's building, had the sign in place, and decided to enjoy the rest of his cigar before he went in.

A car came slowly along the street as if the driver were lost. He went by, and Maxwell sat up, watching the car in his side mirror. It got into an empty space, and a minute passed. Suddenly the driver's door opened, and a man got out. He practically ran to the door of the building in front of which Maxwell was parked. Borloff? Maybe. Whoever it was darted into the building.

Maxwell thought about going in and seeing if that had been Borloff. Then, what the hell, along the sidewalk came Charles Ruskin, carrying a plastic sack. Maxwell had never liked men as good-looking as that. Into the building he went. If that had been Borloff, he and Cy Horvath would have a parlay. He punched Cy's number and told him the story.

"You're having a busy day."

"Maybe it'll get busier."

"Don't go away."

It was nearly half an hour before Cy got there. Maxwell got out of his car.

"Traffic," Cy said.

"Doesn't your siren work?"

"I never use it."

Inside the building they went carefully up the stairs to Borloff's door. They took up positions on each side before Cy knocked. They exchanged a glance. Maxwell nodded and got out his weapon. Cy's hand was on the knob. He turned it. The door opened.

They found the body of Carl Borloff in the bedroom.

THREE

AGNES LISTENED DISTRACTEDLY as the chatter of the police radio filled the car. The monotonous drone of the dispatcher never changed, no matter what incident he was reporting. Traffic accidents, a shoplifter at the mall, a woman dead of a drug overdose in the Pits. That caught her attention, and she slowed the car. Intuition? A hunch? Thank God Cy wasn't with her. At the next corner she turned and headed toward Dirksen Boulevard. She was tempted to use the siren, but that would have been too much like Peanuts.

There was a cruiser pulled up in front of the building and a 911 ambulance. Agnes skipped out of the car and hurried toward the building. An officer stopped her.

"It's okay, Riley." She flashed her badge, but it was her face he recognized.

"Third floor," he said.

"Another ritual murder?"

"Looks more like suicide."

Agnes bounded up the steps to the third floor. The building seemed to reek with the odors of hell. Some kind of linoleum made the floor of the hallway sticky to her shoes. Light flooded from an open door. Agnes went in and saw Dr. Pippen hunched next to the body on the bed. She put a hand on Pippen's shoulder and looked at the lifeless body. "Her name is Louellen."

"Was." Pippen stood and turned to Agnes. "You knew her?"

"Bobby Newman's studio is in this building. This girl posed for her."

There was a liquor bottle on the table beside the bed, along with a needle and a pipe. Louellen must have gone into the next world in a haze. Agnes tried not to think of the welcome she would have received there. Judgment is mine, saith the Lord. "Suicide?"

Pippen said, "Well, she didn't leave a note, but she must have known that the combination of all those things was lethal."

"Can we put off calling it suicide until we check out that stuff?"

Pippen shrugged. Agnes got out her phone and called Cy.

Before she could say anything, he spoke. "Maxwell and I just found Borloff."

"Good!"

"Not so good for him. He's dead."

"Good Lord. Wait." She handed the phone to Pippen. More intuition. "Tell him what we've got here."

Agnes went into the hallway and saw a door close. She went to it and knocked. "Police. Open up."

It took another pounding on the door before a frousled female looked out over the chain. Agnes showed her badge. "Open up."

"What the hell time is it?"

The door closed, there was the sound of a chain, and the door swung open. The woman was waddling back to her unmade bed.

"Louellen's dead."

The woman stopped, and for a moment her broad face was full of horror, but that went away. "Yeah?"

"When did you last see her?"

"I don't know. Yesterday. What time is it?"

"Four o'clock."

The woman glanced at the cracked shade that kept the world at bay as if to discover whether it was a.m. or p.m.

"What's your name?"

"Pearl. What happened to her?"

"Looks like a drug overdose, plus booze."

Pearl shook her head. "Louellen didn't drink."

"Never?"

"Never. She said it made her sick. I think because it gave her an advantage with johns."

Pearl tugged her robe more tightly about her. On a far wall was a religious picture.

"What's that?"

"You know."

"Tell me."

"Our Lady of Guadalupe."

"What's your real name, Pearl?"

"Rosita."

"Tell me about Louellen. When you saw her yesterday, was she alone?"

Pearl snorted. "She was never alone for long. A skinny little thing like that."

Agnes still carried the sketch Louellen had made of Bobby's mysterious boyfriend. She showed it to Pearl.

"What's that?"

"A drawing Louellen made for me."

"Louellen did that?"

"It's pretty good, isn't it?"

"Yeah, that's him."

"Was he with her yesterday?"

Caution glazed Pearl's eyes. "I don't think so."

"I think he was."

Pearl's hand went out to the bedside table for her cigarettes. The first one she shook from the package looked homemade. She palmed it, pulled out another, and started the hunt for matches. Agnes had never smoked. She watched as Pearl inhaled deeply and then sighed forth smoke.

"You saw him yesterday, didn't you?"

"Lady, I don't know one day from another anymore. What difference does it make to me what day it is?"

"You could be doing Louellen a favor."

Another deep drag on the cigarette. "How?"

"Do you want them to call it suicide?"

"It couldn't have been."

"Why?"

Pearl seemed embarrassed; her eyes went to the picture on the wall. "The way she talked. She wanted to be a good girl again, you know." The thought saddened her. "Who doesn't?"

Agnes went to the door.

Pearl said, "She's really dead?"

"Yes."

"May she rest in peace."

On that surprising remark, Agnes went back up the hall to Louellen's room, where Pippen told her Cy was on his way. "The crime lab is busy with Borloff. They'll come as soon as they can."

"What did you tell him?"

"That you didn't think it was suicide."

"Did I say that?"

"You didn't have to."

"You'll do an autopsy?"

"That's my job."

CY CAME AND PRETENDED THAT Pippen was just another pretty colleague. The 911 crew was downstairs in their ambulance listening to a ball game. When the crime crew finally arrived, Cy gave them the usual instructions. When Pippen had gone, Cy said, "You're thinking Charles?"

"Why don't we go upstairs. You can tell me about Borloff."

When they got there, Cy said, "What's this tape doing down?" He tried the door. Unlocked. They went inside to discuss Louellen, and that was when they noticed something sticking out of the coverlet on the waterbed. Agnes took hold and pulled, feeling like a magician. It was a T-shirt. There was a name sewn inside the neck. Carl Borloff.

WHEN THEY GOT BACK DOWNTOWN, an infuriated Captain Keegan handed them a printout of Rebecca Farmer's story on the *Tribune*'s Web site.

FOUR

TETZEL WALKED INTO TUTTLE's office and stood looking bleakly at the little lawyer. Hazel followed him in, standing at his side.

"Scooped," cried the reporter.

He moved toward a chair, lost his balance, and was eased into it by Hazel, who sniffed disapprovingly. "You're drunk."

"Not yet, my dear, but that is my hope."

"What's this all about?" Tuttle asked, lifting his tweed hat, then settling it on his head again.

For answer, Hazel sailed the *Tribune* at him and wheeled to go. Tuttle tried to catch the flying newspaper and almost toppled from his chair. Hazel closed the door on this sordid scene.

Tuttle read Rebecca Farmer's story, his little eyes widening. He whistled tunelessly. The phone rang, but he ignored it. Let Hazel take it. "Who the hell is her 'authoritative source'?"

"Menteur has finally lost it. He'll be sued out of his shoes for running that."

The thought of prospective legal work caught Tuttle's attention. "He's libeled my client," he cried.

"The quirky serial killer?" He was quoting the perfidious Rebecca.

Tuttle read aloud. *"It is not often that a major story walks into the pressroom and all but writes itself. On Wednesday afternoon, your reporter..."*

"Please," Tetzel begged. "Not while I'm still sober."

"Tetzel, she accuses my client Carl Borloff of two murders, without a shred of evidence."

Even if Rebecca was right, Borloff would need to be defended at the trial. This was a win-win situation.

The door opened, and Hazel looked in. "A nut call."

Tetzel turned. "Present."

Hazel ignored him. "Some nut just called. He was breathing heavily, and I braced myself for an obscene phone call. He said one word and hung up."

"What word?"

"Peoria."

"Thank you, Hazel."

"For what?"

For bringing Tuttle the hint he needed as to where his client had gone. He rose from his desk chair, squared his tweed hat, and looked doubtfully at Tetzel. "You coming along?"

"The Jury Room?"

"Not yet, Tetzel. We are going to Peoria."

"Not me."

"You don't want to interview the man who has been libeled and pilloried in your colleague's story?"

Tuttle had to spell it out for the addled reporter. Carl Borloff, under instruction, had made himself scarce, as a safety precaution. That enigmatic phone call alerted his attorney as to where he would be found.

"Peoria's a big place," Tetzel said.

"Not if you know where you're going. Angelo Menotti, my client's hero, lives in Peoria."

It was the thought of countering Rebecca's story with his own on the man she had accused in print that got Tetzel to his feet. The prospect seemed to have sobered him. "I'll settle her hash, Tuttle."

"I've never understood that phrase."

The two men went through the outer office.

"Hazel," Tetzel said, "in case of obscene phone calls."

"Yes?"

"Comply."

Something heavy hit the door that Tuttle closed behind them. On the way down the stairs, he considered calling Peanuts and making the trip to Peoria at taxpayers' expense. On the second flight of stairs, he decided against it. If Borloff had read that story, the sight of a police cruiser would send him into a panic.

"Where's your car?" he asked Tetzel. Maybe they could put the trip on the *Tribune*'s tab.

"Let me think."

"We'll go in mine."

There was a threatening note from the manager under the windshield wiper of Tuttle's car. He removed it, got behind the wheel, and handed the note to Tetzel. "Put that in the glove compartment with the others."

To his surprise, he saw that his gas gauge read FULL. Once they were under way, Tuttle had Tetzel call the paper to get the address of Menotti's studio in Peoria. The reporter wrote down the information with a shaky hand and filed the slip behind the sunshade on the passenger's side.

"We'll never find it," Tetzel said.

"Ha."

On any other occasion, even such a city boy as Tuttle might have enjoyed the fruited plains of Illinois turned golden in the setting sun, but for him the journey was merely a matter of following the concrete, keeping to the right lane of the interstate, allowing maniacs to barrel past at eighty and more.

"Is there a governor on this thing?" Tetzel grumbled. "Can't you keep up with the traffic?"

"Take a nap," Tuttle advised.

"With all this noise?"

Tuttle found the roar of his motor and the rush of wind soothing. It concentrated the mind. His thought in the office returned. No matter which way this thing went, Tuttle would be representing Carl Borloff. Say the guy was a killer; killers had a constitutional right to a vigorous defense. On the other hand, if he was innocent, something that was more difficult to think now, the *Tribune* would pay through the nose. Images of himself humbling the *Tribune* while a crowded courtroom followed his every word started him whistling.

"I'd rather listen to the motor," Tetzel said.

Tuttle had another thought. "Call Cy Horvath, Tetzel."

"What for?"

"Tell him I am on my way to Peoria to meet with my client."

"Isn't that kind of finky?"

"We'll beat him there. If he comes."

"He could call the Peoria police."

"You're right. Postpone the call. We'll make it when we cross the bridge into Peoria."

"He'll tell me to go to hell."

"We'll cross that bridge when we come to it."

When Tetzel made the call, it kept breaking up, but he got through to Horvath. "Tuttle wants you to know that he is on his way to Peoria to talk with Carl Borloff."

"Funny."

"You're easily amused."

"Borloff's dead, Tetzel. He was found dead on the floor in his apartment."

"What did he say?" Tuttle asked eagerly.

"Find a bar and I'll tell you."

FIVE

MADELINE FOUND IT DIFFICULT to write in Susan's studio and had switched to the kitchen table, a table now in use as Amy Gorman ate her breakfast.

"Have you eaten?" Amy asked, forking scrambled eggs into her mouth. She had made toast, which she loaded with butter and strawberry jam.

"All I'm going to."

"Breakfast is the most important meal of the day."

"What do you do, skip lunch?"

Amy licked her lips and looked hungrily at the piece of toast she had picked up. "You're kidding."

"Is lunch the second most important meal of the day?"

"Are you on a fast or something?"

Madeline smiled. She felt awful wishing that Amy would finish and go off to work so Madeline could plunk down her computer on the kitchen table and get going. She was just a guest, but then so was Amy, two refugees. Things were popping out in her galaxy, though, and she was anxious to get at them.

Finally Amy was done. She took her dishes to the sink and rinsed them before putting them into the dishwasher. "When I get old I'm going to sleep the day away like Susan."

"She's up half the night."

Amy turned. "Was he here last night?" Amy herself had gone yawning off to bed before nine.

"Who?"

"Adonis. The beautiful one. Haven't you met him yet?"

"I guess not."

"Susan treats him as if he were a mere mortal."

"She's never mentioned a man to me."

"That's what I mean."

After Amy left, Madeline got ready to go to work. The newspaper lay on the counter. It had been ignored by Amy, and Madeline resisted distractions at this point of the day. Mornings were her most productive times. She settled down, brought up her manuscript on the screen, and soon was plinking away at the keyboard. What is more absorbing than writing fiction? Madeline seemed to drift out of the present, losing all sense of time except that measured by the oddly crimson sun that circled the planet Photon. It was eleven o'clock Earth time when Susan came yawning into the kitchen and broke the spell. Madeline saved her text and closed the top of her computer. "I'll get out of your way."

"Did you see Amy this morning?"

"I watched her eat."

Susan laughed. "She really packs it away, doesn't she? I think her tapeworm has a tapeworm. She says she never gains weight." Susan tightened the belt of her robe.

"She asked if I've met your boyfriend."

Susan looked blank, then made a face. "Fulvio? He's a protégé of my aunt's. When he was here the other day, you were napping, or you would have met him."

"Amy seems gaga over him."

"I know. His looks are his cross. He told me he has considered going to a plastic surgeon to get an ugly face."

"What does he do?"

Susan thought about it. "I don't know. He's between ships, I guess. Want to see what he looks like?"

"Sure."

"Come on." Susan led the way to her studio, holding a cup

of coffee out before her as if it were a divining rod. She went to an easel and threw back the cloth.

"Oh, my God," Madeline cried. "That's him."

"That's my line."

"Susan, he's the one I'm hiding from."

"Fulvio? You've got to be kidding."

"What do you know about him?"

"Not much more than my aunt told me. He likes to talk about my family, don't ask me why."

Madeline dropped the subject. She was a guest here, and she shouldn't be commenting on Susan's friends, but she had a strong urge to leave this house, go somewhere else. She remembered the way the reporter had spoken; she remembered Mintz with his air gun. Maybe it was safe to go home now.

They went back to the kitchen, where Susan ate standing up, just toast, juice, and coffee. She opened the newspaper. "My God," she cried.

"What is it?"

"Fulvio! He's being sought by the police."

Madeline jumped up and stood beside Susan, mouthing the words as she read. Tetzel? That was her reporter.

"Why do they call him Charles Ruskin?" Susan asked.

"That's his name."

"He told me he was Fulvio. My aunt Margaret calls him Fulvio. That amateur sketch could be anybody. Madeline, it's some awful mistake."

Madeline said nothing. In the story, Charles Ruskin was tied to all the dreadful events of recent days—Bobby Newman, Madeline's editor in Kenosha—but the heart of the story was the fact that Charles Ruskin was the last man to have seen Carl Borloff alive. Susan read it all with her mouth hanging open. She turned from the paper with determination on her face. "I'm calling Margaret."

Madeline listened to Susan summarize the story in the

Tribune. "Don't you read the local paper? Well, you ought to. Margaret, have Amos Cadbury do something. You and I know Fulvio couldn't have done these things."

Hanging up the phone, she said to Amy, "She will. Amos Cadbury can do anything." She paused. "Well, almost anything."

Susan went off to shower and, as she put it, to get undressed for work, meaning the jeans and sweatshirt she wore in the studio. Madeline got set up again on the kitchen table, opened the text on her monitor, and stared at the words. That's all they seemed now, words. When she had written them they had been a pure medium that carried forward her story. Now they were clumps of letters, lines, bah.

She went up to the studio to find Susan just sitting on a stool. She had a cigarette in one hand and her lighter in the other, and she might have been Lot's wife for all the animation she showed.

"I can't work."

"Neither can I."

"Madeline, it has to be some horrible mistake."

"I hope so."

The doorbell rang, and Susan went to answer. At the sound of her scream, Madeline dashed to the front hall. A startled young man, impossibly good-looking, much more so than his pictures, stared at Susan. Susan had stopped screaming and was now laughing. "They let you go," she cried. "I knew they would. Did Amos Cadbury take care of it?"

She took his hand and led him into the living room. This was a time for celebration, she decided. "Wine," she cried, and dashed away and came back with a bottle of merlot. "This is Australian," she said. "No cork. Just twist off the cap." She handed the bottle to Fulvio.

"A small point of order, Susan. I don't know what the hell you're talking about."

He uncapped the wine and began filling glasses. Susan glared at him, then went to the kitchen for the newspaper. She dropped it in his lap. "There you are. Read all about it."

He read. He worked his lips. He made noises. He kept on reading. Finally he looked at Susan. "That's not me."

"What did I tell you, Madeline?" Susan said triumphantly.

"I mean it's not a picture of me."

"You just said that."

"Not quite." He lifted his wine and stared at the glass like a scientist in a lab. "It's my brother, Charles."

SIX

AFTER MARGARET'S CALL, Cy Horvath and Agnes Lamb, accompanied by representatives of the Barrington homicide bureau, arrested Charles Ruskin at the home of Susan Devere. Both Susan and Amy Gorman had to be subdued by officers as the arrest was made.

The subject himself was strangely composed. "I'm not Charles Ruskin. My name is Fulvio Menotti."

The cards and ID in his wallet bore this out. They took him in for questioning anyway, ignoring the wariness of their Barrington counterparts. Fulvio Menotti was the spitting image of the man sketched by Louellen, and that was good enough for Cy. Nonetheless, they were faced with the difficulty of understanding how someone named Fulvio Menotti had been calling himself Charles Ruskin.

"Two names are not two people," Cy said.

Maxwell came in and was taken to view the suspect through a one-way mirror. "That's the man I saw with the reporter and the skinny little hooker, the alleged suicide. He's the guy that went into Borloff's building and somehow disappeared by the time Cy and I got to the apartment. Ask the reporter from the *Tribune*."

Rebecca Farmer couldn't believe that the source of her great story was now being held for questioning in the death of Carl Borloff and maybe others as well. She stared openmouthed at him through the one-way mirror.

Agnes said, "Is he the man?"

Rebecca gave her a stricken look.

"Yes or no?"

Her "yes" was almost inaudible. Agnes led her away.

Returned from Peoria, an apparently cold-sober Tetzel was all over the place, going from Cy's office to Agnes's, taking notes like crazy, trying not to grin like an idiot. He had the pressroom all to himself now.

If they had their man, though, there were weird complications. In Borloff's apartment a plastic bag was found, containing the box cutter that proved to have been the weapon used on poor Bobby Newman.

Maxwell said, "I think that's the bag he was carrying when he entered the building."

The T-shirt found on the waterbed in Bobby Newman's studio told another story when Rebecca broke down and related her visit there with the suspect. So they held him now on suspicion of having killed Borloff.

"I can't believe he killed anyone," Rebecca said to Agnes.

A murder charge could not be just a matter of belief. Maxwell's identification and Rebecca's reluctant corroboration were something, but hard evidence was needed.

Miss Pageant, the Kenosha librarian, came down and added her testimony. "That's him, the silent partner."

To that extent, everything looked good, but Jacuzzi the prosecutor posed the puzzling question. "Why? What's the motive, Cy?"

The search for a motive now became the primary task. Agnes went back to Susan Devere.

"He didn't do it. I don't care what you say. You heard him, he's not Charles Ruskin. That's his brother. Ask Amy Gorman."

"That's what he said," Amy admitted, but she no longer seemed to share Susan's conviction that some horrible miscarriage of justice was under way.

Neither Susan nor Amy knew where the suspect lived.

"Didn't you even wonder, Susan?"

"He's a sailor. My aunt met him on a freighter."

If a member of the merchant marine, he had to belong to the union. Cy checked on that and was given an address for Fulvio Menotti. It was a room in a one-star hotel on Dirksen, taken by the month. The clerk listened to their request, then said they had to talk to the manager. The manager's name was Solomon, a tall fellow with a large head on which remnants of hair were carefully distributed. His eyebrows were luxuriant, and his belly hung over his belt. "Let me see your warrant."

"You want a warrant?" Cy asked.

"Absolutely."

"Then I'm glad I brought one."

The elevator was the size of a confessional—Cy's analogy; Agnes let it go—and they rocked up the shaft to the third floor. At the door of number seven, Solomon asked to see the warrant again. He read it as if he were looking for a loophole. He gave it back to Cy and, as he unlocked the door, said, "He was such a nice guy."

Solomon was the first male who had spoken kindly of the suspect.

Menteur was more typical. "I wouldn't buy a used car from that son of a bitch. A real pretty boy."

"You bought a story," Cy had told him.

"We didn't pay him!" Menteur paused, chewing gum furiously. "We did buy a pig in a poke."

Solomon went ahead of them into the Spartan room. The single bed was neatly made; there was a duffel bag lying on the baggage stand under the window. The bathroom was spick-and-span. The rope was looped over a hook in the closet. Cy fed it into a plastic evidence bag. He didn't have to say "Kenosha." There was nothing else significant in the room except the business card of Margaret Devere Ward stuck in the frame of the mirror. That went into another ziplock bag.

"When did you last see him?"

Solomon wasn't sure. Downstairs, the clerk wasn't sure. They had a photograph of the suspect with them, and both men looked at it. The clerk looked to Solomon for a cue, but the manager smoothed his eyebrows and nodded.

The rope proved to match the length cut from it to choke J. J. Rudolph. Even Jacuzzi was impressed. Now it was Agnes who began having doubts. She told Cy she would talk to Margaret Devere Ward.

"We've got enough identifications."

"Another can't hurt."

MARGARET DEVERE WARD was the kind of white woman that made Agnes want to check to make sure that Lincoln had actually issued the Emancipation Proclamation. Tall, patrician, a woman who seemingly hadn't had a doubt in twenty years. So she was surprised at her graciousness.

"Please sit down. You're here about Fulvio Menotti, I suppose."

"What can you tell me about him? Your niece said you met him on a boat."

"That's right. It was a very long voyage, and from the very first moment I met him, he struck me as someone special. Imagine my surprise when I learned that he was a grandson of Angelo Menotti."

"He looked you up when he came to Fox River?"

"At my suggestion. I wanted to introduce him to my mother. She is a lifelong admirer of Angelo Menotti, and I was sure she'd want to meet him."

"Did you introduce him to her?"

Margaret smiled. "Only recently, and got chased out of the

room. My mother wanted to be alone with him. They talked
for over an hour."

"And?"

"That was it. I had already introduced him to Susan. I was
certain that she would be impressed to find that I had such
bohemian friends, and he that I had such a niece."

"We arrested him at her house."

"Poor Susan."

"Did he ever call himself Charles Ruskin?"

"That was his little joke, I suppose. Of course you know
who Ruskin is."

"No, I don't."

"One of the most perceptive art critics who ever lived."

"That was the joke?"

"He adopted the name when I asked him to inquire about
Carl Borloff."

"Inquire?"

"Our family foundation had long supported Borloff's art
magazine, *Sacred Art.* At my mother's insistence. Now she
wanted to give him an enormous amount of money to produce
a book of reproductions of Menotti's stained glass windows.
Menotti again. My mother's obsession. Susan was strongly
opposed, as was my brother, James. When he suggested to
Amos Cadbury that a private investigator should be engaged,
I told him I already had done that. When I mentioned to
Fulvio my misgivings about Borloff, he said he would look
into it for me."

"Amos Cadbury engaged an investigator named Maxwell."

"I didn't know that."

"Did Charles Ruskin report to you about Borloff?"

"He told me he would write up a full report when he was
finished."

"How did you get in touch with him?"

"He came here. We talked on the phone."

"Do you have his number?"

She thought. "He always called me."

"There should be a record of incoming calls on your phone." There was. Agnes jotted down the numbers from which her investigator had called Margaret Devere Ward. There were several, but one occurred often.

Mrs. Ward came with Agnes through the outer office. She extended her hand. "I can't believe that I was such a bad judge of character."

AGNES GOT AN ADDRESS for the frequent number, expecting it would be the hotel on Dirksen. When it wasn't, she tried the other numbers, but they were all public phones. The address she had gotten for the number from which Ruskin had usually called was in Skokie, and Agnes thought of calling Cy before going there. He wasn't in, so she left a message, telling him what she had learned and where she was going.

The address was a house in a neighborhood of little houses whose owners had a strong sense of property—well-kept lawns and shrubbery and a flag flapping at every door but Fulvio's. She got out of the car and had started for the house when she was hailed from the next yard.

"Anything wrong, Officer?"

He was a thin rail of a man, barefoot, playing water over a flower bed from the hose he held. Agnes talked to him over the hedge.

"Just routine."

"He's not home."

"Fulvio Menotti?"

"Is that his name?"

"Didn't he use that name?"

"He's not very friendly."

"How do you know he's not home?"

"He usually leaves his car in the driveway."

"Well, I'll check it out anyway."

"What's he done?"

"We hope he can help us in an investigation."

"Lots of luck."

Agnes rang the front doorbell without result, then went around to the back, following a little walk beside the drive that led to the garage farther back. She stretched and ran her fingers along the ledge above the back door. Nothing, She looked down at the mat on which she stood. She stepped back and lifted it, and there was a key.

She hesitated, then put the key in the lock and turned. The door stuck when she pushed on it but then opened. Agnes went inside. She looked around the kitchen, which had an unused look. Why would Fulvio Menotti have a room on Dirksen in Fox River and a house in Skokie? She went through the kitchen and dining room toward the living room, whose blinds were closed.

There was a sound behind her, and too late she tried to get out her weapon. Something landed on her head, sending shooting stars through her brain, and then she was falling, falling, falling.

SEVEN

EDNA WENT OVER TO THE RECTORY to tell Father Dowling that the story in the *Tribune* must be about the man who had come to the center to ask about Willie. "I told you he lied to me about having attended the school."

"I remember."

"All the awful things he's done, Father."

"Like not graduating from St. Hilary's?" He smiled when he said it.

He went back to the school with her, remembering what Willie had told him of Holloway. Edna went up to her office, and Father Dowling went down the stairs to the lower floor where Willie's room was. He found the maintenance man slumbering in his chair, with the *Tribune* scattered on either side of him. He had cut something from the paper and pinned it up alongside the story of the attempted bank robbery that had put him in Joliet. He jostled Willie's shoulder.

The little man grumbled and turned away. There was an impressive number of empty beer cans scattered among sections of the paper.

"Willie?"

Willie came awake with a start, looked wildly at Father Dowling, and tried to get up.

"Stay in your chair, Willie." He drew up the straight-back chair and sat. "I see you've read the story in the paper."

Willie admitted that he had.

"Is that the man who visited you, the one who wanted to steal a stained glass window?"

"Holloway? Naw, that's Floyd."

"Floyd?"

"Pretty Boy Floyd. It's a good thing he knew how to take care of himself. Even so, the chaplain had him moved."

"Father Blatz?"

Willie nodded. "For his own protection. Joliet is a zoo, Father."

"Tell me about Floyd."

"It's funny they didn't mention Joliet in that story."

"Yes. I wonder if the police haven't arrested the wrong man."

"Oh, that's Floyd, all right. He talked circles around the chaplain, acted as altar boy, the whole bit. Spent most of the day in the library. The son of a gun was a VIP down there."

"Floyd's name wasn't Floyd?"

Willie shook his head. "Charles something."

"When did he get out?"

"Before I did. Months before."

Before calling Phil Keegan, Father Dowling thought he would run down to Joliet and talk with Tubby Blatz.

His old classmate had drawn an assignment few would envy, prison chaplain, but maybe in the Joliet diocese it was regarded as a plum. Tubby was in his office, talking with an inmate, and Father Dowling waited until the man left.

"You've been waiting, Roger? You should have let me know you were here."

"You looked busy."

"They come to me just to break out of the routine."

"Have you been reading about events in Fox River?"

"What events?"

Father Dowling was glad he had thought to bring along the rectory copy of the *Tribune,* over Marie's protests. ("I want to save that.") He opened the paper and showed Tubby the story.

The chaplain shook his head as he read. "So Charles will be coming back."

"Tell me about him."

"Of course he was innocent, like everyone else here. He might have gotten away with it, too. The woman he had robbed changed her story and said she had given him the money. The fact that he had been found with her jewelry and checkbook made that less persuasive."

"That's his photograph?"

Tubby studied it again. "He doesn't look a day older than when he was here. He was known as Pretty Boy. You can see why. I got him out of harm's way and had him assigned to me. He stayed in a little room off the sacristy."

"A Catholic?"

"More or less."

"How more and how less?"

"He knew a lot about the Church, but then he'd say something that rang false. He thought absolution was an indulgence."

"So he practiced?"

Father Blatz was silent for a moment. "Roger, he was a con man. I came to think he wasn't a Catholic at all. I told him he had to stop receiving communion."

"He accepted that?"

"He said he had been about to suggest it himself."

"What was his real name?"

"Menotti. Charles Menotti."

THE DRIVE BACK TO FOX RIVER was one of the times that Father Dowling wished he used a cell phone. Phil Keegan had to be told that they were very likely holding the wrong man. Phil had chuckled when he told the pastor of St. Hilary's that Fulvio had said they were looking for his brother.

"Amos Cadbury called," Marie said when he got back to the rectory.

"Any message?"

"He wants to see you. He actually asked where you were."

"What did you tell him?"

"In prison." Marie never smiled when she was pleased with herself. "I told him I didn't know when you'd be back."

In his study, Father Dowling put through a call to Amos Cadbury.

Amos told him that James Devere and his sister, Margaret, were anxious to talk to him. At the Devere house. "I'll come by for you, Father."

"No need for that. I'll meet you there."

"In an hour?"

Before giving the paper back to Marie, Father Dowling opened it on his desk and studied the photograph. Family resemblance is often a mysterious thing. He looked forward to talking with James Devere—and Margaret, too.

EIGHT

Cy Horvath listened to the message Agnes had left on his phone and sprang to his feet. The message had been recorded almost an hour ago. He bounded from the room and took the stairs to the roof and the police heliport.

Biederbeck was in his little office, feet on the desk, scowling at a television set. "Wouldn't you think reception would be better up here away from all the interference?"

"Warm it up, Beady. We're going to Skokie. You got a map of it?"

"In the copter." Biederbeck, the welcome but infrequent prospect of flying before him, got up and ran out to his craft. Cy picked up the phone and called Keegan.

"You're flying?" Keegan had a horror of defying gravity.

"She called an hour ago."

"Keep me posted."

The great blades of the helicopter were turning lazily when Cy came onto the rooftop. Biederbeck was aboard, grinning in anticipation.

Cy climbed in. "No stunts."

"Have I ever?"

Cy could count the times he had flown with Biederbeck, but every one had been an adventure. Prayer came easily in a copter. Biederbeck revved the rotor and then, magically, effortlessly, they lifted, fifty, then a hundred feet above the great encircled X on the rooftop. At sufficient altitude, they shot ahead, the cabin tipped forward, over the edge of the roof, and then there was the vertiginous sight of the streets below. Biederbeck gained more altitude, and soon they were whirling west.

"You know the place?"

"We'll be looking for one of our cruisers."

"Stolen?"

Cy ignored him, examining his conscience, assuring God he would be good as gold from now on. The only consolation was that he could never have covered this distance in less than an hour by car. He had found a map of Skokie in a leather pocket beside him. Opening it blotted out the swiftly passing scene below. When they got there, Beady identified the main street, and Cy guided him from the map.

"Thar she blows," Beady cried, and they began to descend. The cruiser with FOX RIVER POLICE suddenly legible on its side was parked in front of a house.

"The lawn?"

"Anywhere," Cy said.

Beady brought it down gently on the lawn, and Cy got the door open and ran crouched under the blades toward the house. He had his weapon out before he began beating on the door. Behind him the great blades turned slowly to a stop.

"Around back," he shouted to Beady.

He knocked, he rang the bell, and then, lowering his shoulder as he had playing offense for Illinois, he crashed into the door. It gave on the second try. He stumbled through and had trouble coming to a stop. Agnes stood staring at him. The man who was more behind than next to her held a mean-looking steak knife to her throat.

"Drop that!" Cy barked.

"No, you drop that."

"It's all over, Charlie."

The man considered that. "In that case, what do I have to lose?"

The answer came in multiple form. Agnes turned and

brought her knee into his groin, just as Beady came in from behind and wrested the man away from Agnes. He still had the knife in his hand when Cy got the cuffs on him.

"You all right, Agnes?"

"I am now." If Pippen ever looked at him like that, Cy would be a goner.

BIEDERBECK WAS DISAPPOINTED that he wasn't going to carry Charles whoever back to the heliport. "I could give him a pretty good ride."

It was tempting, but Cy shook his head. "We'll use the cruiser."

"Aw," said Beady.

Cy followed Agnes and the prisoner, giving her the satisfaction. From the next yard, a man yelled, "What's he done?"

"Jaywalked," Agnes called back.

Before putting Charles in the backseat, Cy got leg irons out of the trunk. When those were on the prisoner, Cy put him in the backseat, enjoying it when he pushed the man's head down as he did so.

Once inside, before Cy closed the door on him, Charlie tried to smile. He said in a strained voice, "I don't think I'll ever play the violin again."

"But you'll be able to sing soprano."

Beady had started his rotor, and the man next door backed away. It was a beautiful sight, watching the chopper rise, seemingly orient itself, and then prattle away to the east.

"I'll drive," Cy said. "You keep an eye on your prisoner."

NINE

TETZEL WAS THE EMPEROR of the pressroom in the courthouse. He was hailed when he entered the Jury Room across the street.

Even Lyle Menteur, editor of the *Tribune,* drifted dangerously close to praise. "More interviews," he suggested but it sounded like hip-hip-hooray to Tetzel.

Tetzel flapped his notebook and flourished his tape recorder. "As many as you want."

Menteur chewed a mouthful of gum morosely. Was he picking up the scent of cigarette smoke from Tetzel's clothes? His resentment at the exemption of the courthouse pressroom from the no-smoking ordinance would always be a barrier to fulsome praise.

"I haven't seen much of Rebecca lately," Tetzel said offhandedly.

"She's on sick leave."

"In Amsterdam?" Rebecca's piece on the hookers of Holland had been spiked by Menteur.

"Ho ho." Nicotine deprived as Menteur was, male solidarity survived in the editorial breast.

Success, when it comes late, is a bittersweet thing, and Tetzel grew philosophical. "Gone with the wind," he said to Tuttle. "Look at this monitor. Letters, words, sentences." He punched a key, and the screen cleared. "That's news, Tuttle. Snowflakes on the warm sidewalk of life."

"Have you thought of poetry?"

"It is my consolation. Do you know Kipling?"

Tuttle wrinkled his nose. Never answer a direct question. "After I finish my novel I shall turn to verse."

"I'd keep that quiet if I were you."

"You may be right."

Tetzel's story as originally written had crested with the arrest of Fulvio Menotti in Barrington. The arrest of Fulvio's brother changed all that, and the story as run ended with the look-alike brothers. Tetzel would have likened it to *A Tale of Two Cities,* but at the time he was alone in the pressroom, and talking to himself was something he only did while writing.

He heard that Father Dowling had inquired about Charles, so Tetzel drove out to St. Hilary's to get his take on the man.

"CONFESSIONS ARE SATURDAY," the housekeeper said, sweeping Tetzel with an assessing glance. "Unless it's an emergency."

"I *would* like to see him now."

Mrs. Murkin threw up her hands. Her job did not include the care of souls or the discernment of spirits. Another sweeping glance and she sniffed. "You've been drinking."

"It's my mouthwash."

Frowning, she led him down the hallway and tapped on a door. "Father, a penitent to see you."

Father Dowling looked up, his look welcoming, then puzzled. "Aren't you Tetzel of the *Tribune?*"

"I confess."

"Any other serious sins? Sit down, sit down."

The housekeeper expelled air—"Humph"—and clomped off down the hall.

"She misunderstood me."

"It's when she understands you that you're in trouble. Quite a dramatic story you wrote."

"Thank you. I'm working on a follow-up. We know more of the innocent brother than we do of Charles. I understand you were down in Joliet recently."

"Have you talked with Father Blatz?"

"Not yet."

Father Dowling began to fill his pipe. Tetzel got out his Pall Malls and looked a question.

"By all means. Why settle for secondhand smoke?"

"Father Blatz is the chaplain at Joliet?"

"That's right. Charles was his assistant during much of his stay there."

Having lit up, Tetzel scrambled to get out his notebook. *Accused Murderer Chaplain's Assistant.* "Can you tell me about that?"

"It would be secondhand. Talk with Father Blatz. I was surprised that you made so little of the connection to the artist Angelo Menotti. Both young men are his grandsons, you know."

Tetzel scribbled. "That will be in future articles. Right now I'm interested in the man who tried to shift blame for what he did onto his brother."

"I'm sure you remember Cain and Abel." A smile and then a rising cloud of smoke. "Once at an international conference Graham Greene said that every time he heard the phrase 'brotherly love' he thought of Cain and Abel."

"I'll use that. Have you talked with the suspect, Father?"

"If you don't inquire into my professional secrets I won't inquire into yours."

"Of course, of course." *Pastor of St. Hilary's Invokes Seal of the Confessional.*

"I enjoyed the series by Rebecca Farmer on her adventures in Europe."

"That's been discontinued," Tetzel said evenly. "She went too far when she submitted a piece on Amsterdam."

Father Dowling puffed on his pipe. After a moment, he said, "Angelo Menotti lives in Peoria."

"I was on my way there when I learned of the murder of Carl Borloff."

"His funeral is tomorrow."

"Here?"

"The rosary is tonight at McDivitt's."

Tetzel made a note.

TEN

In the conference with Cy and Agnes, Jacuzzi the prosecutor waxed philosophical. "In trying to lay it on Borloff and then his brother, he provided us with all the evidence we need to get a conviction. The box cutter, the rope. It reminds me of a play."

"Running or passing?"

Jacuzzi was not to be distracted. He couldn't believe that the twins could be so identical that people wouldn't know they were talking to one or the other. Apparently, though, that was the case. Margaret Devere Ward, taken downtown to identify Charles Menotti, couldn't believe her eyes. It helped that Fulvio was standing beside her. She looked from him to the man behind the glass and threw up her hands.

"Was it you I met on the freighter?"

"Of course."

"But how would he know of all that?"

"I told him. I had no idea that he would impersonate me."

"What on earth does he have against you?"

"Do you have any brothers?"

Cy and Agnes had explored that with Fulvio. Seldom had 'sibling rivalry' seemed so apt a phrase.

"He was always in trouble. Many times I was blamed for what he'd done. He ended up blaming everyone else. He wanted our grandfather to support him."

"What did he say?"

"'On the toe of my shoe.' When Charles saw all that Devere

money going to people he regarded as parasites on our grand-father's fame, he must have gone berzerk."

"He did get one hundred thousand dollars of it from Carl Borloff."

Fulvio whistled. "He should have settled for that."

"He had already killed several people."

Fulvio became solemn. "He has to see a priest. Is there a chaplain here?"

"Father Dowling has talked with him."

Fulvio seemed relieved. "Nobody's all bad, you know."

"Are you including Louellen in the indictment?" Agnes asked Jacuzzi.

"That would be hard to prove. I want to stick with the sure ones."

Agnes didn't like that at all. She reviewed everything that had been found in Louellen's room; she went downstairs to the morgue to talk to Dr. Pippen.

"Alcohol and drugs," Pippen said, shaking her head.

"She didn't drink."

"How do we know that?"

"A woman down the hall. If she never drank, others would have known that."

"The trouble is, you can start drinking."

"I don't want her just forgotten."

"Agnes, if they convict that man they will have convicted the man who murdered Louellen. If he did."

Agnes knew what she must sound like, even to Cy, even to Pippen, and there was some truth in it. She didn't think the skinny little hooker was looming large enough on anyone's radar because she was black. She went back to the evidence room and had the custodian get out everything.

"You were just here."

"I may have overlooked something. I'm going to take this to the lab."

"Sign for it."

Winston in the lab seemed to wear glasses so he could look over them. When he wasn't doing that, he put them on top of his head. He groaned when Agnes told him what she wanted. "I checked all that stuff, the syringe, the pipe, everything."

"Do you drink, Winston?"

"Is that an offer?"

"I don't drink. How do you open a bottle of liquor?"

Winston showed her. The cork had a plastic ridged top, and it was twisted off. With both hands? No, you hold the bottle with one hand and twist with the other.

"Where would you grip the bottle?"

"In the middle. There are no prints there, Agnes."

"What if you held the bottom and twisted different ways with different hands?"

"I've never seen it done that way."

"I've never seen it done any way."

Wearing gloves, Winston placed the bottom of the bottle in the palm of one hand, got a grip on the bottle, then put the other hand on the cork. He checked where a bottom grip would have made prints. There still were no fingerprints on the bottle.

"Of course, it was wiped. All this stuff was."

"Why is the bottle dented on the bottom?"

"So are wine bottles."

"Did you check in there?"

Winston checked in there and found a print. He grinned as if it had all been his idea. "He must have carried it that way."

The print matched Charles's. Agnes went back to Jacuzzi with the news. He still didn't want to add Louellen's name to the list of victims.

"I'll picket your office unless you do."

Jacuzzi had a crooked grin that many jurors found charming. "You're kidding."

"Try me."

Louellen's name was added to the list of Charles Menotti's victims.

Cy congratulated her. "I think you've discovered a new right, Agnes."

"It's only justice."

"The next time I'm the victim of a mass murderer, I'll insist on equal billing."

From Cy such kidding was okay. Don't ask her why.

THE DEVERE FOUNDATION was indeed the link between all the recent murders, and it had generated the second link that was Argyle House. Charles, infuriated by his grandfather's disinterest in him, had irrationally determined to become the executor of his estate, the heir of Angelo Menotti's fame. He had followed the dispersal of Devere money, all of it connected, as he thought, with Angelo Menotti. That his resentment would turn him into a murderer surprised even him, if you could believe him.

"Bobby? The poor girl refused when I went there to take away the portrait she had done of me. She said it was one of the best things she had ever done. She intended to show it. I couldn't have that." He looked around the room, but his eyes returned to Agnes. "If only I had known then that Fulvio was back."

"Your twin brother."

"Separated at birth. We never got along."

Charles became uncomfortable when Agnes asked him why he had desecrated Bobby's body as he had.

"Who would think I would do a thing like that? She didn't die of hanging, you know."

"It wasn't the exhaust, Charles."

"I know. She was dead when I brought her there. She died in her studio."

Their struggle when he had tried to remove his portrait had seemed just jostling at first. Bobby had climbed onto his back to prevent him from taking the picture. That had angered him.

"I threw the canvas on her waterbed and grabbed her by the throat. Not meaning to do more than frighten her." Again he looked away. "It was as if I couldn't remove my fingers from her throat."

He looked at Agnes as if expecting sympathy.

Was it possible to strangle someone inadvertently? Maybe if it was your first attempt.

"So you hung her stripped body in Amy Gorman's garage and cut it up a bit."

"I am sorry about that."

"Why make her body seem that of Madeline Schutz?"

"It confused you, didn't it?"

"How did you get hold of her purse and clothing?"

"I talked a man named Mintz into letting me into her apartment. I was her publisher; she had sent me to pick up a manuscript."

"I'm surprised you didn't get rid of Mintz, too."

"By then I had thought of turning suspicion onto Fulvio."

"Brotherly love."

"My grandfather thought the world of Fulvio."

Louellen had to go, of course, because she would know about him and Bobby. Carl Borloff?

"That son of a bitch. Can you imagine making a career out of someone else's work?"

"Your grandfather's."

"Yes!"

"Wasn't that more or less your own plan?"

"It's not the same thing. My grandfather opposed what he was doing. Not that anyone gave a damn."

"What about J. J. Rudolph?"

"Bobby told me about her. So I went to Kenosha and joined the firm."

"Just like that? Do you feel any guilt at all?"

He thought about it. "I'm trying to explain how it happened." Does anyone ever stop seeming innocent in his own eyes? That was a problem Agnes would leave to God. Meanwhile, she was glad that Charles would go on trial for all the murders he had done.

"He won't die in prison," Cy predicted. "He did pretty well in Joliet the first time. He will be free before he loses his looks."

ELEVEN

At the trial, Amos Cadbury himself sat with defense counsel, unsettling Jacuzzi. When had Amos Cadbury ever appeared in criminal court? Or sat next to Tuttle, for that matter. That patrician presence at the defense table had no effect on the outcome of the trial. The best Tuttle could do was argue mistaken identity and go on and on about the unreliability of fingerprints, citing instances.

"He doesn't take advice," Amos told Father Dowling afterward.

"It was good of you to give moral support."

"Moral? To Tuttle." A wintry smile. "I did it for Jane Devere."

"Of course."

Willie and Holloway followed the trial with interest. Pretty Boy, as they still thought of Charles, had a lazy arrogance throughout the proceedings of which Holloway approved.

"He doesn't have a chance, so why not enjoy it?"

Willie shook his head. "Can you imagine going back to Joliet?"

"Phyllis would never permit it."

"Your parole officer?"

"Willie, have you ever wondered about the way we attract females?"

"No. You going to marry her?"

"If she proposes."

When Father Dowling visited the upper floor of the Devere mansion, Jane seemed to have aged. "I don't know which of them Margaret brought to me."

"The grandsons of Angelo Menotti."

A long silence. "I have never gone to confession to you, Father Dowling."

"You told me you had a confessor."

"I do. Sometimes I want to confess sins that were forgiven long, long ago. Sins whose effects don't go away."

"You and Angelo Menotti?"

"How did you know that?"

"You put a case to me once."

She nodded. "It *was* a kind of oblique confession."

Sun slanted into the room as she spoke. Father Dowling listened to her anguished story. A young wife having an affair with an artist on whom she'd had a crush as a student at Rosary College. She had persuaded her father-in-law to engage Menotti to do the stained glass windows for St. Hilary's church. She had visited him in his studio in Peoria.

"What a seducer he was."

"You became pregnant?"

She took a very deep breath. "You must have seen the Menotti traits in James."

"Are you certain Angelo was the father?"

"Yes." She nodded. "Oh, yes. In compensation, I developed an exaggerated pride in the Devere family. Dear God, how I have tainted it."

"Your husband never guessed?"

"Father, he was so happy at the prospect of becoming a father. Dear God, how could I have done that to him?"

"I think you handled it well."

"You do?"

"What was the alternative?"

"I could have told my husband!"

"You could have, yes. I think you were wise not to."

She subsided into silence. Her eyes went to the Menotti Madonna above her prie-dieu. "Angelo would not have married me if he could have."

Father Dowling could think of nothing to say to that.

"He was only a seducer. I knew that, and that made it easier for me to deceive my husband."

Father Dowling had taken a little stole from his pocket and put it over his shoulders. "I'll give you absolution now, Jane."

"I confessed it long ago."

"Think of this as a general confession."

She bowed her head then, and he said the words of absolution, tracing the sign of the cross over her. He rose to go. "I'll bring you communion next Tuesday."

"Thank you."

When he had reached the door, she called his name. He turned. "Father, Susan and Fulvio...I think they're in love." He waited. "They can never marry."

Consanguinity? No need to discuss that now. "Let's cross that bridge when we come to it."

PART FIVE

ONE

AGE IS A MYSTERIOUS THING, or so Amos Cadbury found it to be. Or perhaps the mystery lies in memory and its selective retention of the past. After the trial, the venerable lawyer had flown off to Florida and the condo on Longboat Key that a client had put at his disposal. It had been Amos's practice over the years to discourage clients who wanted to buy rather than rent when they went south in the winter, but his advice was seldom taken. He did not understand this compulsion to multiply the nuisances of ownership—a home in Fox River, perhaps a condo in the Caribbean, boats both in a Lake Michigan marina and in the Gulf. The complications of taxes should be enough to make renters of us all. Now, though, he was glad that his advice in the matter was seldom followed. He sat on a patio under a pergola, smoking a pensive cigar and thinking of Jane Devere, trying to relax.

The old woman's long-ago affair with Angelo Menotti preyed on his mind. Finally she had put aside indirection and discretion and told Amos of her conviction that her son, James, was the fruit of her affair with Menotti.

"Jane, he is his father's son."

"What have I been telling you?"

Amos had meant Jane's husband, William, but her confidence soon had him seeing, or thinking he saw, Menotti traits in James. Suddenly the specter arose of the claims that might be made on the Devere fortune by Menotti or his descendants. What a scandalous case it would be if the whole Menotti menagerie felt that they had a plausible claim on the fortune begun by August Devere and subsequently considerably enlarged by James. Such thoughts robbed Amos's stay of the relaxation he had sought, and after five days he flew back home.

His driver met him at O'Hare, and Amos immediately called Father Dowling.

"You're in Florida, Amos?"

"I have just returned. I must see you, Father."

"Of course."

"Could I come to the rectory?"

"Now?"

"Yes."

"I'll have Marie set another place at table."

"Will there be others?"

"Phil Keegan might stop by later."

"POTLUCK," AS MARIE MURKIN dismissively described the meal she prepared, consisted of veal, potatoes au gratin, and asparagus. The housekeeper came and went throughout the meal, muttering apologies, blaming Father Dowling for not telling her that Amos Cadbury was coming.

"Marie, I just landed. I telephoned Father Dowling on my way here. I would have come if only for this wonderful meal."

An equivocal wave of the Murkin hand—was she trying to stop flattery or encourage it? After cherry cobbler, the two men adjourned to the pastor's study.

"Jane Devere," Amos said when they were settled. "You remember that I told you of the legal puzzles she liked to pose?"

"I remember."

"They were hints, of course. Now she has made it clear." Amos paused. "Of course, this is in the deepest confidence."

At Father Dowling's nod, he went on. The priest did not react as Amos had expected when he told him Jane's con-

viction that her son, James, had Angelo Menotti for a father.
"Has she told you this, Father?"

The priest looked away, and Amos immediately regretted the question. Jane's confidence to him had been more
one between old friends than between lawyer and client, but
whatever Jane had told Father Dowling came under the most
solemn of embargos.

"Let me just say what she has told me."

Father Dowling nodded, almost with relief.

So at last Amos was able to lay out the potential complications—legal complications, to say nothing of emotional
complications—that would follow if Jane was right.

"Surely she doesn't intend to make an announcement,
Amos."

"She thinks she owes the truth to James."

"Good Lord."

"Indeed."

"How can she be sure, Amos? I don't understand these
matters, but at the time she had a husband as well as a lover,
did she not?"

Amos lifted his eyes.

"It could be decided, of course. Verified or falsified."

Amos thought, sat back. "Ah."

"We can put the matter to Phil Keegan when he comes."

PHIL LISTENED, SIPPING BEER. He began to nod before the story
was complete.

"I can have the lab do it. A routine test. I can tack it on to
the Menotti case. That's still open."

Amos undertook the task Phil assigned him with enthusiasm, taking strange pleasure from bringing the necessary
samples to the police lab. While he was at it, he decided to be
thorough. Jane's DNA would be compared both with James's

and with Fulvio's. While he was at it, he added Susan to the list.

"Uncle Amos, he hasn't even proposed."

"It's just a matter of tying up loose ends, Susan."

SOME DAYS LATER, PHIL KEEGAN and Father Dowling came to Amos's office, and the venerable lawyer tried to read their expressions to see what lay ahead.

"Adam and Eve, maybe," Phil said when Amos had put the two men in chairs facing his desk.

"Adam and Eve?"

"There's no later connection, Amos."

Phil handed the lab reports to Amos, and he paged through them, waiting to feel a sense of relief that did not come.

Father Dowling understood. "I'll talk to Jane, Amos."

TWO

FATHER DOWLING BROUGHT holy communion to the Devere home and was led upstairs to Jane's apartment, where the old woman reverently received and then as usual spent some minutes at her prie-dieu while Father Dowling sipped coffee in the next room. When she joined him, she poured herself a cup of coffee, looking thoughtful. "I told Amos Cadbury my story, Father."

He nodded.

"The question is what I must do now."

"What does Amos advise?"

"Of course, he sees everything as a lawyer. It is your advice I want, Father Dowling."

The tests, Phil's mention of Adam and Eve, quoting the lab technician, brought on long thoughts on the vast concatenation of destinies that stretched back over the centuries, over millennia, the uncountable generations of human beings, succeeding one another, parents, children, grandchildren, on and on into ever more distant prefixes. The unity of the human race was a theological as well as a biological truth. In that sense, we are all blood relatives to one degree or another. Of course, Jane Devere had something far more specific in mind. It occurred to Father Dowling that the decision he faced was at least as complicated as hers.

"Do I have the right to withhold the truth, Father?"

That was akin to the question he put to himself. Did he have the right to keep from Jane what all the testing had brought to light? Or not brought to light. Throughout her long life, Jane had lived in the conviction that her affair with Angelo Menotti had wrought a permanent effect on her children and grandchildren. James and James's children, Susan and Hugh, were, she thought, descendants of Angelo Menotti and not of her husband and thus not true Deveres.

"Imagine being told such a thing about yourself, Jane."

"Doesn't the truth set us free?"

After a silence, Father Dowling leaned toward her. "Jane, this is my advice. Keep your secret. Saying what you think would have most unwelcome consequences, and what would be gained?"

She looked at him, and gradually an expression of relief came over her face, seeming to smooth away the wrinkles. "I think I hoped you would say that."

"It's best."

"The secret can go with me to the grave?"

They sat on for a time while Father Dowling considered the secret that would indeed be interred with her. The secret that there was no secret. On the drive back to the rectory, he told himself he had been right not to tell Jane her lifelong suspicion was unfounded. Would she even have believed him? The thought of bringing those lab reports to the old woman seemed grotesque. Let it remain one of the infinity of truths that will come to the light on the last day.

THE LETTER FROM THE CHANCERY was lying on his desk when he returned to the rectory. Marie watched warily from the doorway as he picked it up. He looked at her.

"And the winner is…"

After he read it aloud, he let Marie's joyful cry suffice for them both. Off she went then, to spread the good news. Father Dowling lit his pipe. *Not my will, O Lord, but thine be done.* Of course, it is easier when they coincide.

* * * * *

REQUEST YOUR FREE BOOKS!

2 FREE NOVELS
PLUS 2 FREE GIFTS!

WORLDWIDE LIBRARY®
Your Partner in Crime

YES! Please send me 2 FREE novels from the Worldwide Library® series and my 2 FREE gifts (gifts are worth about $10). After receiving them, if I don't wish to receive any more books, I can return the shipping statement marked "cancel." If I don't cancel, I will receive 4 brand-new novels every month and be billed just $5.24 per book in the U.S. or $6.24 per book in Canada. That's a saving of at least 34% off the cover price. It's quite a bargain! Shipping and handling is just 50¢ per book in the U.S. and 75¢ per book in Canada.* I understand that accepting the 2 free books and gifts places me under no obligation to buy anything. I can always return a shipment and cancel at any time. Even if I never buy another book, the two free books and gifts are mine to keep forever.

414/424 WDN FEJ3

Name	(PLEASE PRINT)

Address	Apt. #

City	State/Prov.	Zip/Postal Code

Signature (if under 18, a parent or guardian must sign)

Mail to the **Reader Service:**
IN U.S.A.: P.O. Box 1867, Buffalo, NY 14240-1867
IN CANADA: P.O. Box 609, Fort Erie, Ontario L2A 5X3

Not valid for current subscribers to the Worldwide Library series.

Want to try two free books from another line?
Call 1-800-873-8635 or visit www.ReaderService.com.

* Terms and prices subject to change without notice. Prices do not include applicable taxes. Sales tax applicable in N.Y. Canadian residents will be charged applicable taxes. Offer not valid in Quebec. This offer is limited to one order per household. All orders subject to credit approval. Credit or debit balances in a customer's account(s) may be offset by any other outstanding balance owed by or to the customer. Please allow 4 to 6 weeks for delivery. Offer available while quantities last.

Your Privacy—The Reader Service is committed to protecting your privacy. Our Privacy Policy is available online at www.ReaderService.com or upon request from the Reader Service.

We make a portion of our mailing list available to reputable third parties that offer products we believe may interest you. If you prefer that we not exchange your name with third parties, or if you wish to clarify or modify your communication preferences, please visit us at www.ReaderService.com/consumerchoice or write to us at Reader Service Preference Service, P.O. Box 9062, Buffalo, NY 14269. Include your complete name and address.